Praise for Ronica Black

Freedom

"This is a great book. The p... ...led throughout but what I found cap... ...growing affection between the two main characters. Although they are both very different women, you find yourself holding your breath, hoping that they will find a way to be together."—*Lesbian Reading Room*

The Practitioner

"*The Practitioner* by Ronica Black is the angsty sort of romance that I can easily get lost in. I wanted to fill a tub and bathe in all the feelings. Hell, if I had one of those fancy, waterproof Kindles, I just might have."—*Lesbian Review*

"The beginning of this novel captured my attention from the rather luscious description of a pint of Guinness. I cannot tell a lie, I almost immediately wanted to be drinking it...The first scene with the practitioner also pulled me in, making me sit up and pay attention to what was happening on the digital page. The relationship was like a low simmering fire, frequently doused by either Johnnie's personal angst, or Elaine's. This book was an overall enjoyable read and one which I would recommend to people wanting characters who practically breathe off the page."—*Library Thing*

Under Her Wing

"From the start Ronica Black had me. I loved everything about this story, from the emotional intensity to the amazingly hot sex scenes. The emotion between them is so real and tear jerking at times. And the love scenes are phenomenal. I feel I'm raving – but I enjoyed it that much. Highly recommended."—*Kitty Kat's Book Review Blog*

The Seeker

"Stalkers, child kidnappers and murderers all collide in this fast-paced, dual-plotted novel. This is not Black's first novel, and readers can only hope it will not be her last."—*Lambda Literary Review*

Lambda Literary Award Finalist *Flesh and Bone*

"Ronica Black handles a traditional range of lesbian fantasies with gusto and sincerity. The reader wants to know these women as well as they come to know each other. When Black's characters ignore their realistic fears to follow their passion, this reader admires their chutzpah and cheers them on…These stories make good bedtime reading, and could lead to sweet dreams. Read them and see."
—*Erotica Revealed*

Chasing Love

"Ronica Black's writing is fluid, and lots of dialogue makes this a fast read. If you like steamy erotica with intense sexual situations, you'll like *Chasing Love*."—*Queer Magazine Online*

Hearts Aflame

"Sleek storytelling and terrific characters are the backbone of Ronica Black's third and best novel, *Hearts Aflame*. Prepare to hop on for an emotional ride with this thrilling story of love in the Outback…Along with the romance of Krista and Rae, the secondary storylines such as Krista's fear of horses and an uncle suffering from Alzheimer's are told with depth and warmth. Black also draws in the reader by utilizing the weather as a metaphor for the sexual and emotional tension in all the storylines. Wonderful storytelling and rich characterization make this a high recommendation."
—*Lambda Literary Review*

"I like the author's writing style and she tells a good story. I was drawn in quickly and didn't lose interest at all. Black paints a great picture with her words and I was able to feel like I was sitting around the campfire with the characters."—*C-Spot Reviews*

Lambda Literary Award Finalist *Wild Abandon*

"Black is a master at teasing the reader with her use of domination and desire. Black's first novel, *In Too Deep*, was a finalist for a 2005 Lammy…With *Wild Abandon*, the author continues her winning ways, writing like a seasoned pro. This is one romance I will not soon forget."—*Books to Watch Out For*

"This sequel to Ronica Black's debut novel, *In Too Deep*, is an electrifying thriller. The author's development as a fine storyteller shines with this tightly written story...[The mystery] keeps the story charged—never unraveling or leading us to a predictable conclusion. More than once I gasped in surprise at the dark and twisted paths this book took."—*Curve*

"Ronica Black, author of *In Too Deep*, has given her fans another fast paced novel of romance and danger. As previously, Black develops her characters fully, complete with their quirks and flaws. She is also skilled at allowing her characters to grow, and to find their way out of psychic holes. If you enjoy complex characters and passionate sex scenes, you'll love *Wild Abandon*."—*MegaScene*

Lambda Literary Award Finalist *In Too Deep*

"Ronica Black's debut novel *In Too Deep* has everything from nonstop action and intriguing well developed characters to steamy erotic love scenes. From the opening scenes where Black plunges the reader headfirst into the story to the explosive unexpected ending, *In Too Deep* has what it takes to rise to the top. Black has a winner with *In Too Deep*, one that will keep the reader turning the pages until the very last one."—*Independent Gay Writer*

"[A]n exciting, page turning read, full of mystery, sex, and suspense."—*MegaScene*

"[A] challenging murder mystery—sections of this mixed-genre novel are hot, hot, hot. Black juggles the assorted elements of her first book with assured pacing and estimable panache."—*Q Syndicate*

"Black's characterization is skillful, and the sexual chemistry surrounding the three major characters is palpable and definitely hot-hot-hot...if you're looking for a solid read with ample amounts of eroticism and a red herring or two you're sure to find *In Too Deep* a satisfying read."—*L Word Literature*

By the Author

In Too Deep

Deeper

Wild Abandon

Hearts Aflame

Flesh and Bone

The Seeker

Chasing Love

Conquest

Wholehearted

The Midnight Room

Snow Angel

The Practitioner

Freedom to Love

Under Her Wing

Private Passion

Dark Euphoria

The Last Seduction

Olivia's Awakening

A Love That Leads to Home

Passion's Sweet Surrender

A Turn of Fate

Visit us at www.boldstrokesbooks.com

A TURN OF FATE

by
Ronica Black

2021

Credits
Editor: Cindy Cresap
Production Design: Stacia Seaman
Cover Design by Jeanine Henning

Acknowledgments

It was August, 1987 when the call came. I was eleven years old; my younger sister, Robin, was eight. The call came from Robin's teacher, which we thought was odd, given that it was summer. When my sister answered the phone, she thought she was in trouble, as her little eight-year-old mind couldn't understand what the phone call could be about. She handed the phone to my mother, and based on her reaction, we knew that whatever it was, it wasn't good.

My mother hung up and sat us down. She told us there had been a plane crash and that Robin's classmate and friend had been killed, along with all the others on board.

I remember sitting there shocked. We cried. My mother did her best to console us and we did our best to grieve as only children can, with a lot of confusion and questions. And I remember thinking that if we're this hurt and confused, how must the loved ones and family members of those on board be feeling?

I'll never forget wondering about that. So when this idea came up for this book, naturally my mind traveled back all those years to that hot summer day in August. I called my sister, and we relived a bit of the past. And it was still just as sad and tragic today as it was then. That's when I knew I had to write this book.

I can only hope, however, that I've done justice to what it must've felt like for those families whose loved ones were so tragically taken.

Thank you, Robin, for helping me remember.

And thanks, as always, to the entire Bold Strokes team for all their hard work.

Thank you to my editor, Cindy Cresap. Cindy, every time we work together I learn something new. Thank you.

For my sister, Robin, who helped me remember the past.

And for Flight 255. RIP

PROLOGUE

I don't care what Viv says," Kinsley said as she dealt the playing cards like one of those professionals in Vegas. "NSYNC is so not better than the Backstreet Boys."

Nev watched her best friend in wonder, only half listening. She was too focused on the lightning quick flick of her wrist and fingers as she dealt those cards. How did she do it? Nev didn't know. She just knew that when it came to Kinsley, not much surprised her anymore.

Kinsley finished dealing and cocked her head, "They're good, sure. But better? Nuh-uh. No way. I really think she's just saying that because she's seriously crushing on Justin Timberlake."

Nev picked up her cards and drew her legs in lotus style. She and Kinsley were in her bedroom playing bullshit and listening to one of Kinsley's Backstreet Boys CDs. Currently, Kinsley was singing along to "I Want It That Way" as she studied her hand. It was her turn to go first, but she seemed to be taking her time, pausing momentarily to grab a handful of popcorn from the holiday tin Nev had snatched from the kitchen. They'd already finished off the caramel corn section. Now they were munching on the cheddar cheese, having both agreed to save the white cheddar portion for Nev's twin sister, Vivian, who was due back from volleyball camp in Wisconsin in a few hours. The last week of Christmas break just hadn't been the same without her, and they were both excited for her return.

Kinsley hadn't said so or anything, but Nev sensed she felt the same. It was the main reason why she'd come over to spend the night. So they could both welcome her home. Sure, she and Kinsley got along great and Nev considered her her best friend, next to Viv of course, but they were used to being the Three Musketeers, not two peas in a pod. And lately, something was different when it was just her and Kinsley.

Something unspoken. She'd noticed it back in August when they'd started the sixth grade. Kinsley had walked into class on the first day of school a little more womanly, with a stylish new layered haircut, newly developed curves, and a shimmering golden tan from her vacation in San Diego. All the boys' heads had turned at her entrance. And Nev had to admit, hers had too. She, of course, hadn't told anyone. She'd kept to herself her admiration and the funny feelings she'd get in her stomach when Kinsley laughed or when they'd playfully roughhouse. She wanted to figure out what those feelings meant before she shared them with anyone. Even Viv, who she told absolutely everything to, didn't know. Actually, when it came to Viv, most of the time she didn't even have to tell her. Viv just knew. And vice versa. Her mother said it was a twin thing. She wondered if Viv was aware of her funny feelings for Kinsley. If she did, what did she think? If she didn't, what *would* she think?

"I mean, he's cute and all," Kinsley continued, "but he doesn't knock me off my feet or anything," She finally discarded. "Two aces."

Nev searched her hand for some twos.

"What do you think?" Kinsley asked.

"'Bout what?"

"About what I just said. Duh."

Nev shrugged, not really having followed her train of thought that closely. "I really haven't thought about it."

Kinsley eyed her. "You don't have an opinion?"

Nev plucked a card from the deck. "Nope. One two."

"At all?"

"Nuh-uh."

"Well, which group do you think is cuter?" She snuck her tongue out to touch her top lip as she examined her hand once again.

Nev looked at her over her cards. "I don't really like any of them."

Kinsley slumped like she was exasperated. "I'm not asking you to marry them. Just tell me who is cuter. Come on. You must think at least one member is hot."

Nev returned her attention to her cards. "I don't even really like pop music. I'm more into country."

"That has nothing to do with what I'm asking."

Nev eyed her. Waiting. "It's your turn."

Kinsley sighed and shifted her hand around before discarding. "Three threes."

Nev shook her head as she located two threes in her own hand. "Bullshit."

Kinsley groaned and slapped her hand down on the discard pile to scoop it up. "Damn it, Nev. You're too good at this."

"Not really. You're just really bad."

Kinsley gave her the finger. "It's better with three people."

Nev just grinned and grabbed some popcorn.

The CD ended and the room fell heavy with silence. She found Kinsley staring at her as she chewed.

"What?"

"You didn't give me an answer."

Nev fought groaning and stretched out a pajama clad leg. Her black fuzzy sock had a piece of orange popcorn stuck to the toe, and just as soon as she noticed it, her plump cocker spaniel, Posh, snuck by and snatched it before waddling over to her bed in the corner.

Kinsley laughed. "That's so gross."

Nev smiled. "She's done worse."

Kinsley's eyes grew wide. "Oh my God, I know! Remember last summer when Viv laughed so hard the spaghetti she just ate came out of her nose and Posh ate it?"

Nev cracked up. "Yes!"

"And Viv said it burned because she'd had Dr Pepper too, so Posh was eating like, spaghetti, snot, and Dr Pepper all mixed together."

"Stop!" She was laughing so hard it hurt. "You're gonna make me ralph."

"Well, don't worry. If you do, Posh will eat it before your mom sees it."

They fell over with giggles and Nev laughed until her eyes watered.

"Remind me to never, ever let that dog kiss me again," Kinsley said.

"Aw, you're hurting her feelings," Nev said, looking back at Posh all curled up on her bed. Posh was considered the family dog, but she was really Viv's. Viv had named her after one of the Spice Girls and Posh had bonded with Viv more than she had anyone else.

"She misses Viv," Nev said. "If she were home, she wouldn't even be in my room."

"Yeah," Kinsley said, eating some popcorn. "I miss her, too."

Nev examined her hand and discarded. "Three fours." She was

hoping to catch Kinsley off guard. It didn't work. She actually took the time to painstakingly search her hand.

"Bullshit!"

"Damn it!" Nev retrieved the cards and returned them to her hand.

"Girls!" Mom yelled from the living room. "Language!"

They laughed again, Kinsley covering her mouth.

"Sorry, Mom!" Nev called out.

"Sorry," Kinsley whispered.

"Don't worry about it."

They laughed some more and Kinsley discarded. "Two fives."

Nev searched her hand. "You're right, though. This game is better with three people. Where's Viv when you need her?"

She set down some cards. "Two sixes."

"It was nice getting a break from her pain in the butt annoying singing and all, but I do miss her." She looked at Kinsley. "If you tell her that, I'll kick your ass."

Kinsley grinned. "Ooh, you said ass. You must mean business, you rebel, you. I'm so scared." She grinned as she leaned over and fumbled with the buttons on the stereo. She switched on the FM radio to her favorite pop station. Then she refocused on her cards.

"I really wish I could've gone to camp with her."

Nev sipped from her can of Orange Crush. "You got sick. You can't help that."

"I know, but maybe I should've hidden it and toughed it out. So I could go, you know?"

"Um, you were chucking up a storm. Don't think you could've exactly hidden that, Kinny."

She shrugged. "Still, I wish I could've gone. It was my idea and everything. I feel bad Viv had to go alone." She put down a card. "One seven."

"There's always next year. And you never know. Viv could come home and tell us it sucked balls. Then you might be glad you didn't go."

Kinsley laughed a little. "Good point. But I hope for her sake it didn't. I hope she had fun."

"Mom said she sounded like she was having fun."

They grew quiet and Kinsley glanced around the room as Nev rearranged her cards. She appeared to be taking in Nev's posters of horses, the US Women's Soccer team and her autographed photos of Mia Hamm and Brandi Chastain, which Nev had waited in line for hours to get. Kinsley and Viv were into volleyball. But Nev's thing was soccer. She was obsessed and determined to someday make the US women's team.

Kinsley's eyes lingered on Nev's poster of the Spice Girls behind her bed.

"Nev?"

Nev swallowed some more popcorn. "Yeah?"

"Do you think any of the boys at school are cute?"

Nev felt herself redden. They were back to this. "I don't know."

"No, for real. Give me an answer."

Nev shrugged.

Kinsley looked at her. Pegged her with a powerful stare from her hazel blue eyes. "Because I don't."

"What?" Nev about spit out her drink. "But you have a boyfriend and everything."

"Conner's okay, I guess. He's nice and the other girls think he's cute."

"Kinny, he's the most popular guy in sixth grade. Viv has the total hots for him."

She dropped her gaze. "I know," she said softly. "So, why am I not into him?"

"Maybe you just like someone else," Nev said half-heartedly.

Her eyes came back up. "I do like someone else," she said.

Nev swallowed and suddenly that funny feeling was back in her stomach again. Her mind went to a couple of hours from then when Viv would be home and they'd all be asleep together on the floor, snuggled in blankets and laughing until they fell asleep. Would she be able to roll over and smell the apple scented shampoo of Kinsley's hair? Would she feel the warm press of her body against hers? Would it keep her up like it did the last time she spent the night?

Would she wake the next morning to find Kinsley looking at her like she was right now? Looking at her in the way she'd been looking at her for a few months now?

"Oh," Nev said, pretending to study her cards. Sarah McLachlan started singing "Building a Mystery" on the stereo. Nev loved that song and she burned hotter as she listened to the lyrics and thought of Kinsley.

"Don't you want to know who?" Kinsley asked.

Nev almost closed her eyes at the words. *Are you going to say it's me? Could that be possible?*

"Nev?"

"Hm?"

"You know, you never did answer my question about the boy bands."

Nev groaned. "God, that again?"

"Why won't you answer?"

"I did. You just didn't like my answer."

"Your answer gave away nothing."

"Gave away nothing? What are you wanting me to give away?"

Kinsley looked away. Nev saw *her* blush this time and Nev couldn't bear to look at her, suspecting the blush was because of her. They sat quietly as the song played on until eventually, as the song faded out, Kinsley spoke.

"What about the Spice Girls?" she asked softly. "Do you think any of them are hot?"

Nev glanced at her quickly, burned so hot she thought she'd die, and then stared down at her cards.

"Because I do."

Nev didn't respond. She was having trouble breathing, much less speaking.

"I like Sporty Spice. She reminds me of you."

Nev forced down a swallow and felt her heart beating in her ears. She glanced up at Kinsley and saw a look she'd never seen before in her eyes. It was similar to the one she'd been giving her, only this one was ten times as powerful, ten times as fierce. She looked like she wanted to lean in and kiss her, and for a long, incredible second, Nev wondered what that would be like. It nearly made her dizzy she swooned so hard.

The normally upbeat deejay came on over the radio, interrupting the heavy moment. She sounded distressed.

"We have some breaking news this evening out of Milwaukee. We are getting reports that a commercial airliner crashed soon after takeoff about twenty minutes ago. We will keep you updated on the latest details as they come in."

Nev stared at the stereo as the deejay went to commercial. Kinsley didn't speak for a long moment. Neither did Nev.

"Isn't Viv taking off from Milwaukee?" Kinsley asked in a soft voice.

"It isn't her," Nev said firmly. No way. No how. Viv probably hadn't even taken off yet. Probably wasn't even on the plane yet. She didn't even like to fly, so she was probably putting off even getting on until the last second.

But something in her gut wouldn't allow her to buy into that. Her mouth went dry and she struggled to swallow down the last two swigs of soda. She closed her eyes as her heart pounded. She searched for the familiar sensation she'd had since birth, the one that came over her every time she thought of Viv.

She clenched her eyes and then her hands. Tried harder.

She opened her eyes as panic set in.

Something was wrong, terribly wrong. She could no longer feel her twin sister.

Another commercial commenced and the house phone rang, causing Nev to jerk. Kinsley came to sit next to her and she squeezed her arm.

"I'm sure you're right," she said.

The commercial ended and another started. Nev heard movement coming from the living room. Raised voices. Shuffling, hurried feet.

She could sense her parents' unease.

Oh, God.

The deejay came back on.

"Some tragic news out of Milwaukee tonight. We've just received confirmation that a commercial flight en route from Milwaukee to Phoenix crashed shortly after takeoff. Rescue workers are at the scene, but so far there has been no word on survivors."

Nev turned the stereo off and shoved it over, wanting it to shut up. They weren't right. They didn't know. How could they know? She leaned forward and yanked the plug from the wall, ensuring it would never come back on.

"Nev," Kinsley said, gently tugging on her. "It'll be okay. I'm sure Viv is fine. We don't even know if that's her flight—"

The bedroom door flew open and Dad rushed in looking ashen.

"Nevaeh," he choked. "Oh, God."

Mom hurried in, took one look at her, and fell to the floor and burst into tears. She fell upon Nev sobbing, and Nev knew then it was true. The feeling in her gut was real.

Viv was gone.

CHAPTER ONE

Twenty Years Later

"So, what you're saying, Ms. Padovano, is that there are different flight rules for flying into fog?" the pretty but very professional news anchor asked. Kinsley nodded, feeling at ease with the question, and kept her eye contact with the newswoman rather than the camera as she answered.

"That's correct. When you fly into fog you have to fly under IFR."

"And what's IFR?"

"Instrument Flight Rules. In other words, the instruments guide you rather than your own vision, which is known as VFR or Visual Flight Rules."

"That explains so much of what we've been hearing on the cockpit voice recorder. It's all beginning to make sense now." She glanced down at her notes. "Can you tell us what IIMC is? The pilot refers to flying into IIMC."

"Sure. IIMC stands for Inadvertent Instrumental Meteorological Conditions. The pilot is reporting that he has inadvertently flown into fog and is now requesting to fly under Special VFR, or Special Visual Flight Rules."

"Special Visual Flight Rules?"

"Yes. And to be able to fly by Special Visual Flight Rules you have to be IFR rated and your plane has to be IFR capable. This pilot was, but unfortunately the fog was just too much for him."

"Unfortunately, yes, it seemed to be." She paused. Sighed. "Such a terrible tragedy." One of the producers gave the signal to wrap things up. The newswoman looked at the camera. "I'm afraid that's all we have time for this evening." She glanced back to Kinsley. "Thank you so much for your time, Ms. Padovano, for helping us make sense out of the cockpit voice recording and for shedding some light on this tragic accident."

"Thank you for having me."

The newswoman turned to face the camera once again. "That's all for this special report on last month's small plane crash in Denver. We'll see you again for the news at ten."

"And we're out," said one of the producers. "Rachel, fabulous job as always, and, Ms. Padovano, you did great, thank you."

Kinsley rose from behind the desk and shook his hand. "My pleasure."

Rachel approached her next, hand outstretched. "Great job."

"Thanks."

They rounded the news desk and a young man handed Rachel an iPad, which she immediately began messing with.

"You handled that like an old pro," she said, smiling over at Kinsley.

"I do this a lot."

"It shows." She winked and walked off, young man talking in her ear. Kinsley rubbed her temple and stopped at the refreshment table for a bottled water. She eyed the food but decided against it, her growing headache too prominent. What she really needed was a damn Diet Coke. The caffeine, she knew from experience, would help her headache. As she grabbed her things and headed for the exit she tried to remember the last time she'd had any caffeine. Or even eaten for that matter.

She thought maybe it had been on that morning's flight in from Phoenix, but now she couldn't recall. That was how things were lately. Her mind too busy playing catch-up to her frantic lifestyle rather than focusing on silly everyday things like eating. And sleeping. And doing anything required for basic survival.

So how was she surviving?

I'm barely hanging on, that's how.

But she reminded herself that that's how she preferred things now. Working long hours, traveling most of the week, spending very little time at home in Phoenix. It was easier to stay distracted and avoid the reality of her life.

She inwardly cringed as she thought of her ex-girlfriend.

It had been six months since Gabby had ended things, and yet her harsh words sounded like they were being spoken right into her ear.

You're going to die alone. You'll be so busy nitpicking everyone

*else in your life about how they aren't good enough, that you'll end up
all alone. And that's the way you'll die. Alone.*

She rubbed her temple again and fumbled in her purse for some
Advil. The headache coming on was so bad she was ready to crush the
damn pills and snort them.

She laughed at herself, finding it funny that she was considering
snorting Advil. Could one even snort Advil? Why did anyone snort
anything? Didn't it sting? She shook her head, regretted it, and gave
up on her quest for the painkiller. She entered the newsroom lobby and
went to slip into her coat when she realized she was still wearing the
mic.

"Oh, my God." She sighed and turned to head back, but a young
intern was already chasing her down. The young woman smiled,
breathless as Kinsley removed the mic and handed it over.

"Thanks."

"What can I say? I'm a space cadet."

The intern laughed. "That's pretty funny considering you're an
aviation expert."

"Right? You'd think outer space would be in my wheelhouse."

The young woman laughed again and wished her a good evening
as she walked away. Coat on, Kinsley once again headed for the door.
She was pushing it open when her cell phone rang. She fumbled for it
in her purse as she crossed to step inside the elevator. But it, like the
Advil, was elusive. When she finally found it, she quickly answered.

"Hello?"

The call had ended.

She checked the number, didn't recognize it, and tossed it back
into her purse. It rang again almost immediately. She decided to let it
go to voice mail and exited the elevator and then the building, stepping
out into a chilly Denver evening. She tugged her coat closed and waved
at her driver, who was pulling up alongside the curb. The news station
had provided her with transportation to and from the station, and she
couldn't have been more grateful. The chill of the oncoming night was
already biting into her bones, and she cursed her pantyhose, wishing
they were warmer. She crawled into the car and debated removing her
heels.

"Back to the hotel?" the driver asked.

"No, I think I better get something to eat first. Any suggestions?"

"A ton. What are you in the mood for?"

"I don't know." She rubbed her temple again and thought of the silence and loneliness she'd find back at the hotel and said, "Surprise me." She dropped her hand from her temple and began to massage the silk fabric of her blouse. It was a habit she'd developed recently. Her own silent way to self-soothe. At the moment, however, it wasn't doing much good.

They pulled into traffic and her phone beeped with a text message. She checked it and her heart sank. It was her cousin Marty's wife, Diane.

"Oh, great." First the headache and now this. She had no idea what she could possibly want, but she knew it couldn't be good. Diane had never been a big fan of Kinsley's. Mainly because Kinsley had something in common with Marty that she didn't. A love of flying.

Kinsley returned the call and she answered on the third ring. Her voice was tight, like she'd been crying.

"It's Marty," she said by way of greeting.

"Marty? What is it? What's wrong?"

"His plane. Your plane. That stupid plane."

"What's wrong with the plane?" Why would Diane be calling her about the plane she and Marty co-owned?

"It crashed, that's what." She started to cry, and Kinsley struggled to breathe.

"What?" Her heart plunged to her feet, yet she could feel it pounding in her ears. "Is he—"

"He's alive. But he's hurt. Bad. You need to come home."

"I'll catch the first flight back to Phoenix."

"We're in Flagstaff. He was flying out of Flag."

"Okay."

"Hurry, Kinsley. The NTSB has questions about the plane, about Marty, things I can't answer. Questions that I have, too. Understand?"

She more than understood. She'd been consulted on dozens of crashes over the years. So, she knew the routine. Only now, she was going to be one of the ones under the microscope as the investigation into the accident got underway. That only added to the anxiety already flooding through her veins.

She closed her eyes. "I'm on my way."

She ended the call and spoke to the driver. "Forget dinner. Take me back to the hotel."

❖

The doors to the hospital whooshed open as Kinsley rushed inside and headed straight for the main desk. She waited anxiously, checking her aviator's watch for the time as the woman in line in front of her got the information she needed. When it was Kinsley's turn, she was still breathless, but now it was mainly from nerves.

"Can I help you?" the young woman with the volunteer name badge asked.

"Marty Miller."

The young woman typed on her keyboard and Kinsley eyed her watch again. Diane's call had come more than three hours ago.

"He's here," Kinsley said hurriedly. "At least that's what I was last told."

Come on, come on. I'm freaking dying here.

"Yes, just one moment." She typed some more. She looked up at Kinsley. "ICU. Follow the signs down the hall to your left."

"Thank you." Kinsley hurried off toward the hallway. She'd been out of the loop, without any information, on her two flights in from Denver. Diane had stopped answering her texts, and the local news wasn't as up-to-date as she would've liked.

She'd seen what little news footage there was on her phone while she was in the air. The plane had come down over the Coconino Forest, on the outskirts of Flagstaff, near I-17. She'd seen a plume of white smoke rising from beneath the trees, a black scar marking the earth, a trail leading up to the smoke. Emergency vehicles had been on scene.

That was all the information she had other than what Diane had provided, which was very little.

Now she was in Flagstaff and about to find out firsthand just how bad things were.

She felt sick.

Not just nervous sick, but terrified sick. Like this couldn't be reality kind of sick.

She'd only felt that way one other time in her life and she'd thought she'd never feel that way again. Had hoped she'd never feel that way again. It was, if she were being honest, the whole reason why she'd gone into aviation. To help prevent others from having to feel this way.

It was eerily quiet as she made her way down the hallway, following the signs to ICU. When she arrived, she checked in with a voice that was threatening to fail her. The nurse asked if she was family. She told her she was Marty's cousin and the nurse directed her back. Kinsley walked slowly, suddenly in no rush whatsoever. In fact, she wanted to run in the opposite direction. Flee the scene like a madwoman being chased by imaginary adversaries.

But she kept on, knowing she had to face what was before her.

She found the room number for Marty. Only it wasn't really a room. More like a section with a glass partition separating it from the center area. She could see right in, and her heart lodged in her throat. Marty was lying there with his eyes closed, his head wrapped, his face red and purple and swollen. A tube was taped to his mouth, feeding him air. The machine hissed as it breathed for him, his chest rising and falling in perfect rhythm.

She swallowed and winced from the pain. Her throat felt tight, almost too tight to breathe. It was like she could feel how Marty felt. It terrified her. She stood there for several minutes, silently watching him, wondering what the hell could've gone wrong. Wondering if it was something she could have prevented.

"Kinsley."

Kinsley turned and found Diane.

Her eyes were red-rimmed, her cheeks scarlet with emotion. She'd been crying. A lot.

"Hi."

She went to hug her, but Diane stood stiffly.

"You can't stay long. They only let one family member back at a time and they just let me back in. I told them I'd see you out."

They stared into Marty's room. Kinsley didn't say anything though she had a million questions. She was just too damn afraid to hear the answers. She brought her hand up and began to absently massage the cuff of her shirtsleeve.

"He has to have facial reconstruction and surgery on his leg," Diane said. Her voice was flat, completely void of emotion. "That's if he lives."

Kinsley drew in a shaky breath. The urge to flee came again, but she fought it, telling herself she could leave soon. That she had to leave soon. It was the rule.

Thank God for rules.

"They keep telling me he's a hero, though. That he somehow managed to put that plane down somewhere away from people. That he purposely went between those trees to shear the wings off so there'd be no big fire. He landed somewhere safe is what they keep saying. But it wasn't safe. Not for him. But that's Marty, isn't it? Always thinking of others. Even in his last—moment." She began to cry and Kinsley stepped to her, but she waved her away.

"Don't."

"Diane—"

"No. No, Kinsley. I don't want your comfort. I don't want your words of sympathy or whatever. What I want is my husband back. I want him back." She slammed her fist against her thigh and cried again.

"I'm—" Kinsley stopped herself from offering sympathy.

"You knew how I felt about this little venture of yours," she said, searing daggers into her with her eyes. "You and Marty buying these old planes and fixing them up. I don't care that you weren't doing it for profit, that it was just for fun. It was dangerous. I knew it was. Damn it, I said it was. But you and Marty wouldn't listen. And now look." She motioned toward Marty. "Look what happened, look where he is."

"We don't know what happened," Kinsley said softly, reaching, grasping for any sort of reason.

"It was engine failure, Kinsley," she snapped. "That's what happened."

"What? How do you—?"

"That's what they're saying. What Marty told air traffic control."

Kinsley's chest tightened like it was in a vise, and she leaned against the glass partition as she struggled to get control of herself. She tried desperately to recall recent conversations with Marty about the plane. What they were working on, what needed to be tested out. She couldn't concentrate, Diane's words and accusations stabbing her brain instead. Just like Gabby's had earlier.

Diane began to cry again, and Kinsley lifted a hand to touch her, but then dropped it, defeated.

"I'm sorry," she whispered. She remained a second longer and then walked away when she got no response. She wiped tears as she rounded the half circle of the ICU unit.

The nurse who checked her in was headed toward her. She saw Kinsley and spoke. "Leaving so soon?"

Kinsley hitched her thumb back toward Diane. "His wife is here now, so she said I had to leave. Only one family member at a time."

The nurse shook her head. "No, that's not right. You can stay. For as long as you want."

Kinsley's heart sank. Diane didn't want her there. So, she'd lied.

"I probably should get going anyway."

"Are you sure? Because I can go talk to her."

"I'm sure. But—can you tell me—is Marty going to be okay?"

"Hard to say. The next twenty-four hours will tell us a lot."

She gave her a soft smile and left her. Kinsley rested her hand on the counter, wishing like hell she could help her cousin. He was hurt and hurt badly. A damn machine breathing for him. His face and leg broken.

And worse, it could all be because of her. Because of something she and Marty didn't do right.

If that were true, how would she ever get past it? How would she ever be able to forgive herself?

The answer is simple.

I won't.

CHAPTER TWO

The late evening sun emerged from behind a smear of pewter clouds and shone through the changing leaves of the trees as Nev pulled off the highway to head farther into Cypress Creek Canyon. She slid on her sunglasses and adjusted the visor as she accelerated a little in her Nissan Titan, wanting to get back to the ranch in case the clouds decided to unleash a downpour. The truck sped along the dirt road, kicking up a mist of red dust as she worried about the three horses she'd left out in the corral. Rain wouldn't kill them, no. But these weren't average horses. They were rescues, and some of them didn't do too well in storms. People often teased her about helicopter parenting her horses because things like that concerned her, but she didn't care.

She gladly owned the title of helicopter parent and represented it well.

She was proving that by driving faster than she normally would in order to get back to check on them. She didn't usually approve of speeding, and truthfully, it made her anxious, regardless of who was in control or what sort of vehicle or craft she was in. It was just an accident waiting to happen was what she always said. So the fact that she was currently disobeying her own rule meant her worry meter was nearing off the chart levels.

And worrying was something else she didn't approve of and did her best to avoid doing. But it seemed to be just one of those days.

She turned up the volume on the stereo and tried to relax. George Strait was on and he usually did the trick, but "Amarillo by Morning" didn't last long enough to be effective. The news broke in with the local weather. Sixty percent chance of rain, off and on throughout the night and into tomorrow.

"Great."

Adrianna, her friend who ran Peace of Life, the nearby spiritual retreat, had wanted to bring her new clients by tomorrow for an introduction to the horses for their upcoming therapy sessions.

There was nothing like a little mud to welcome the newbies. From her experience, she figured there'd be at least one or two who were already uneasy around horses to begin with. So, some thick, sticky mud and sporadic rainfall would surely put them more at ease.

Her focus went back to the news as the latticework of shadows from the leaves played on the hood of the truck.

"The investigation into the small plane crash just outside of Flagstaff last week is still ongoing. The pilot remains in critical condition. The NTSB is—"

Nev switched off the radio and swallowed against the rising emotion in her throat. News like that still affected her, even after twenty years, but she convinced herself she was more concerned over her horses than anything else, and she chided herself for the needless worry.

Everything was going to be fine.

That was what she always told herself and, for the most part, it usually ended up being true.

She hoped today would be no different.

After all, Arthur was there at the ranch, so there was a chance he'd keep an eye on the horses. Deep down, though, she knew that was unlikely. Her friend and mentor hadn't been having one of his better days when she'd left him. Yet he'd insisted she take the trip into town for supplies.

"I don't need a babysitter, Nevaeh," he'd said. "I'm seventy-eight years old, not seven."

On one hand, she was glad she'd gone. They'd been in dire need of scrap metal for the blacksmithing business she now solely ran, but on the other hand, with his advancing Parkinson's disease, a bad day sometimes meant he could hardly function at all.

She shouldn't have left him. Not today. He was having one of those bad days, and his home care nurse could only hold him back so much, meaning he was probably out in the corral trying to bring in the horses.

Reluctantly, she pressed harder on the gas pedal and took one of the turns she'd taken for more than five years now. Only this time instead of an easy turn, she felt the tires on her truck slide over the dirt and gravel, causing the back end to fishtail before she righted herself.

She was busy looking in the rearview mirror to make sure everything in the bed was still secure before she happened to glance ahead again. And there, partially blocking the road, was another vehicle.

She slammed on her brakes and jerked the wheel to the left, thankfully missing the vehicle and its occupant by several feet.

She sat gripping the wheel, breathing hard, heart racing.

The occupant of the vehicle, a woman, climbed out and came to stand at the front of Nev's truck. Nev clenched her jaw. She was furious at the woman for parking like she had and just after a turn to boot, not giving another driver much of a chance to swerve to avoid her. Nev pushed open her door and shoved her cowboy hat on her head as she crossed to the stranger.

"Any reason why you decided *not* to pull all the way off the road?" Nev asked.

The woman, who was slight in build and considerably shorter than Nev's five-foot-nine frame, placed her hands on her hips and grimaced. Or at least Nev assumed it was a grimace. It was difficult to tell with her aviator sunglasses covering a good portion of her face.

"I didn't *decide* to do anything," the woman said. "My tire blew and this is where I ended up."

Nev sidestepped and took a look at the woman's small SUV crossover. She couldn't see the flat so she assumed it was on the front right.

"You could've pulled off the road a little more, don't you think?"

The woman cocked her head and Nev felt a rush of familiarity she couldn't explain.

"It literally just happened a few seconds before you came barreling around the bend. I didn't exactly have much time to examine where I was on the road, or to take into consideration that some lead-footed maniac would come racing around the corner at any moment. Is there some reason why you decided to go so fast you nearly lost control?"

Nev almost cracked a smile at her witty retort. But she rarely cracked a smile for anyone these days, and she wasn't about to start with this feisty stranger. Smiling, like laughing, seemed to hurt more than it helped lately. And both seemed to take more energy than she seemed to have.

When did smiling become such a chore?

"I'm in a bit of a hurry."

The woman crossed her arms over her chest. The wind whistled through the pines and blew the woman's shoulder length brown hair across her face. She hurriedly swiped at it and then seemed to try to arrange her bangs. "Well, do you think you could at least help me out a little before you go on your way? *Please?* I'm pretty sure it will take Triple A a lifetime to find me out here."

She wasn't wrong about Triple A. This was a private road leading to one of only two places. The ranch, where she lived and worked, or Adrianna's retreat. She was guessing the woman must be one of Adrianna's latest new age gurus. Even though she didn't mind working with guests of the retreat when it came to her horses, she rarely wanted anything to do with them outside of that. And at the moment, she really didn't want to take the time to start.

You can't change a tire?

Nev bypassed her to examine her SUV. She found the blown tire on the front right wedged against a large rock along with part of the frame.

"Seems I'm not the only one who lost control on that turn."

"I didn't lose control on that turn. The tire blew and I skidded off the shoulder into the rock."

"Uh-huh."

"Look, I don't have to explain myself to you. I don't owe you a damn thing."

Nev crossed back to her. She pulled off her hat and ran her hand through her hair before returning it to her head, "No, but you'd think you'd be a little nicer if you wanted my help."

The woman scoffed, shook her head, and whipped off her sunglasses. She burned Nev with a fiery stare from a pair of hazel blue eyes. Nev took a quick step backward.

What the hell?

No.

It can't be.

She got her bearings and cleared her throat.

"Kinsley?" Her voice sounded as rough as the gravel beneath her feet.

The woman shook her head again as if she hadn't heard her correctly. "What?"

"Is your name Kinsley?"

"Yes, how did you know that?"

Nev sank a hand in the back pocket of her jeans. She took a deep breath and eased off her own pair of sunglasses. Then she pulled off her hat.

Kinsley reacted instantly. Only she didn't back step. She nearly fell over.

Instinctively, Nev reached out to steady her.

She looked incredulous. "Nev Wakefield?" She backed away a step, finally able to stand on her own. "Oh, my God. It is. It's really you."

"'Fraid so."

"I don't understand. I—what are you doing here?" She took in their surroundings as if she'd just landed on a foreign planet and Nev was one its mysterious inhabitants.

"I was going to ask you the same question. But I'm pretty sure I already know the answer. You're headed to Peace of Life, aren't you?"

"Yes. Are you?"

"I live on the ranch next door. Adrianna, the owner of Peace of Life, is a longtime friend."

"Oh." She squinted back toward the sun. Nev noticed that her cheeks were flushed and her eyes puffy and red-rimmed. If she wasn't mistaken, she appeared to have been recently crying. And she wasn't exactly dressed like someone escaping to a spiritual retreat in the heart of the canyon. Most of Adrianna's guests came decked out in yoga pants or cargo shorts and hiking boots. Not pencil skirts and high heels. Something about her presence was totally off, but Nev couldn't place it.

She kicked absently at the ground with the point of her cowboy boot. Should she ask if she was okay? She'd just been in a small accident, was that why she was so upset? Nev sensed that maybe it was more than that. But she decided to leave it alone.

She wanted, however, to keep looking at Kinsley, totally captivated by the familiarity of her, but more than that, she wanted to study her beauty. Kinsley had grown into a very beautiful woman, and though she hadn't gotten much taller, she had a very prominent presence that left Nev intrigued if not somewhat intimidated.

"You aren't going to be at the retreat, then?" Kinsley asked.

"No."

She met her eyes again, and Nev could swear she saw a flicker of relief in them.

"Well, maybe we'll still get a chance to catch up some."

Is she being sincere or merely polite?

Considering she looked as uncomfortable as hell, Nev assumed it was the latter.

"Maybe." Nev wondered what all they would have to talk about should they actually get together. Seeing her again was alluring, but the pain of their past was already pushing through the surface of their friendly facade. Nev couldn't forget, regardless of how attractive Kinsley was, that had she not mentioned the volleyball camp to Viv, her sister would still be alive. It was something she thought of often, wondering what could have been. Something that had been engrained in her by her parents and extended family. To the Wakefields, Kinsley and her family might as well be dead. They wanted nothing to do with them, and Nev suspected Kinsley's family felt the same about hers. Her father had, after all, fired Nev's father soon after the accident when the families began to accuse and argue. The Wakefields had struggled financially for a good while after that.

Was Kinsley aware of that?

Was she aware of just how catastrophic the actions of her family had been?

It didn't matter. Nev wasn't about to tell her or discuss it with her. No, at the moment, Nev just wanted to get back to the ranch and see to Arthur and the horses. Rehashing old, painful wounds wasn't on her list.

"You got a spare?" Nev asked, gesturing back toward her vehicle.

"I should."

Nev waited at the back as Kinsley opened the hatch. Then Nev searched and found the lug wrench and the jack, but no spare. She dug around some more, removing Kinsley's luggage.

"Where's the donut?" Kinsley asked as she joined her.

"You tell me." Nev wiped her hands off on her jeans.

"I don't know."

Nev gave a sardonic laugh. "Of course not. It's only your car."

"It's a rental," Kinsley shot back. "So, no, I don't know where the donut is."

A rental? Does she not live in Arizona anymore?

Nev grabbed her luggage and started for her truck.

"What are you doing?"

Nev hoisted first one, then the other, into the extended cab. She closed the door and faced Kinsley.

"You got anything else?"

"I'm—riding with you?"

"Doesn't look like either of us has much of a choice."

Kinsley started to speak, but then seemed to change her mind. She hurried back to the SUV and retrieved her purse and keys.

Nev retrieved a couple of emergency flares she had and placed them back at the curve so any oncoming vehicle would slow and pull to the side and hopefully avoid Kinsley's vehicle. Then she climbed back into her truck, buckled her seat belt, and put the truck in drive, all without saying another word to Kinsley, who was now sitting next to her.

The woman whom she thought she'd never see again.

Chapter Three

Patsy Cline?" Kinsley asked, glancing over at Nev. They'd been riding in silence for a long while, Nev with an elbow resting on the door, hand massaging her brow. Her distress was obvious, but she kept the rest of her posture lax and even hummed along to the music every now and then. Her hand, however, never left her brow.

Kinsley was positive that Nev was just as thrown by their encounter as she was. In fact, Nev had almost been friendlier when she'd thought Kinsley was just another stupid tourist. Now, it seemed, she was tainted with an even darker label. She might as well have the bubonic plague the way Nev was leaning toward the door and all but ignoring her. It was becoming very clear that the disdain that had torn their families apart was still present as far as Nev was concerned. It was just as well, though. She now had other problems that she somehow had to wade through.

"You can change it if you want," Nev eventually said.

Kinsley rubbed the cuff of her shirt, her nerves getting the better of her. "That's okay. I quite like her actually. Though her music makes me sad. And it's sad what happened to her—" She caught herself and swallowed the lump in her throat. She'd just gone where neither of them should go, and her thoughts immediately went to her cousin and what had happened days before. She felt sick and wondered if Nev felt similarly when thinking about Viv. "Sorry."

Nev dropped her hand and straightened. "No need." She reached out and killed the radio.

The ensuing silence was maddening.

So much for my attempt at small talk.

Just as well, I was struggling to even do that.

She couldn't get her mind off Marty and the crash. Nearly every waking second, she was going over and over the process they'd gone through with the plane. The research, the purchase, the repairs. What had they missed? What would the NTSB find? God knows they were certainly looking hard enough. She'd helped as much as she could, turning over documents and answering questions. That is until the stress had nearly eaten her alive and she was pretty much good for nothing as far as recalling details and forming rational thought. Her mind was now toast, her heart completely broken.

She hoped coming up to Cypress Creek Canyon would help ease some of those qualms.

Kinsley tried to push it from her mind and focus on the breathtaking scenery around her. Golden sunlight illuminated the fall colors of the oaks and the junipers and the cypress. The trees blew in the breeze and made for a beautiful backdrop against the red rock walls of the canyon. They rounded another bend, and Kinsley inhaled at the sight of the sparkling creek snaking through the canyon on her left.

"God, this place is beautiful," she let out.

Nev seemed surprised.

"Have you never been to Cypress Creek Canyon?"

"No."

Nev didn't respond. Kinsley couldn't bear the silence.

"So, you live up here, then?" she asked.

"For a few years now."

"You like it?"

Nev looked at her. "I wouldn't live anywhere else. Not if you paid me."

Kinsley smiled and refocused on the view. "I can see why."

"You're next to the retreat, then?"

"You mean resort?" She raised her eyebrows. "Sorry, bad joke. Adrianna likes to call it a retreat, but really, to me anyway, it's a resort. And yes, I'm next to it, though not exactly right next door so to speak. I'm about a ten-minute drive to the west. More forest, less canyon."

"Oh. And you have a ranch?"

"A small ranch, yes. My friend and I run our business from there."

Kinsley waited for her to explain. She didn't. She wondered if by friend she meant partner.

"You aren't going to tell me what you do?" She cocked her head at her.

Nev wrung her hand on the steering wheel after she took a quick glance at her.

"We, uh, have a blacksmithing business and I also run a small horse rescue."

"That all sounds really interesting." Kinsley turned to face her and studied her closely. Nev seemed to redden under her stare. Kinsley's heart sped up as she recognized her blush as nervousness and recalled times long ago. Nev might have grown up and changed, but the eleven-year-old girl who grew uneasy with personal questions was still there. Her hair was just shorter and her body…longer and…

She turned away, upset at herself for going anywhere near assessing her attractiveness. Nev was way off-limits for several reasons. For one, there was the family animosity that they obviously both still felt. Nev seemed about ready to jump from the vehicle in order to escape, and Kinsley's own feelings on the past were threatening to surface as well. Did Nev know how badly it had hurt when her parents had told Kinsley to stay away? When they pretty much told Kinsley and her family to fuck off? And that's *after* they did the unthinkable and blamed them for Viv's death. Did Nev have any clue whatsoever just how badly her folks had handled the whole thing? If she did, she didn't seem to be objecting to their behavior. If anything, she seemed to be agreeing with it.

Kinsley shifted in her seat, ready to jump from the truck herself. She stole another quick glance at Nev and assessed the other reason why Nev was off-limits. She didn't even know for sure if she was a lesbian. There had been hints of it when they were kids, but lots of young tomboys turned out to be straight. Kinsley noted Nev's closely cropped sun-streaked hair, her muscular build, her dirty jeans, cowboy boots, and T-shirt. The way her jaw flexed when she seemed to be thinking about something. She was gorgeous, and if she wasn't gay, then Kinsley definitely needed to get out more. Because Nev Wakefield appeared to be one hot butch.

Nev slowed the truck as they came to an elaborate wrought iron sign that said Peace of Life.

"Here we are," Nev said as she turned into a circular drive and headed toward a beautiful tan stucco building with large floor to ceiling windows. Numerous bungalows with matching stucco stretched out to the left of the main building, all of them nestled into the backdrop of trees and canyon.

Kinsley leaned forward. "Wow, it's right on the creek."

Nev laughed. "You really are clueless, aren't you?"

Kinsley pressed her lips together. "I'm just surprised is all. I didn't really look into this place much before I made the reservation."

"Why not? Why stay somewhere you haven't checked out? That seems sort of ludicrous, don't you think? Especially for the money you had to cough up to stay at this place?"

Nev put the truck in park and turned off the engine.

"I was in a hurry and—I just needed to get away, okay?" She wasn't about to explain, and even if the reason why hadn't been so traumatic, she wouldn't have shared anything further with Nev. She was seriously rubbing her the wrong way.

Nev removed her sunglasses and studied her. "Okay."

Kinsley couldn't stand to be under her stare, her eyes too alive and mesmerizing. And at the moment, seeking. She released her seat belt and crawled from the truck.

"Don't worry about my bags, I can get them." But Nev was already out and pulling them from the cab.

Kinsley hurried to her and grabbed the luggage. "I got it, thank you."

"It's no problem," Nev said. "I don't mind helping."

"I don't need help," Kinsley said quickly. "But thank you."

"Okay," Nev said again. She held up her hands. "I'll leave you be." She didn't leave, however. Instead, she put her cowboy hat back on and closed her door like she was planning on staying a while.

"Thank you for, you know, everything," Kinsley said, hinting to her that she was fine and could, indeed, go.

Nev only looked at her.

"Well, Nevaeh, what a nice surprise," a woman said, coming out the glass doors. She crossed to them with open arms and enveloped Nev in a long hug. "Mm, I love me some Nevaeh hugs." She drew back. "So strong." She touched Nev's arms and grinned at Kinsley. "Don't you think? Have you ever seen a more beautiful specimen of a strong female?"

Kinsley stammered. "Sure, uh—no. I mean, yes, she's—strong."

"It's all that work she does with metal. Bending it and pounding it until she gets her way." She winked and came to Kinsley. "And you must be Ms. Padovano."

"Kinsley." She stuck out her hand.

"Adrianna," she said, swooping her long white braid away from her shoulder to take Kinsley's hand in both of hers. "Welcome, friend, welcome."

"Thank you."

"Did you have a nice ride in?"

"She had some trouble around Dead Man's bend," Nev said. "You need to call Bradley and have him come get her car."

"Oh, no," Adrianna said, looking to Kinsley. She touched her shoulders. "Are you all right?"

"I'm fine. Just had a tire blow on me."

"More than a blown tire. Her frame is jacked. She hit a boulder," Nev said.

Kinsley eyed her. "Thank you, Nev. I'm pretty sure I got it from here."

Nev seemed to ignore her, speaking to Adrianna. "Let Bradley know he needs the tow truck. It's far from just a flat."

Adrianna nodded.

Nev tipped her hat at them. "Have a good night, ladies."

Adrianna smiled. "See you soon, love."

Nev climbed in her truck and drove away, leaving Kinsley alone with Adrianna, who led her past a magnificent fountain and into the tall, glass-fronted building.

Kinsley warmed instantly at the roaring fire burning in the large stone hearth in the corner. Wind chimes sounded in the distance as the logs crackled in the fire, putting Kinsley at ease immediately. She stilled, closed her eyes, and inhaled the scent of eucalyptus as Adrianna rounded the polished wood counter to gather Kinsley's keys and paperwork.

"I see you met Nevaeh," she said, causing Kinsley to open her eyes.

"Yes."

She spread some papers out for Kinsley to sign and handed her a pen.

"She's a good apple," Adrianna said, twisting one of her numerous turquoise rings. "Invaluable around here."

Kinsley glanced up at her. "She...is? I didn't think she'd be around here much."

Adrianna raised her brow. "She pops in from time to time to fix things. That won't be a problem for you, will it?"

Kinsley shook her head, surprised she'd picked up on her discomfort. "No, I—"

"Most of my guests are rather curious about her and some even... interested. Never had anyone who had a problem with her before."

"I don't—I—"

"Is it because she's gay?"

"What? No. Of course not."

"Because if it is, then you might as well tuck your tail and get right on out of here."

"I'm gay," Kinsley said with a small smile. She was a bit amused at Adrianna's protectiveness. Nev obviously meant a lot to her.

She closed her mouth. "Oh."

"And I don't have a problem with her being around. I just…I know her."

"Ooh." Her eyes widened.

Kinsley hurried to explain. "We…we were childhood friends."

"Oh, well that's nice." She beamed. "How wonderful. You get to reconnect."

"It's not exactly like that." She sighed and pushed the completed paperwork to her. "We aren't exactly on the best of terms."

Her smile faltered. "I see."

"But it won't be a problem. I'm pretty sure we'll mostly avoid each other."

This time it was Adrianna who gave her a small smile. "Not so sure you'll be able to do that as much as you think." She put away the paperwork, handed Kinsley a folder full of information and a keycard. She then led the way to the back door with Kinsley's luggage in tow.

"Why?" Kinsley asked, hurrying after her. "Because she will need to fix things?"

They emerged onto a vast patio that led down to a stone path illuminated by soft, solar lights. The sound of the creek water was considerable and even more soothing than the crackling fire and wind chimes. Kinsley could smell the earthy water, and the air coming off it was cool and crisp. The sky was now painted scarlet and pink as the sun slowly sank behind the walls of the canyon. The whole scene was breathtaking but subtle. So moving in its simplicity. So very different from cement and sidewalks and airplanes and engines and simulations and explanations.

"Nevaeh runs the horse therapy group," Adrianna said, leading them off to the right of the main building where more bungalows were nestled back into the canyon. "So, you'll be seeing her a good bit if you plan on following your itinerary." They bypassed hidden bungalow after bungalow and eventually came upon some on the other side of the creek. They crossed a small wooden bridge and Kinsley's excitement grew. She was thrilled she was in one of the more secluded buildings. A little extra solitude would help even out the dread she felt in realizing she would be dealing with Nev more than she'd hoped.

She looked back to the pink sky.

Nev and horses.

Not exactly my two favorite things.

"I'm actually a little afraid of horses," she said as they turned toward the bungalow on the far end and walked up to the front patio adorned with decorative Mexican pottery. A motion sensing light came on when they neared the door.

"A lot of my guests are," she said as if she'd heard it all before. "But Nev will put you at ease. She's wonderful. Helped every one of my guests so far."

Kinsley bit her lower lip. "Yeah, I don't know."

"At least come with the rest of the group and give it a try. See how you like it. You never know," she said, raising her eyebrows playfully. "They just might grow on you."

Who? Nev or the horses?

Kinsley didn't dare ask. She could tell by the glint in her eyes what she meant. And she wasn't just speaking of the horses.

"This cabin is you, dear," she said, unlocking the door. She pushed it open and allowed Kinsley entry first and then followed. "You've got everything you need," she said, moving about. "Fresh towels and linens are in the closet, there's more wood for the stoves on the back patio. We do have Wi-Fi, though most guests prefer to unplug while they are here. I recommend it. You've got a full kitchen with some complimentary snacks and drinks in the fridge to get you started, and the Jacuzzi on the back patio heats up quickly should you want to use it. Breakfast is at seven, and we have our first group session at eight. From there you will follow your own personalized itinerary, which you will find in your folder." She placed a warm hand on her shoulder. "Think you'll be all right?"

"I'll be fine." But her voice didn't hold much conviction. Adrianna was looking at her with such kindness and sincerity, it had caught her off guard.

"You sounded so distraught over the phone."

"I'm—I'll be okay."

She smiled warmly at her, and it reached her deep brown eyes.

"I don't know what you've got going on, Kinsley. But you can find the peace you seek here. You just have to be sure you're ready to let it in when you do." She headed for the door.

"Enjoy your evening and I'll see you in the morning."

"Thank you, you too."

Adrianna left, closing the door behind her. Kinsley stood looking at the log-cabin-like interior of her new temporary home. The wood beamed walls were light with rich, colorful artwork. The floors matched the walls, only they were accented with handwoven rugs. The living room was cozy and decorated in warm reds and browns. The dark leather sofa and matching chair sat close to the wood burning stove.

The bedroom was decorated similarly and also had a wood burning stove. The bed was large and framed by a hand carved headboard. An impressive painting of an elk standing creekside at dawn was above it.

It would be easy to relax here, and she could already imagine herself curled up in her cabin for days, doing nothing but reading and sipping hot cocoa. She closed her eyes and listened to the rushing creek.

This place is amazing. Please let it help.

Chapter Four

Nev wiped the sweat from her brow and sang along with Ray Charles as she stood at the forge in her long leather apron, steel toed work boots, and jeans. She was waiting for a half-inch stick of metal to heat up in the orange coals, but the fire wasn't hot enough for her liking. She increased the air flow from down below, and soon the tip of her stick began to glow and she slid it in a little farther, ensuring the first four inches would get the heat she wanted. When she was satisfied, she moved the piece over to the anvil with her tongs where she began establishing the tip of the blade by hammering out a four-sided point.

She worked quickly, wanting to beat the heat of the metal before it cooled. When it did, she brushed the hot scraps off the anvil and returned to the fire where there was another short bout of heating and singing along to Ray Charles. Then she came back to the anvil, hammered her piece some more, turned it ninety degrees, and pounded again. And then back to the fire she went, heating and singing, before returning once again to the anvil. It was a routine she knew well. A routine that assured peace from the stresses of life outside the shop. Like Kinsley Padovano, for instance.

Her unexpected reappearance had done more than knock Nev for a loop. It had kept her up at night, to the point where she was beyond tossing and turning, and instead was up pacing the halls, thinking about the past and all that had transpired. How could she just reappear? And act like everything was fine?

The endless questions Nev had played on her nerves, and she'd all but given up on any restful sleep. So, it was off to the shop she went, beginning at dawn and working for as long as she possibly could, needing to keep her mind and hands occupied. Luckily for her, the work was lined up and she was even a little behind.

She eased up on the strength of her blows to start flattening the end of the blade just as Ray Charles gave way to Otis Redding, and she was just about to join in and sing with him when she heard someone come in behind her. She returned to the fire without needing to see who it was. The familiar humming she heard made her smile. She walked back to the anvil and found Arthur waiting, holding her cross pein hammer in his left hand, already knowing it was what she needed next. He handed it to her and continued to hum as she set to work enhancing the blade with the smaller hammer.

"Another letter opener," he eventually said. He stood watching her in his hunched posture, right hand shaking uncontrollably. She could tell by the eager look in his eyes that he wanted to grab hold of her hammer and do the work himself. It was very difficult for him to have to stand by and watch, which, she assumed, was why he'd stopped coming into the shop so much.

"Yep."

"You're going to have to be careful what you give Adrianna," he said softly, pausing to get some of the words out. "Her guests go crazy for your fancy stuff. Next thing you know, you've got a million orders for letter openers."

"Not quite a million. Not yet." She looked up at him through her protective eyeglasses and smiled. "Only seven."

"Give it time. Soon it'll be more than you can handle."

It's already getting there.

"That would be great." She refocused on the blade. "You know I love doing the more creative work."

She heard him scoff.

"I do know. You're getting all—artsy-fartsy on me."

She laughed. Arthur was not fond of her newfound interest in creating the more artistic pieces. Even if he did like some of the things she made. He was old-fashioned in nearly everything he did, and he preferred smithing things that people needed. Things that helped people through life and lasted for life.

"I still get the important stuff done," she said, referring to the jobs he considered important. The ones that paid the bills. Though if he knew how much she was getting for some of her creative pieces, letter openers included, he might just reconsider his negative attitude. And if he knew she was using a lot of it to help with his care and to keep things running smoothly, well…some things she knew were better kept to herself. "You don't have to worry."

"I'm not. I just…"

She glanced up at him and swept away the hot scraps so they wouldn't melt into the anvil. "Miss it."

He swallowed and didn't bother answering. She could tell by the tears welling in his eyes just how deep his longing was. She crossed back to the fire and took her time with the heat, giving him some time to recover. He'd had to give up smithing months before due to his progressing Parkinson's. Ten years after his diagnosis, his body was finally turning on him in ways he could no longer ignore. Now he could no longer hold a steady hammer or hold much of anything steady, for that matter. And that was what was killing him. Not necessarily the disease, which was indeed affecting him, but the fact that he could no longer do the things he loved to do. In particular, smithing.

His hand was still trembling when she returned to the anvil. He was hastily trying to wipe his eyes with it. She continued to work and waited patiently for him to guide her on spreading and developing the curve of the letter opener. But he remained a few feet away and watched quietly.

Adrianna had asked if his hovering bothered her a couple of weeks before and she'd readily told her no. She loved having him in the shop. Missed having him in the shop. He'd been her mentor and he'd taught her everything she knew. His absence there was notable and the real reason why she kept playing the music. Arthur was a huge blues buff and he'd always had it playing when they worked. Smithing without the blues would be to her like swimming without the water. You wouldn't get very far, and neither did she without his presence. So, she'd remedied that by playing his music, and when he did come around, he seemed pleased to hear it and seemed to feel more at ease. Maybe the music was helping to lure him in. She hoped so. She really loved having him around.

"You wanna do the basket weave on the handle?" she asked as she finished up the blade.

His eyes brightened.

"All you have to do is twist."

He started to come to her, but then stopped short, a look of doubt on his face.

"Come on," she said. "You can do it."

She heated a cluster of one-eighth-inch steel pieces and secured them in the leg vise. Then she held out the wrench for Arthur and gave him a wink. "Come on."

He hurried to her, took the wrench, tried to grab hold of the cluster, but he had trouble. Nev gently took the tool and secured it for him, then carefully led his trembling hand to the handle. There they gripped together and gave the metal pieces a good, slow, cable twist.

"Perfect." She took the piece to the fire and came back to the vise. They repeated the procedure, only this time twisting in the opposite direction.

"Beautiful," she said when they finished. "Told you you could do it." Arthur smiled shyly and it tugged at her heart. This once strong, confident, tough as nails, but gentle as a lamb man had withered down to mere skin and bones and now stood looking at her like a boy who'd just helped his father with something for the first time. What had happened?

And why?

Why Arthur?

She didn't understand the reasoning behind things sometimes and didn't like to accept that maybe there just really was none to begin with. That maybe everything was just random, a roll of the dice. None of it sat right with her, but trying to find the answers to such questions almost made her as crazy and pissed off as the events that made her question things to begin with. She couldn't win. That was why she didn't allow herself to think about it much anymore. That kind of thinking only led to trouble, and she was more often than not left swimming in a sea of painful questions with no answers in sight. And she'd grown tired of drowning.

There was one thing she was certain of, though. She hated death and refused to accept that it just happened and happened to everyone. That was unacceptable, and it wasn't going to happen to Arthur. Not anytime soon. Not if she could help it. She'd keep researching for the latest medications and treatments. She'd keep making sure he did his therapy and exercises. Together they'd stop the progression. She knew they could.

She waved Arthur back over and had him help her as she MIG welded the decorative ball to the basket weave handle and then the handle to the blade. He seemed pleased with her work, and she turned to put the final touches on it with the wire brush. She was just about finished with the final polish when she heard it.

A clang and then curses.

She turned as Arthur fell to the floor, grabbing his foot.

"Arthur!"

She hurried to him, kicked the hammer next to him out of the way, and knelt to check on him. He was wincing and cursing, clinging to his foot.

"What happened?" She tried to ease his hands away as he rocked in obvious pain. "The hammer fell on your foot?"

"Dro-dropped it."

"Okay," she said softly. "Let me see." She carefully untied his sneaker, wishing he'd been wearing his work boots while in the shop. The sneakers, though, were easier for him to get around in, and since he no longer worked in the shop, he usually wore those. That, however, was something they'd need to talk about. Maybe he could keep his boots by the shop door and she could help him change into them when he came in.

Maybe. If he'd go for that. He hated to be any trouble.

She carefully removed his shoe and sock. She didn't have to ask him where the hammer hit. She could see the red mark on the top of his arch. She hoped like hell he hadn't fractured anything, but she didn't voice her concern. She didn't chide him for handling the hammers either. He knew better than to pick up anything bigger than the cross pein hammers and had been purposely avoiding doing so due to his instability. Why he'd chosen to pick one up today was unknown.

"I was put-ting it away—for you," he said. He was upset on top of the pain. His speech was often affected when he got upset.

"I appreciate that," she said. "I know you were just trying to help."

She gently touched the red mark. He whimpered.

"Okay, big guy." She helped him stand. "I think we better get this checked out."

He started shaking his head. "I'm fine."

He hated going to the doctor, hated hospitals. Hated anything medical. She couldn't blame him at this point.

"We'll let Louise decide."

"There you are," a woman's voice said from the doorway. Arthur's nurse, Louise, hurried toward them as if she'd heard her name. Her purple scrubs swished as she moved, and the closer she came, the more alarmed she looked. "What happened here?" she asked, her voice growing high in pitch.

"It was an accident," Nev said, giving her a look, letting her know she wasn't going to elaborate in front of Arthur. Louise, who didn't tend to mince words, shook her head and directed her words to Arthur.

"Where did you get to? I was making us lunch and turned around with your tuna salad and you were gone."

"Lunch?" Arthur said. He looked confused. "I already ate. Didn't I?"

Louise took his arm and tucked it protectively in hers. "No, no you didn't, Mr. Sneaky. Come on, let's go back inside and eat. You've got to be hungry. You didn't finish your breakfast."

"Yes, I did. I had corn flakes."

He suddenly pulled away from her. "I don't—need your help—Louise. I can walk myself."

"Okay, honey. You go right on ahead."

Louise came back to Nev and they watched him slowly make his way to the door, one shoe on, one shoe off.

"He dropped a hammer on his foot. You'll need to check it."

Louise tsked. "He's getting worse. He shouldn't be in here."

"I'll keep a better eye on him."

"You didn't today. And he got a hammer."

"He knows he's not supposed to handle the big ones. I don't understand."

"Nev, honey." She crossed her arms over her ample chest. "It's his dementia. He forgot he wasn't supposed to handle the hammers. I bet you anything."

"I think he was just trying to help."

"Well, good intentions or not, he got hurt. We both need to do better."

Nev sighed. "Yeah. You're right."

"He needs to stay out of here."

"No, I can't do that to him, not yet."

"Okay. But don't say I didn't warn you."

"Just please. Check his foot." She checked her watch. "I've got a therapy class in fifteen minutes. I need to get ready."

They both headed for the door behind Arthur.

Louise picked up her step and hurried to him to help him walk. "Don't forget, you need to eat too," she called back to her.

Nev waved her off and handled it the way she'd been handling everything lately.

"Later. I'll think about later."

CHAPTER FIVE

K insley stepped out of the passenger van and snuggled deeper into her hoodie. The sky was overcast with a shy sun peeking out every once in a while to shed some warmth. But mostly it stayed hidden and left her and the others exposed to the chill of the sporadic sprinkling rain. Kinsley had assumed that the grim weather would've been enough to cancel today's meeting with Nev and her horses. But Adrianna had persevered with a comment about a little rain never hurting anyone and off they'd gone with the Ramblin' Blues Ranch their destination. Now they were here and Kinsley's nerves gave way to awe. The ranch was open and vast with endless green fields, two large barns flanking a ranch-style house, and stables across from that. Thick forest surrounded the property, and the distant canyon beyond took her breath away as the red rocks contrasted with the changing leaves of the trees. The place was surreal. She understood at once why Nev was so content living there.

She inhaled the fresh air, caught the scent of horses, and followed Adrianna and the small group toward the stables and corral. Her pulse accelerated a little as she thought about interacting with the horses and with Nev Wakefield. Neither sounded very appealing at the moment, but she'd promised Adrianna she'd come along and at least check things out. The four others in her group seemed to be very excited, leaving her feeling like a bit of an outsider. Horses were not her forte. But then again, neither was Nev. And yet she was here.

To face her fear.

That's what Adrianna and her other spirit counselor, Holly, had said. So far, however, she wasn't liking it, despite their praise and encouragement. And as she got closer to the stables and caught sight of a couple of horses in the pen, everything rushed back at her and she realized she didn't really give a damn whether this was an opportunity for growth or not. She wanted to sprint back to the van and go back to the resort and sit by the creek with a good book and try not to think about horses and Nev, and airplanes and crashes, and friends in the hospital, and whose fault was what. New opportunities and facing her issues be damned. She wasn't up for it.

But then an androgynous, muscular cowgirl walked out of the stables, and her racing pulse dead stopped. She tugged off her sunglasses and blinked as the cowgirl glanced over at the approaching group and gave a nod.

It was Nev.

And boy, was she beautiful.

"Kinsley, you coming?" Adrianna had turned and was waving her over. Perhaps she sensed Kinsley's hesitance. Or perhaps she sensed her sudden heart attack at the sight of Nev. Whatever the reason, she now had her arm around her and was walking with her to the pen.

"You doing all right?" she asked, giving her a little squeeze.

"I'll be fine." Would she? Or would her heart keep racing and slamming to a stop, leaving her feeling woozy and light-headed?

Nev was leading a horse into the pen, and Kinsley found looking at the both of them to be difficult. They were both so strong and sinewy and beautiful, yet dangerous for her to get too close to. She'd never been afraid of something beautiful and alluring before. And now she was faced with not one, but two things.

"Don't you worry," Adrianna said. "Nev knows these horses like the back of her hand. She's the best I've ever seen. She'll take real good care of you."

That's what I'm afraid of.

They reached the pen and leaned on the railing, all of them watching Nev closely as she brought over a large red horse.

"Welcome to Ramblin' Blues Ranch," she said, tipping her cowboy hat. "I'm Nev and I, along with my good friend Deena…" She glanced around as if looking for her. "Who doesn't seem to be around at the moment, run this therapy group."

Just then another woman walked out of the stables leading a white horse. She was dressed similarly to Nev in jeans, boots, and cowboy hat, but she was shorter and slighter in build. She smiled at the group as she approached.

"Here's my MIA," Nev said. "This is Deena. She's my right hand around here. If you ever need anything or have a question, she's the one you want."

"Hi," Deena said.

The group voiced their hellos as Nev continued.

"We're a rescue ranch funded solely by donations, and our volunteers are the ones who help keep us up and running. So you'll also see a few of them around from time to time. Feel free to say hello and to ask them for help if needed. They've been with us for years and know the ins and outs of the ranch too."

"Almost better than us," Deena said with a laugh.

Nev cracked a smile at her. "True."

They continued, but Kinsley found herself focused on the body language of Nev and Deena. They were very relaxed with each other, completely at ease. And the way they interacted and joked suggested a long-standing relationship. Just what kind of relationship had Kinsley curious. Based on the grin Deena had easily elicited from Nev, Kinsley wondered briefly if Deena could be Nev's girlfriend, or maybe a casual lover. A friends with benefits type deal. The thought bothered her, and she began to scrutinize Deena's appearance, searching for clues about her sexuality. But Deena looked to be an average woman, with long blond hair and pretty brown eyes that almost matched the color of Nev's horse. Sort of an amber.

The group laughed, bringing Kinsley back to the conversation. Nev patted her horse.

"This here is Willow. She's just one of the horses you'll get to work with while you're here. Currently, we have eight. You'll get to work with six of them. The other two aren't quite ready yet."

"All of your horses are rescues?" one of the women asked. Her name was Stephanie, and Kinsley had met her earlier at their morning yoga session. She was a young mother of four from San Jose, who, according to her, had desperately needed to get away.

"Every last one," Nev said.

"But then how do you know they'll be able to work with people? I mean, if they've been hurt or abused?" a man named Matthew asked. Kinsley had yet to talk personally to him, but he seemed to be a very inquisitive man, having grilled Adrianna with questions about the retreat the entire ride over.

"For exactly that reason. We've all been hurt at some point and these horses are no different. They need therapy just like humans do.

They need to work with us just as much as we need to work with them. Therefore, we help to heal each other."

"But—"

Nev held up her hand. "Deena and I work with all of these horses one-on-one for weeks before we decide who's ready to work with people and who isn't. And those that are, are only allowed to do certain things based on their personalities and needs. Willow here, she can do it all. But a couple of the others still have limits."

Matthew nodded like he understood. Nev continued.

"So, you see every horse is an individual and you'll get to know their personalities and their preferences. I try to match you up with the horse I think you'll do best with at first, and then as you and the horses get more comfortable, we'll change things up a bit."

"What about her? Do we get to work with her?" one of the other women whispered to her friend as they stood next to Kinsley. "She's the best looking cowboy I think I've ever seen."

Her friend laughed and whispered back. "You're into women now?"

"I'm into her."

They both laughed and Nev welcomed them into the pen to meet the horses. Kinsley remained where she was, allowing the others to go first. There would be plenty of time for her to meet the horses after the others had spent some time with them. At least, that's what she was telling herself. It sounded like it could be true so she was going with it.

She stood leaning on the rail, watching as Deena introduced the group to Baby, the horse she had. She encouraged them to pet her, one at a time, showing them how and explaining a little about equine behavior and ground manners. Nev had walked off a ways with Adrianna, and Kinsley suspected they were discussing her based on the concerned look Adrianna gave her, but she did her best to ignore it. Willow the horse however, wouldn't allow her to totally zone out. She edged closer to her and snorted. Kinsley backed away, able to feel her breath on her skin. She had come a little too close for comfort.

"Whoa, manners," Kinsley said.

Willow just looked at her. Then she came even closer, stuck her head over the railing, and snorted again.

Kinsley backed up some more and wiped her cheek. She wasn't sure if it was rain or specks of snot from Willow's snort, but both had her rubbing her face furiously. More rain sprinkled down on them as if to mock her. Willow, too, seemed to be giving her a look of contempt.

"I thought you were one of the polite ones," she said as she gave up with the face cleaning.

"She is," Nev said, walking up to pat Willow on her neck. "She's almost bombproof."

"Bombproof?" What in the world did that mean? And where had Nev come from? Kinsley hadn't even seen her walk over.

"Means she's calm. Wouldn't startle if a bomb went off."

"Oh."

"You don't know anything about horses, do you?"

I know I don't want to get near one. Does that count?

"Not a thing. Guess that's just something else I'm totally clueless about." She emphasized the word *clueless*, making sure Nev knew she was repeating the word she'd chosen to describe her.

Nev continued to pet Willow, her face giving away nothing. If she'd picked up on the reference, she didn't seem to care.

"Willow's a two on the temperament scale. One being bombproof. Ten being hot-blooded. So you can relax, come closer if you'd like."

Kinsley remained where she was, a couple of feet away.

"I'm good."

"Ah, you're not so bombproof," Nev said.

Kinsley wasn't sure why, but she took offense to the statement. It ranked right up there with clueless. "I'm fine."

"I'm thinking maybe a seven. Possibly an eight if you're startled."

Kinsley cocked her head. "Right, because you know me so well."

"I know what I see."

Kinsley glanced down. She'd unknowingly backed away some more. She quickly took a few steps forward. "I—" She stopped.

Nev wasn't paying attention. She was busy stroking Willow's neck and speaking softly to her, and for a moment, Kinsley got lost studying the strength of her arms as they glistened with movement under the sprinkling rain. It was cold and wet out and yet Nev was clad only in a dark T-shirt and jeans. Even Deena had on a jacket.

"She only wants to say hello," Nev said, looking back to her. "She doesn't just walk up to anyone, you know. She likes you. Senses something about you. That's all. She's no threat."

Kinsley took another step. She was torn between coming toward Willow and coming toward Nev. She didn't really want to interact with either, but she was tempted and somewhat dared to say hello to Willow. Which left her half wishing Nev would go and leave them be, but then again she was also afraid for her to leave. She wasn't ready to be alone with Willow. She wasn't ready to be alone with Nev, either. God, it was too early in her reprieve to be this confused and distressed.

"Come on," Nev said. "Come say hello."

Her tone had softened and the way in which she was stroking Willow seemed to lull and calm Kinsley as well. She came closer and approached the rails. She stood eye to eye with Willow and stared into her large, dark brown eyes. They were so dark and deep they appeared to be almost liquid.

"There you go," Nev whispered. To whom, Kinsley didn't know. Perhaps she was calming and soothing them both. Whatever. It was working.

"Go ahead," she said. "You can touch her."

Kinsley reached up and paused. She closed her eyes as she recalled being thrown from a horse when she was a small child. She remembered the jolt, the flailing, the screams of her mother. The whinny of the horse before she heard it thunder away after she'd slammed to the ground.

She hesitated and felt her hand shake. And then, just as she was about to lower it, she felt another hand on hers. She opened her eyes. Nev had taken hold of her hand. Kinsley swallowed at the warm, wet feel of her palm. At the gentle strength she could feel harbored in her grip.

"It's okay," Nev said. "I got you."

Kinsley looked into the light green eyes that used to mesmerize her as a kid. So full of life and joy and mischief. The color remained the same, but their depths told a different tale now. The life was still there, but the joy and the playful mischief were gone. Now she could only see a calm sort of sadness. A soft melancholy that spoke of great loss and endless seeking.

"It's okay," Nev said again. Kinsley pulled herself from her heavy gaze and looked back to Willow. The soft rain made a ticking noise as it fell upon Nev's hat. Silver droplets plopped and then ran down Willow's coat. Somewhere beyond them Kinsley heard the others laugh. She closed her eyes again and focused on the rain, on the sound of it, the cool feel of it on her face and the way it smelled as it dampened the grass and earth around them.

"Doesn't the rain bother them?" Kinsley asked.

"Light rain doesn't hurt anyone. Thunder and lightning, however, they can be sensitive to. So if there is a chance of that, the horses remain indoors."

Kinsley reached farther then, her hand in Nev's, and allowed Nev to lead her to Willow's snout. Kinsley shuddered as she felt her. Firm and velvety. She opened her eyes and remembered to breathe.

"Good," Nev said. She stepped closer and helped her stroke Willow, who also remembered to breathe, snorting once again. Kinsley laughed nervously and her hand shook again, but Nev was quick to reassure her. "You're doing great."

"I'm scared to death," Kinsley managed.

"I know," she said. "I remember your fear. But that's the great thing about working with horses. You can just forget everything and focus on them. On the now."

"I wish I could," Kinsley said. "Forget. But some things are too powerful to just forget." *Like my cousin. And whether or not he will live, and if so, with what repercussions.*

"I know what you mean," Nev said, her face hardening. "Some things are unforgettable and unforgivable." She grew quiet and Kinsley took the statement to heart.

She's talking about me and my family and the past.

She started to back away, but Nev held on to her and spoke.

"You can just do what I do and follow Willow's lead. She knows how to forgive and forget. And she's aware of your fear. It's why she came to you. She understands."

"She does?"

Nev stopped the movement of their hands and met her gaze once again.

"Would you like to know her story?"

CHAPTER SIX

"Our vet said she'd never seen a horse that had ever survived the condition Willow was in before," Nev said.

Kinsley covered her mouth, horrified. "Oh God, it was that bad? Wait. Don't tell me. I don't think I can—was she abused?"

"She was malnourished," Nev said.

Kinsley slowly dropped her hand.

"The man who had her couldn't afford to feed her like she needed, and after a few phone calls from myself and local law enforcement, he finally decided to let us have her."

"He didn't mean to do it?"

"Nah, I think he really loved her. He was just struggling financially, and he didn't realize that the best thing for her would be to let her go to someone who could properly care for her. We see that kind of thing all the time around here."

"That's so sad. Poor Willow. So, she was starving?"

"Her condition was very serious. She was emaciated and anemic. She had dermatitis. And she was depressed, scared. She was always well behaved, though. She stood well for the vet and she let us trim her feet, though I don't think they'd been trimmed before. We got her on some good quality senior feed, and she had access to good quality hay twenty-four-seven. She slowly started to recover, and she regained her weight. Her long coat blew out with a shiny new undercoat, and her dermatitis cleared up. She looked like a brand-new girl in a fairly short amount of time."

"And her depression?"

Nev smiled and it actually made Kinsley's heart skip a beat. She still had that dimple on her right cheek. When they'd met as kids that dimple had been the only way she could tell Nev and Viv apart at first.

"What do you think?" She leaned into Willow and kissed her, wrapping her arm around her. "Does she seem sad to you?"

Willow snorted again and turned toward Nev. She flicked her tail.

"I don't think so," Kinsley said with a smile of her own.

"She forgave and forgot. Moved on. Lives in the now. Think you can try and do that while you work with her? I think she'd really like you to work with her. What do you say?" Nev asked, rubbing her snout.

"I—"

Would it mean more of this? More one-on-one with the two of you? Would it mean that you will try to forgive and forget too?

She inhaled.

"Sure."

"Wonderful."

The rain started pelting down and Nev looked up at the darkening sky. "Would you like to see the stables? See Willow's pad?" She grinned.

Kinsley had to swallow again. She shrugged to try to seem like she wasn't being affected at all by her strong, wet, androgynous looks.

"Sure."

She followed Nev into the stables, and the rest of the group helped Deena bring in the other horses. Kinsley stayed with Willow, just outside her stall. Nev gave her a handful of small carrots so she could feed her as she dried her off with hand towels.

Kinsley laughed as Willow ate from her palm. "It tickles a little."

Nev looked at her and paused. She seemed to be as captivated by Kinsley's laughter as Kinsley was of her smile.

"I haven't heard that laugh in a long time," she said.

They both fell quiet.

"It's really nice to hear it again."

They held each other's gaze for a long moment, and then Nev continued to rub Willow down.

A few more moments of silence ensued as the others worked around them, getting all the horses settled in. Nev offered to introduce her to the other horses, but Kinsley politely declined. One horse was enough for today. She did, however, want to keep the conversation going with Nev.

"How did you get her dermatitis to go away?" It was an odd question, she knew, but she was curious. Nev seemed to take really good care of these horses, and she knew she'd be happy to explain.

"We have lotions that help. And neem oil. And of course, lots of

TLC and careful grooming. We had to cover her while her long coat blew out to help protect her from the sun and the dirt. Little things like that helped her along nicely."

"You really care," Kinsley said.

Nev paused for a second as she removed her halter. "Of course I care. I love them."

"I can tell. I think everyone can."

Nev kissed Willow on the snout and exited the stall door. She gave Kinsley a wink. "Just wait. You will too."

"What? Care?"

Nev turned to look back at her. "Love."

Kinsley stopped following and stood there staring after her.

Love?

Who? You or the horses?

Kinsley blew out a breath and opened her eyes. "I don't understand. I'm not supposed to be thinking about anything? How is that possible?"

Holly offered her a smile, the wind blowing strands of her dark hair across her face. They were sitting lotus style on the large patio outside the main lodge at Peace of Life. They were engulfed in silence save for the wind chimes, the trickling rain, and the rushing creek. If Kinsley hadn't been so frustrated with their current undertaking, she would've found the moment beautifully serene.

"Thoughts will come," Holly said. "Let them."

"But you said—" She sighed. "I'm so confused."

"Think of them like clouds." She glanced out at the overcast sky. "Allow them to come, but imagine them as clouds drifting by in the background."

Kinsley rubbed her forehead. *Clouds? What the fuck?* When she closed her eyes her mind conjured up everything from airplanes, to Marty's face, to Nev, to her job. It was endless. And this woman wanted her to imagine all that as clouds?

"Clouds," Kinsley said.

"Yes."

Kinsley shrugged. "Okay."

"Let's try again."

Kinsley repositioned herself with her hands on her knees. She took in the lit candles, the flames dancing against the backdrop of the rain. She felt the thin mat beneath her, giving her just enough cushion to ward off discomfort. She looked at Holly sitting across from her wearing gray yoga pants and a navy Adidas jacket with white stripes running down the arms. She allowed all of it to seep in and relax her and then she closed her eyes.

"Breathe in," Holly said softly. Kinsley inhaled. "Hold it for four seconds. Now exhale for four seconds." Kinsley did as instructed. "Again. Inhale, hold for four, and then exhale holding for four. Imagine blowing all your troubles away, allowing your body to relax more and more with each exhalation, until you feel like you're light, unburdened, ready to float away."

Kinsley kept breathing. Her brow furrowed. She was feeling light all right. Light-headed.

"Now, I want you to focus on the breath. Nothing else. Just your breathing. If anything else comes, simply acknowledge it and send it away on a drifting cloud."

Kinsley focused on her breath. Or tried to.

How does one focus on their breath?

Say to myself in and out, and in and out? Is that all? Or am I just supposed to feel it and not put words to it?

God, this meditation thing bites.

Did I sign up for this?

I did, didn't I?

Just like the horses.

She saw Nev's face again. The heart-stopping smile with the dimple. The cowboy hat angled across her face. The rain glistening off her bare arms.

Then she saw the Cessna one-eighty. The one she co-owned with Marty. She saw the crash site, both wings torn from the body of the plane. Saw Marty in the ICU through the glass partition.

"No!" Her eyes flew open and she stood. Holly looked up at her with wide eyes.

"What is it? What's wrong?"

Kinsley shook her head, her breathing now out of control, her heart pounding with panic.

"I can't do this." She hurried down the patio steps and into the rain. Her bare feet slapped against the wet stones of the path. She began to run, ignoring Holly as she called out after her. She raced across the bridge and sprinted up to her cabin door. She tried to enter, but it was locked. She reached for her pockets but realized she'd left her hoodie back at the lodge with Holly. Along with her key.

"Damn it." She exhaled and ran her hand over her damp head and loosened the tight ponytail, allowing her hair to spill onto her shoulders. She sank into a patio chair and stared out at the rushing creek. It looked like whisky flowing over gray slabs of stone beneath the overcast sky. It sounded like heaven. Had a mineral smell to it. Every time she looked at it she was amazed by it, captivated by its beauty and the magic spell it seemed to cast over her, leaving her feeling resolute and calm. If only she had this in her backyard. Life wouldn't seem so troublesome if she could come home to this every day.

What was she going to do? She couldn't hide away here forever. She'd have to go back eventually. She'd have to face the repercussions of the crash, deal once again with her job…if she could get any work after this. That was worse-case scenario, though. Even if, for some reason, she was found partially at fault for the crash, chances were she'd eventually be called upon once again for her expertise in aviation. She was one of the top experts in the field.

Right?

But this time she couldn't comfort herself with an answer.

She couldn't fool herself, not today.

She sighed and leaned forward to rest her elbows on her knees. She ran her hands through her hair and stared down at her cold feet. She wasn't even a week into what was supposed to be a peaceful reprieve and she'd already had a meltdown.

And in front of someone.

Wonderful. Fan-fucking-tastic.

Had she made a mistake in coming? In trying to escape Phoenix and her home for the majesty and calm of the canyon? After all, everyone raved about this as a place you go to for spiritual awakening and soul rejuvenation. And it was absolutely beautiful and serene. But she couldn't seem to relax. She couldn't yet let go.

If she couldn't relax here, then where could she?

Nowhere. There's not a place on earth I can escape to.

"Thought you might be needing this," a voice said.

Kinsley looked up and found Adrianna at the entrance to the patio, holding her hoodie and key card.

"Yes, thank you."

Adrianna brought it to her and then motioned toward the chair next to her.

"Mind if I join you?"

"Please."

She sank into the chair with a long sigh and then stretched out her denim clad legs and crossed her pointed toe boots. Turquoise stitching in the shape of angel wings ran along the sides of both boots. An elaborate turquoise cross sat in the center of the toe. Kinsley had never seen anything like them.

"Love your boots," she said.

Adrianna looked at them as if she'd never seen them before either.

"Thanks. Good friend of mine made them for me."

"Are you…religious?"

Adrianna chuckled. "Would it shock you to learn that I am?"

"No, not really."

Adrianna patted her arm. "I'm not religious. But I consider myself a very spiritual person."

"Mm. But you like angels. And crosses."

"I like lots of things. Especially things that represent peace and love and forgiveness." She took a deep breath. "I don't have all the answers, young lady, and, in my opinion, no one on this earth does. So, I don't like to go around pretending I do and telling everyone who thinks differently than I do that they're wrong. I believe what I believe and that is this. I believe in everything." She spread out her arms. "No one religion is right and no one religion is wrong. Everything just is. Made especially for us to enjoy while we're on this earth and in these bodies. Who made us? I don't know. What's beyond this life? I don't know. I'd like to think there's more. I hope there's more. But until I find out firsthand, I spend my time taking in what's been given to me. This earth and its creatures. The people around me. I just sit back and take it all in. And I appreciate every single moment and every single detail."

Kinsley stared out at the creek with her, listening to every word.

"Wow. I…that's really beautiful."

"Life is beautiful."

Kinsley dropped her gaze.

"You don't agree?"

"I wish I could. But, no, I can't."

"You took the first step in making that wish come true, didn't you? You came here."

Kinsley looked at her. "Can I really find peace here? Someone like me?"

"Someone like you?" Adrianna turned toward her. "What do you mean by that?"

"I—" She shook her head, stared back at the creek, and rubbed the fabric of the hoodie in her hands. "Never mind."

"How do you like Holly?" Adrianna asked.

"What do you mean? I like her fine. She's very nice."

"Have you spoken with her about your goals? Told her why you are here?"

Kinsley searched for an answer. "I—yes, but I don't really want to get into it." She'd told Holly about the crash but no one else. She wasn't ready yet to discuss it and had only told Holly the bare minimum.

Adrianna chuckled. "Love, the whole reason why you're here is to get into it."

"No, it's not. Not totally. I came here to escape. To find peace. Tranquility."

"And those things can be found. Here better than anywhere because it is peaceful and tranquil and breathtakingly beautiful. But you have to face what's ailing you first. You can't just ignore it and work around it. You won't find true peace that way. You'll only find a distraction. A temporary state. What you're after is real peace. Real inner calm. And that doesn't come without some hard inner work."

"Why wasn't that on the damn brochure?"

Adrianna laughed. "I don't think you read the whole thing. Or maybe you just didn't see it because you didn't want to."

"It wasn't written like that, that's for sure. I would've noticed."

"Would you have? Or did you really only see what you wanted to see? Or maybe you just wanted to get away so badly, you didn't really take the time to read like you should have. You did call and make those reservations rather fast. You were lucky I had a vacancy. Most people make their reservations months out. But I…well, to be honest with you, Kinsley, I didn't exactly have a vacancy."

"You didn't?" She searched her face, confused. She had no idea where the conversation was headed.

"This cabin hasn't been used in a while. Not since my daughter last came and stayed. But when you called and I heard the tremor in your voice and then heard your name, well, I couldn't resist. I sensed you needed to be here and you needed to be here now."

"Heard my name?"

Adrianna nodded and looked over at her wearily. "I've been reading about the plane crash in Flagstaff. Your name...it's unusual and, well, it's been in all the papers."

Kinsley swallowed the ball in her throat. She might as well have swallowed a billiard ball it hurt so badly.

Adrianna reached out and squeezed her forearm. "I'm sorry, I guess I should've told you that sooner. It's just...Well, I was afraid to scare you off. Because like I said, I think you need to be here."

Kinsley felt her eyes begin to burn with rising tears. Adrianna knew her secret, her shameful reason for running away. And she was being so kind about it. So empathetic. Kinsley wanted to burst into tears and cry the tears she'd been crying for days. But she held back. Forced them down as she stood.

"I need to go lie down," she said, hugging her hoodie to her chest.

Adrianna rose alongside her. "I'm sorry if I upset you, love. I hope...I hope you'll still stay."

Kinsley nodded slightly but gave no reassurance. Then she unlocked her door and walked inside without looking back.

CHAPTER SEVEN

N ev was sitting in her favorite chair in the living room attempting to read the latest book by one of her favorite authors, but her racing thoughts made it impossible. Arthur was lounging next to her in his chair, snoring. He had snored for as long as she'd known him, but lately his snoring had been louder, and his sleep seemed more disturbed.

She stood and crossed to him, took the remote from his limp hand, and turned off the football game. She covered him with a soft blanket and extinguished his reading lamp. She usually helped him to bed when he started to doze, but tonight her mind had been elsewhere and he'd fallen asleep on her. She considered waking him to help him down the hall, but since he was sleeping so peacefully, she decided to let him nap quietly in the chair for a while. She wasn't yet ready for bed herself and wouldn't mind the company of his rhythmic snoring. Anything to help ease the loneliness and sense of sadness resonating in her chest.

After tucking the blanket in snug around him, she walked to the simmering fire and retrieved one of the framed photos from the mantel. Then she returned to her chair and sighed as her body relaxed into the cushions. Her throat tightened as she adjusted her reading light and examined the photo, running her thumbs across the three young girls smiling at the camera.

The picture had been taken soon after her and Viv's eleventh birthday. Kinsley and her family had come over to celebrate and the girls had escaped to Viv's room to play games, listen to music, and gossip. They'd been having a ball when her mother had knocked on the door, wanting to take more photos. The girls had groaned but then complied, only they'd been silly and made faces and stuck out their tongues for a few before her mother got one of them smiling. That was the one she now held in her hands.

They were holding each other tight in the photo, Viv in the middle. Posh stood at their feet, looking up at them. Nev could almost envision her little butt wiggling as she did so. Nev cleared her throat at the emotion that came. She hadn't studied the photo in a long while, and when she had, she usually focused solely on Viv. Trying to recall her face, feeling ridiculous, knowing that it was the same as her own. She never had been able to explain it to people, but to her, Viv was very much an individual and very different from herself. Face included. And as the years had gone by, she seemed to lose the details of her sister's face. The way her smile was slightly crooked. The small beauty mark she had on her cheek where Nev had her dimple. The way her eyebrows rose when she was feeling mischievous. And often times, after Nev had studied photos of her and refreshed her memory, she'd begin to wonder what Viv would look like today. Most would tell her to go look in the mirror if she wanted to know. But they'd be wrong. She wanted to see Viv. Not herself. She wanted that beauty mark, those raised brows, that crooked smile. And Viv would no doubt have her hair long and her face fully made up. She'd be the feminine woman Nev wasn't. She'd be Viv.

Nev touched her own lips with a trembling hand as she fought tears. Then her gaze traveled over to Kinsley and her breath hitched.

She was so beautiful. So vibrant.

The light inside her glowing so bright.

So very different from now.

She wondered when that had happened. When her pilot light had gone dim and all but extinguished. Was it a recent thing? Or had it happened when hers had?

Nev touched her face on the photo and began to recall times long ago. Times when she knew for certain her own light had been extinguished.

"Nev, I'm telling you right now. Get out of this car and come with your mother and me." The door to the limousine was open and Dad was leaning in, doing that loud whisper thing he did when he was pissed but didn't want anyone else to know. It was a voice usually reserved for public places. Like the grocery store or one of Viv's dance recitals when Nev was doing something he disapproved of in the audience.

Currently, though, they were in a big fancy car, and most of the passersby had already made their way to the graveside service, where Mom was sitting under a tent with her shoulders hunched, surrounded by other family members. That's where Dad wanted Nev to go. To sit there at the graveside service and listen as some preacher said things about her sister, a girl he didn't even know, so they could put her in the ground.

Forever.

"I'm not going," she said, her voice barely audible. She was trying not to cry and trying not to scream at him for being such an asshole to her. She'd lost Viv too. Couldn't he see that? And she couldn't, under any circumstance, go watch her be put into the ground.

Forever.

"Nevaeh. If you don't get out of this car—" He shook his head, cursed under his breath. His eyes grew big. "This is your sister's funeral, for Christ's sake! Now get out of the goddamned car!"

Nev crossed her arms across her chest and felt her lips quiver. She didn't want to square off with him. Never really had before. But this was different. Viv was gone, she was in a freaking box a few hundred yards away, and she was never coming back.

So, honestly, she just didn't give a fuck if Mom or Dad were pissed. In fact, she was surprised they'd even noticed her missing. They'd spent the last week after they'd returned from the crash site in Milwaukee holed up in their bedroom. Mom wailing and crying and Dad throwing stuff around and then talking softly trying to calm Mom down. They'd said hardly two words to her.

It was like she no longer existed either. Only they didn't seem to be grieving her.

Nev sat very still as her father bored his bulged eyes into her. She decided not to say anything more. She didn't think she could without crying and she didn't want to do that in front of him. She didn't feel he had the right to see her do that now. Not when he'd missed her doing nothing but that the past week.

No.

Screw him.

And screw Mom, too.

Screw everybody.

She was staying put and she was going to remember Viv like she was when she was alive and not have her last memory of her be about that big coffin where they'd put her, all cold and alone and about to go into the ground.

Forever.

She shivered and felt sick. She covered her mouth and turned away. She heard Dad cuss again and the door slammed. She turned back around and found herself alone.

Thank God.

She wiped the tears that came and then smoothed down her black dress slacks. That was another thing that had pissed Mom and Dad off. She'd refused to wear a dress. She'd always fought them on that, but they'd usually won by bribing her with something as a reward. Not today, though. Nuh-uh. No more dresses. Not ever. Not for a million bucks and a chance to hang with Mia Hamm. Okay, maybe Mia Hamm. But Mia would definitely let her change into jeans and sneakers as soon as she got there. Yeah, she totally would. She was super cool.

But she wouldn't do it for Mom and Dad anymore.

A knock came from the window and the door opened. She braced herself for another verbal onslaught from Dad or maybe Grandma. But to her surprise the person who ducked inside and closed the door was Kinsley.

"Hey," she said softly. She was wearing a dress and she looked so pretty in it, even if it was black.

"Hey." Nev continued to smooth out her pants. They weren't hers. The dress slacks. They belonged to Eric, one of Kinsley's brothers. They'd lent them to her when they'd learned Nev was refusing to wear a dress. "Tell Eric I said thanks for the pants."

"Sure." She began smoothing her dress, like she was nervously mirroring Nev. "You can keep them if you want. They're too small for him now."

"Okay."

She glanced out the window. "Are you...gonna go to the service?"

"No."

"Yeah, I don't really want to either." She looked back at her. "Okay if I hang here with you?"

Nev shrugged. "Sure, if you want."

"I do."

Nev wiped her face again, conscious of the tears that had been falling. She didn't want to cry in front of Kinsley either. But for totally different reasons.

"How have you been?" Kinsley asked.

Nev stared down at her pants. "Okay, I guess."

Other than Grandma, no one else had asked. Everyone had just rushed to Mom and Dad and cried with them and consoled them.

How awful to lose a child, everyone kept saying.

Well, they still had one. Couldn't anyone see her?

"I'm not okay," Kinsley said. "I'm a wreck. I—miss her so much." Her voice caved and she straightened her spine and rubbed her face as if trying to get control. She was always so honest. No matter the topic. Kinsley was not one to mince words, Viv always said.

"I do, too," Nev whispered. "I miss her a lot." She took in a deep, shaky breath. "And I can't watch them put her in the ground. I can't. I won't."

"Me neither."

"How can they do that?" she said. "How? It's Viv. Viv. My sister. Their daughter."

"I think they feel like they don't have much of a choice, Nev. I mean, what else can they do?"

"I don't know. Not that, though. Not the ground. Where she'll be cold and alone and in the dark. I can't imagine her there—can't—" Her voice gave and she began to quietly sob. Kinsley scooted next to her and took her hand.

"I understand," she said. "I don't want her there either. I want her here. With us. Alive. But she isn't, Nev. She isn't. And somehow, we're going to have to accept that."

"I can't. I won't." Nev shook her head. "I won't, Kinsley. I won't. I'll never let her go."

Kinsley squeezed her hand and looked at her with tears welling in her eyes. "Okay then. I won't either. We'll keep her together, okay? Here with us."

"Where?"

Kinsley reached up and touched Nev's chest. "Here. In our hearts. And no one will know. And we'll still talk to her and laugh with her. She'll still be here and we'll be together, always. The Three Musketeers."

Nev covered her hand with her own and then reached out and touched Kinsley's chest.

"Promise?"

Kinsley nodded. "Promise."

Nev began to cry again as she felt the gentle thud of Kinsley's heart beneath her hand.

"Hey," Kinsley said. "It's okay. She's here. We're here. I'm here. All of us together. Okay?"

"'Kay."

Kinsley touched her face and softly brushed her cheeks with her thumbs, wiping away the tears.

"I'm not going anywhere," she said. "I'm right here. Always."

Nev looked into her eyes and knew she was swearing the truth. Knew she'd never break that promise. And then Kinsley drew closer, warm hand still cupping her face, and softly kissed her.

Nev froze, the kiss as warm as her hands, as soft as her skin. And they remained, lips fused, carefully and gently kissing.

Nev was so caught up in the feel of her, in the taste of her that she didn't hear the car door until it was too late. *Didn't see Grandma stick her head in until it was too late.*

And that's when her world had come crashing down all over again.

Nev set the photo aside and wiped her cheeks. Tears had streamed down her face as she relived the memory and now she wondered if they'd ever stop.

Or if they, like the pain of her loss, would just keep coming.

Forever.

CHAPTER EIGHT

Today's the first day she's been out," Adrianna said as she squinted into the sun, looking to where Kinsley stood leaning against the rails across the corral. "She's been hiding away in her room for the past two days. Hasn't spoken to anyone."

Nev adjusted her hat and kicked at the dirt. "What are you getting at, Adrianna? I wish you'd just spill it." Adrianna had been skirting the subject of Kinsley for fifteen minutes now, tossing hints and suggestions that she was obviously hoping Nev would notice and respond to. But she should know Nev better than that. She should know it was better to be frank. She'd get a lot further that way. Now, with this latest statement, it seemed she might finally be remembering that.

"I want you to talk to her."

And there it was.

Truth was, Nev should've already been over there working with her and Willow. But after the flashback she'd had, she felt wary about approaching Kinsley, afraid that somehow she, too, was reliving some of same memories and experiencing the same heartache all over again. And by the look of her, standing all alone outside the pen with a pinched look on her face, Nev didn't think she was far off the mark. How could she be expected to deal with Kinsley's pain when Nev wasn't even sure how to handle her own? And why should she have to when Kinsley was one of the reasons why she was in pain to begin with?

Nev pushed out a breath. "I knew it." She looked up at the sky, cursing the fact that Adrianna was ruining her plan of avoidance. "I knew it. You want me to come in and try to save her." It was a familiar story. Adrianna had often nudged Nev into helping guests with deeper issues. Most of the time Nev didn't mind, her horses doing most of the healing work for her. But this, this was something that went deeper. This was territory she'd already been to and didn't want to revisit.

"Well, you do know her, Nevaeh. It's not like she's a stranger."

"She'd be better off if she was. We aren't exactly on the greatest of terms, you know."

"Things went well with her on Monday. You even smiled. I remember because the earth shook a little."

Nev ignored the sarcasm. "Things went well because you personally asked me to work with her and because you know I'll help anyone when it comes to horses."

Otherwise, I would've tried to keep my distance.

"Well, I'm asking you again. Go talk to her. Please. There's a reason why she came today. And I have a feeling it might be you."

Me?

Nev propped her arm up on the rail and glanced at Kinsley, who seemed to be staring endlessly off into the forest.

"She probably just wanted some fresh air."

"She could've gotten that by stepping out of her cabin."

Nev didn't respond, too busy trying to come up with an excuse as to why she couldn't help her.

"Come on, I'll go with you." Adrianna grabbed her arm and tried to pull her away from the rails.

"What's gotten into you?" Nev asked, yanking her arm away.

"Please, Nev."

Nev studied her closely. She was hiding something. Avoiding a truth Nev could sense and see all over her face. "Tell me the real reason."

"I can't."

"Can't?"

"It's for her to tell."

"It's bad?"

Adrianna sighed.

Nev scratched her temple. "Great. Thanks. More drama. As if I don't have enough, Adrianna. The ranch, the horses, the business, Arthur. You know, Arthur? My closest friend in the whole wide world? Remember him? Yeah, he's sick. And he's losing his damn mind on top of it."

"I know, Nevaeh, and I'm sorry. You know I'm not trying to be insensitive to your situation. I'm just really worried about her and I thought since you know her and you both seemed to get on so well on Monday…"

"You thought I could swoop in and save the day again. God, woman, I wish I was the incredible superhero you seem to think I am. I really do."

Adrianna smiled and touched her cheek. "Thank you, love." She started to walk away.

"I didn't say I'd do it." But she didn't look back. "Hey, I didn't say I'd do it!"

Nev slapped her hat against her thigh. "Goddamn it." She looked over at Kinsley and then stalked across the pen, securing her hat back on her head. She walked past the others, wove through two horses, and reached her without garnering her attention. She was still staring off into the distance, her aviator sunglasses absent. Nev noted the dark circles beneath her eyes that weren't so prominent just days before.

"Hi," Nev said.

Kinsley's eyes slid toward her but didn't linger long before returning to the trees. "Hi."

"How are you today?"

"I've been better."

So have I.

She looked so lost, so sad, Nev found herself wanting to reach out and touch her. Smooth her thumbs over the dark patches below her eyes. Bring the vibrant life back to those beautiful irises. Watch them dance with wit and mischief like they used to.

"How are you, Nev?"

"I'm doing all right." Nev was surprised she asked. She was having trouble holding her gaze.

"Yeah?"

"Yes."

"I don't know. I thought you looked kind of pissed at having to come talk to me at Adrianna's insistence."

"Come again?"

Her eyes slid back to her and this time remained, with a hard, serious look.

"You heard me."

"I didn't—"

"Bullshit."

Nev clamped her mouth closed.

"Isn't that what we used to play all the time as kids?" She cocked her head. "I've gotten a little better at the game of lying since then, Nev. I can smell bullshit from a mile away."

Nev didn't speak. She wasn't sure what to say. Something was obviously wrong. Yet the urge to comfort her remained, despite the hard indifference, which only caused her more confusion.

"I put up with it on Monday, figuring you and Adrianna were just concerned for me, so I decided to be polite in return for your thoughtfulness and kindness. But today I'm just not up for nice. Get my drift?"

What the fuck?

"Loud and clear."

Nev started to walk away. Gladly so, the urge to comfort her finally gone. But Kinsley's attitude really pissed her off. She stopped and returned to her.

"Then why the hell did you come?"

Kinsley casually reached in the pocket of her hoodie, retrieved her sunglasses, and slid them on.

"I don't know. Why did you come over here when you obviously didn't want to?"

Nev opened her mouth but had no answer.

"Guess we're both a little *clueless* today, aren't we?"

Nev felt herself heat all the way up to the tips of her ears. She stormed away, leaving Kinsley standing alone along the outside of the pen.

"Goddamned rude woman," Nev said as she stalked through the stable to get Willow. "Come on, girl," she said, opening her stall door to caress her. She tacked her up and then led her out slowly, trying to calm herself so she wouldn't distress her. Willow, however, seemed to sense her dismay because she neighed and jerked against the lead.

"Sorry, girl," Nev said. "I'm a grump, I know. Come on. Let's get you some sunlight and exercise." They headed out into the corral and Nev walked her around, greeting some of the others. All of them were friendly and eager to meet Willow, and two of them seemed more than eager to meet her.

"Hi, I'm Judy," the petite blond one said. She offered her hand along with a broad smile. "And this is my best friend, Kathy. We're from Tucson."

Nev shook her hand. "Welcome, ladies. We're glad to have you."

"We're glad to be here," Judy said. "Especially Kathy here." She nudged her friend, who nervously adjusted her trendy straw cowboy hat. "She really needed to get away, and working with you and these horses is just what she needs."

"I see." Nev looked at Kathy, who smiled at her shyly. "It's nice to have you, Kathy." She offered her hand and Kathy shook it and Nev swore she blushed. She dropped her hand and looked away and Judy beamed.

"She can be a little shy."

"So can I," Nev said, hoping to comfort her. She patted Willow. "But Willow here is a big help. She's the resident icebreaker around here."

"She's beautiful," Judy said. She nudged Kathy again to get her attention. "Right, Kath?"

"Yes, she is. Very beautiful." She held Nev's gaze as she spoke. "So smooth and strong. She's magnificent."

Judy made a noise that sounded like she was stifling a laugh.

"Kath really appreciates strength and beauty."

Nev smiled, unsure if the innuendo she was picking up on was intentional and aimed at her. She suspected it was and it made her somewhat uncomfortable. The women were nice enough and even attractive, but Nev had no interest. Her mind was still on Kinsley, and she could almost feel her eyes on her from across the pen.

She snuck a glance and confirmed her feeling. Kinsley was watching her, and she didn't bother to look away as Nev stared back.

"Ladies, how are we doing?" Deena asked as she came to stand next to Nev. "Have you fallen in love with Willow yet?"

"Oh, we're falling in love all right," Judy said, and again sounded like she was stifling laughter. "Especially Kath. She's almost head over heels and not just for Willow."

Deena raised her brow. "Really?" She stole a glance at Nev and Nev rolled her eyes. Judy and Kathy hadn't seen her do it, but Deena had and the message was clear. "Since you two are so in love with Willow, I'm going to steal Nev for a few."

She cupped Nev's elbow and led her away, out of earshot.

"What's the deal with the housewives? They really coming on that hot and heavy?"

"That's the vibe I'm getting."

Deena shook her head. "Oh, to be you, Nev. I can't even imagine."

"Stop."

They walked over to Juno, who was being fed some hay by one of their volunteers.

"We got it, Zachery, thanks," Deena said, taking the handful of hay from him. She fed Juno while Nev rubbed her down.

"It has been a while since one of the guests drooled over you, but nevertheless, it never fails to amuse me when it does happen." She laughed. "Especially when it's one of those desperate housewife types. What is it you call them? Bi-curious?"

"I don't call them anything other than annoying."

"You know what I mean. And I believe more than once you've gone down that path and helped two or three with their so-called curiosity. Generous and helpful woman that you are and all."

Nev wanted to roll her eyes again. "I am that," she said instead, eliciting another laugh from Deena.

"What's the deal with short, dark, and brooding over there?" Deena asked, nodding back toward Kinsley. "She a head case or just afraid of horses?"

"I believe she's a little of both," Nev said. She dumped a nearby wheelbarrow of hay and Juno slowly migrated to it. Baby soon followed, and she and Deena made their way to the railing to observe their guests and volunteers as they interacted with the horses.

"Both?"

"Yeah, and she doesn't like me much."

Deena looked at her. "Why not?"

"We have…a bit of a history."

"Oh, no. Nev —"

"Not that kind of history." She squinted at her. "God, why do you and Adrianna think I get around like that? You know the majority of my time is spent here. Just when is it that you two think I'm out galivanting around?"

"Hey, I don't keep tabs on you. And you're so introverted and private I don't know where the hell you get to when you aren't helping me with the horses."

"I'm in the house. Or in the shop. You know that."

Deena threw up her hands. "Sure, okay. Like I said, you're like a ghost."

"You really think I'm out sleeping around?"

"Everybody has needs, Nev. Even you. And I'm assuming you can only take being here alone with Arthur so much. I've always assumed you went out and took care of your…urges."

"Urges?" Nev laughed. "Good God."

"I'm not judging. God knows I have my needs too."

"Oh, please spare me those details. I don't think I can handle hearing that at the moment."

Deena leaned back against the rails and propped her heel up on the bottom one. "I think you need to take one of those housewives out on a private trail ride and take care of business. You're cranky."

"And you're hilarious."

"Or go make up with short, dark, and brooding over there. She looks just as cranky. What's the history there, anyway?" She looked at Nev. "If it's not romantic?"

"It's complicated, that's what it is." Nev pushed off from the rails to head back to the horses. Baby needed her foot checked, and Nev suddenly didn't feel like waiting until the guests were gone to do it.

"So, uncomplicate it," Deena said.

Nev walked away and called back over her shoulder. "Easier said than done."

And at the moment, neither of us has any interest in doing so.

Chapter Nine

Kinsley sat curled up on the sofa in front of the burning wood stove in her cabin, writing a letter to her parents. Though she'd been fighting Adrianna and Holly on a lot of their suggestions, she'd decided to take them up on one and sit down and handwrite a letter, the old-fashioned way. It saved her from having to call and having to dodge her mother's questions and her father's concerns. This way, she was totally in control and she didn't have to worry about their reaction.

Trouble was, she wasn't sure what to say. She'd never had trouble speaking her mind before, but now she found that she was hesitant to say anything at all beyond pleasantries. She felt too guilty and responsible to mention the crash or Marty. Besides, she'd made her brother Eric promise to call her the second anything major changed with his condition. She didn't want to count on Diane doing it, seeing as how she'd already made up her mind as to who was to blame. Even if the verdict wasn't back yet on whether or not she and Marty were somehow responsible.

Little did Diane know that regardless of whether or not the NTSB cleared her of any wrongdoing, she was, and probably always would worry, that it was her fault. Diane could rest easy as far as that went. Because she'd been right. Had it not been for her and Marty's hobby, none of this would've happened.

She gripped her pen tighter as a long familiar dread washed over her. Words from long ago echoed in her mind, taking her back. Back to a time she'd rather forget.

"That was total slop," Nev said in response to Kinsley's loud clack of a shot, which had sunk the six ball in the corner pocket.

"Was not." Kinsley rounded the pool table in the large game room of her home and lined up her next attempt.

"Was so, you didn't call it."

Kinsley rolled her eyes. "Do I need to turn up the music? So I don't have to hear you whine?"

Nev shrugged a shoulder. "It's Shania Twain, so go for it."

"Right, I forgot how much you like her. Never mind."

Nev preferred country music to pop. And at the moment anyway, Kinsley was humoring her. After all, she hadn't seen her in days and she had just lost her sister and all.

Kinsley ached at the thought of Viv. There was no way she'd let Nev get away with playing country music while they played pool. No way she'd put up with her whining either. But Kinsley wasn't Viv, and Viv, like it or not, wasn't there to put in her two cents. So Kinsley let it go and appreciated that Shania Twain's songs were awesome and sounded more like pop. If that old, sad stuff came on, though, she wasn't sure she could keep her mouth shut.

She leaned forward and lined up her shot.

"Aren't you forgetting something?" Nev said.

"Fine. I'll call this one. That ball. In that hole right there." She pointed with great elaboration with her cue, then curled her tongue up over her top lip as she concentrated. With careful deliberation, she pulled back on her stick and then smacked the cue ball hard but missed her shot.

"Damn."

"Ha, serves you right for being a smart-ass."

"Better than being a dumbass."

Nev shook her head. "I wouldn't know."

"You sure about that? You have your moments, ya know."

Nev grinned a little as she examined the table. Kinsley's heart rate kicked up at the sight despite the paleness of her skin and the sadness around her eyes. She was suddenly recalling vividly the kiss they'd shared in the limousine. It had been such a monumental moment at such an awful time, she wasn't quite sure she felt right in enjoying the memory of it.

But she couldn't help it.

She thought about it all the time.

Nev's lips had felt…amazing.

Never had she felt anything so warm and soft and tender. And the way Nev's lips had made her heart beat…like it was going to jump right out of her chest and flop around on the floor like a crazy fish out of water. She wondered how Nev felt about it. If it was a good memory for her. A moment to remember or a moment to try to forget.

If Nev's family had anything to do with it they'd insist she'd forget. They'd been up in arms over the whole thing after Nev's grandma had yelled at them and yanked Nev from the limousine, dragging her over to the graveside service, looking back and cursing Kinsley as she emerged from the car, shocked and confused.

Things had been mostly quiet after that, with her own parents coming into her room to question her about the incident the day after the funeral. She'd told them the truth, minus the warm, soft, tender thing and heart jumping out of her chest thing. They'd nodded softly and given each other silent looks and then suggested that she not call Nev for a while. Give things time to cool down. Her family going through so much and all. So, Kinsley had done as they'd said and she'd kept her distance.

Nev, however, had shown up at her door today, breathless, wearing cutoff jeans and her old soccer jersey, having ridden her bicycle over a mile to hang out. Said she couldn't stand to be at home any longer. And she'd wanted to know why Kinsley hadn't called or come around. Kinsley had yet to give her a straight answer. While usually she had no problem in doing so, she wasn't sure she should this time. She didn't want to put any more stress or worry on Nev as it was.

Her parents hadn't said, but they'd implied that Nev's family was not okay with the kiss, and honestly, she wondered if her parents were either. The radio silence that had ensued after their brief talk spoke volumes.

But how could it be wrong when it had felt so right?

She didn't want to kiss Conner like that. Or any other boy. So, what did that mean? Shouldn't they be happy she wasn't going around kissing on boys? Didn't they love Nev?

Did they think she was gay for kissing her best friend? Was that the problem?

Was she gay?

She didn't know. She only knew that she'd done what she'd been compelled to do. And honestly, she wanted to do it again.

"Your shot," Nev said.

Kinsley had missed Nev's turn altogether. She must've spaced out while thinking about the kiss. That had been happening a lot lately. Her spacing out while reliving that kiss. Her brothers had been having a field day with her at dinner the past few nights. Making smart-ass remarks, calling her a space cadet, giving her painful nudges.

She stalked the table, searching for her next attempt. When she found it she pointed again, called it, and snuck out her tongue. She took the shot. Missed.

"Shit."

"Language!" David said as he emerged from his dark hovel of a bedroom and hurried past them.

"Shut up," Kinsley shot back.

"Eat me," he retorted and hustled up the stairs to the main floor.

"I hate having brothers," Kinsley said as Nev moved, now searching for her next attempt. Kinsley instantly regretted saying it, knowing that she was lucky to still have her siblings, but Nev didn't seem to be bothered by it.

"Yeah, they suck."

"They stink too."

Nev laughed.

"Seriously, Eric's BO is so bad it makes me wanna puke."

"Gross."

"Yeah, I know. And you wore his pants." She giggled and Nev gave her the finger.

"Hey, you wanna spend the night tonight?" Nev asked.

Kinsley didn't respond. She wasn't sure how.

"I'm not sure if I can."

"Why not?"

"Um, you know. My parents. They're acting weird over the whole limo thing."

"Oh."

"Aren't yours?"

She shrugged. "Yeah, but who cares? I don't."

"I think they do, Nev. I don't think they'd want me to spend the night. And I don't think my parents would let me."

Nev took her shot and missed. Her face reddened and she flung the pool cue onto the ground.

"Screw it! And screw them!" She hurried to the landing at the bottom of the stairs and sank down with her hands in her hair. She started to cry.

Kinsley hadn't ever seen her cry like that before. She walked to her slowly, worried about approaching her too quickly. Nev was seriously angry and upset, and Kinsley knew the situation was delicate.

"Hey," she said as she eased down next to her. "What's going on?"

"My freaking parents, that's what. They—they're telling me I can't see you anymore. And they're feeding me all this bullshit about why."

Oh, no.

Kinsley swallowed. "What are they saying?"

Nev looked at her with pain filled eyes. "They're saying what we did was unnatural and wrong and that—that Viv would still be here if it wasn't for you. If you hadn't suggested the camp in Wisconsin—if your parents hadn't been so gung-ho about you and Viv going." She shook her head. "It's so messed up what they're all saying. I—I can't take it."

Kinsley touched her shoulder, her own skin burning with rage and shame. Was it her fault? Did she kill her best friend because she'd wanted to go to volleyball camp? Her stomach tightened and she winced from the pain, from the mental anguish.

"I—"

"It wasn't your fault, was it, Kinny?" She looked at her with large, watery eyes so full of questions and pain Kinsley lost her breath looking at them. "You didn't mean for anything bad to happen, right? I mean, you love Viv. Love her like I do."

"I love her very much," Kinsley choked.

"Then why are they saying that? Why are they telling me to forget about you and your family? To just write you off."

"I don't know."

"Well, somebody figure it out!" She stood and bolted up the stairs. Kinsley ran after her, but Nev beat her to the front door. She yanked it open and hurried outside. Kinsley reached her just as she was pulling away on her bike.

"Nev, wait! Stop!"

"I can't, Kinny," she called back. "I can't."

Kinsley wiped a tear from her cheek as the memory finally relented and the vise grip on her heart eased. She'd felt responsible for something totally out of her control at age eleven, and now she was feeling it all over again. Rational thought couldn't seem to penetrate the guilt and shame, for the past or present. And now somehow, with Nev's presence, the two events were colliding and spinning out of control inside her, threatening to eat her alive. How could she get past this? Not one catastrophic event, but two? All the spiritual healing in the world didn't seem near enough to combat this.

She glanced back down at the notebook in her lap. She began her letter to her folks and decided not to try to sugarcoat her feelings. Her mother would worry, but that was what she did. She was a mother and Kinsley her only daughter. Worrying about her seemed to be in the motherhood manuscript.

She told them she'd gone away on a retreat to help with the stress of dealing with the crash. She told them she felt responsible and that she'd never forgive herself for the pain she'd caused Marty and Diane and their loved ones. She said she was staying for the duration of her reservation, which was another week, but that she might request privacy beyond that due to the amount of inner work she needed to do. Then she told them she wasn't going to call but that she'd keep in touch by letter and she asked that they please respect her privacy in this matter. She ended the letter with love and signed off.

Then she sat back and stared out the window at the glittering creek. The sun was setting, and she was once again captivated by the beauty of it. Sunsets were so magnificent and yet she'd missed thousands of them, too caught up in her busy life to pay attention. It made her sad for all that she'd missed and would never get back.

She didn't want to suffer any more regrets like that. She wanted to be present, like Adrianna had said she lived her life. Like how Nev said Willow did. She hoped she'd taken the first step in doing just that by admitting that she had a lot of inner work to do.

Adrianna and Holly would be pleased if not downright surprised at that declaration as well as her deciding to stay for the duration of her reservation. But what if it was too late? What if nothing could be done to help her? Events had already unfolded, and now she was forever tainted. Those beautiful sunsets would forever be susceptible to the darkness that now clouded her insides. She'd never have peace. Never again just get to relax and take in the brilliant colors without worrying about that darkness creeping in to haunt her.

And yet, she still wanted it. She still wanted that peace that Adrianna and Willow seemed to have. Was she crazy for wanting it? Crazy for staying when it seemed so impossible to attain? She'd been uncomfortable from the get-go when it came to her itinerary and some of the healing work Adrianna and Holly had suggested. But the scenery and the environment were what was so alluring. She couldn't bring herself to pack up and drive away, no matter how uncomfortable the spiritual healing made her. Because frankly, nothing was more uncomfortable than the feelings of shame and responsibility she felt regarding the crash. And she couldn't imagine facing them alone back in Phoenix, staring at the walls of her home.

Like it or not, she needed the comfort and consolation of the creek and the majestic canyon.

She was just going to have to suck it up and wade through the suggested healing process, and maybe, just maybe, do some actual healing while she was at it. She wasn't going to hold her breath, though. Because having to accept and process her feelings, even just the ones currently lingering on the surface, was something that was scaring her to death.

She wished again that she were more like Willow. That she could somehow work through her pain gracefully and learn to forgive and forget. But unfortunately, she wasn't like Willow. She wasn't bombproof. So when the feelings she'd been trying to keep shoved down did finally surface, she was likely to startle and downright run.

CHAPTER TEN

S orry about that," Nev said as she reentered the living room. "Just wanted to get him settled."

She'd just helped Arthur to bed, and with the way her body was protesting every single move she made, she knew she wouldn't be far behind. She hoped for her sake her guest wasn't planning on staying too long.

But Adrianna was standing in front of the fireplace, seemingly clueless to her fatigue, having arrived without warning, or apparent purpose. She was staring at the photos on the mantel. Nev grew a little nervous, hoping she wouldn't key off one in particular.

"How's his foot?" Adrianna asked.

"Okay." She didn't want to go into details. She hoped Adrianna would pick up on that. She didn't.

"You said something about a fracture." Her focus remained on the photos.

Nev nearly sighed with tired frustration. It seemed every additional word she spoke exhausted her all the more. "That's what we were worried about. Turns out he's fine."

"Ah. Good." She grabbed the photo, the one Nev had hoped she'd miss, and turned with it in her hand.

"Why didn't you tell me?"

Nev picked up the remote and turned off the television. She wished she could turn off the current conversation. "Tell you what?"

"Don't play coy with me, young lady. You know damn well what."

Nev extinguished the lamp next to Arthur's chair, and then made her way to the kitchen where she fixed them both some brandy.

"There's not a whole lot to tell." She was trying her best to remain calm, but her pulse was going off like a jackhammer. For there was nothing like the wrath of Adrianna.

"Oh, no. Not a whole lot at all. Kinsley's only the mysterious best friend you used to speak of when you talked about Viv. It's no big deal at all that she happens to be one of my guests now. Silly me to think otherwise."

"You said you knew we had a past."

"A past, yes. A fucking past life together, no. She was your best friend, Nevaeh. The one who suffered the loss of Viv with you. The one who—"

"Whose fault it was that I lost Viv to begin with? Yeah. She's the one."

"You don't really believe that, do you?" Adrianna approached the bar, retrieved her brandy, then made her way to the couch. She sat on the end, her usual spot, and crossed her legs. She absently played with the feather that was woven into her hair as she studied the photo.

"It's the truth," Nev said, reluctantly following. She eased down on the armrest opposite Adrianna. She'd rather be discussing anything but this, but if Adrianna insisted on going there, she wasn't going to mince words.

"You were all so happy," Adrianna said softly. "So full of life and adventure."

Nev sipped her brandy. "That was a long time ago."

"Mm. Seems so, yes. To look at the two of you now, that is." She skimmed the photo with her thumb. "I thought she seemed familiar, but I thought it was because of the news and the—"

Nev waited for her to finish, but she didn't.

"What news?"

"Nothing."

Nev laughed. "Oh, okay. Now who's being evasive?"

"I told you, it isn't my story to share."

"Has something happened? Something I should know about?"

Adrianna set the photo aside and drank her brandy. She nearly finished the glass.

"Adrianna?"

"I've made a decision you should be aware of."

Nev blinked, surprised and curious by the statement. "Okay."

"I'm going to let Kinsley stay for a while longer."

"Okay. Why do I need to know that?"

"I'm going to let her stay as long as she wants."

"Okay."

"Free of charge."

Nev lowered her glass. "Come again?"

"I'm not going to charge her for the room beyond her reservation."

"But why? And how can you—those cabins are booked months in advance." She shook her head. "I don't understand."

"I'm letting her stay in Isabella's cabin."

Nev nearly dropped her glass. "In Izzy's cabin?"

Adrianna stared into her drink. "It's time I move forward. Izzy's been gone two years now, and I can't keep that cabin like it's some kind of shrine. She wouldn't want that, and she wouldn't want me letting it go to waste when someone like Kinsley needs it so badly."

"Are you sure about this, Adrianna? Izzy—that cabin. It was her favorite spot. Her favorite refuge." Adrianna's daughter had been an artist. A very successful painter, and she'd traveled the world, visiting friends and seeing the sights. And when she wanted to come home, to relax and unwind, she'd always come home to Adrianna and Peace of Life. Until she couldn't come home anymore. The leukemia had taken her two years before. She'd died in Paris, with friends, unable to travel home. Adrianna had made it to her bedside just in time to say good-bye, to kiss her cheek and watch her breathe her last breath, unable to mutter any last words.

"It was. But she isn't here anymore, love. She no longer needs it. But your friend does."

Nev stood, reeling from all that she was hearing. Kinsley was staying in Izzy's cabin. Izzy's sacred cabin. Adrianna was letting her stay as long as she wanted. For free. What was going on? And what news was Adrianna referring to?

She took Adrianna's glass and poured them both a refill. She returned to the living room and stood by the fire, poking at the cracking logs in her dirty jeans and stocking feet. She'd yet to clean up for the night, having worked in the shop past sundown until Louise left. She was putting in long hours, worried about falling behind but also wanting to keep up with the demand for her more creative pieces. Common sense told her she should stop with the creative work for now and just focus on their usual jobs. But she didn't want to do that. She didn't want to give up the only thing that was keeping her sane, keeping her head above water. The creative work had become her sanctuary of sorts, and if she gave that up, she wasn't sure she'd find a reason, other than Arthur, to keep doing the usual work at all. No, she needed the creative work. Needed it now like she needed air. And she hoped, that if she kept working hard at it, that it would someday pay all the bills and she could do only that. In the meantime, she had to keep doing both to keep things running smoothly. She just hoped she could hold out.

She downed more brandy and stared into the fire.

"I don't understand what you're doing," she finally said, her mind back to the present issue. "With Kinsley. Izzy's cabin. Adrianna, you haven't let anyone set foot in there for years. And on top of that you're letting her stay for free. Why? What the hell is going on?" She knew there was more to the story. Adrianna wasn't one to make rash decisions. Everything the woman did in her life was carefully thought out, premeditated. So Nev knew there was something she wasn't telling her. Getting it out of her, however, would be easier said than done.

"You know how much I charge for these little retreats. It's a small fortune."

"Exactly. So how can you—why would you—" It didn't make sense. None of it did. Those cabins were reserved months in advance, and people were willing to pay top dollar for them. Peace of Life was the most popular spiritual retreat in Cypress Creek. So what was going on? If Adrianna was going to use Izzy's cabin now, she could make bank on letting other guests use it. Why let Kinsley use it for free and for as long as she wanted?

Adrianna held up a hand and stopped her. "Because she needs to be here, Nevaeh." She said it so softly and so matter-of-factly, Nev had no retort. She waited for her to continue, but she seemed satisfied with her statement, settling back into the couch and sipping her brandy.

"That's it? She needs to be here? That's all you've got?"

What the hell is going on?

"If I don't charge her, she'll have no excuse to leave. She'll be able to stay for as long as she needs."

"And how long will that be? Weeks, months, years? I mean what the hell, Adrianna?"

Adrianna smiled. "That will be up to her."

"I was exaggerating," Nev said, nearly tossing the poker down as she walked away from the fire.

"I know."

Nev came back to the couch but stopped to stare at her.

"Why are you smiling?"

"Because you're freaking out."

Nev started to argue but stopped.

"You're all flustered, completely beside yourself at the prospect of Kinsley staying for a while."

"I am not. I'm just confused. This isn't like you. I mean, why her? Why Kinsley? What makes her so goddamn special?"

Adrianna looked at her. "You tell me, love."

"What?" Nev sank down onto the couch and finished her drink. She didn't drink very often, but she suddenly wanted another. And another. Anything to stop this madness with Kinsley. "I think you've finally lost your mind, old woman."

"Have I?"

Nev looked at her. "Yes."

"Maybe I have."

"There's no maybe about it."

Adrianna laughed. "If I'm the one who's lost my mind, then why are you the one losing control?"

"Because I'm going to have to suffer the consequences!" The words just came out, and Nev flushed at being so exposed. She was usually so reserved, calm and in control of her emotions. This, this craziness going on inside her was unusual, unprecedented, and she hated herself for it.

Get control, Nev. Jesus.

Adrianna laughed again and sipped her drink. "Oh, Nevaeh. This drama of yours is so unusual I'm nearly at a loss for words. I've never seen you freak out like this. Quite honestly, I was beginning to wonder if you had it in you. With the ranch, the business, and Arthur, and the way you've held all that together just as cool as a cucumber, I thought for sure you didn't have anything human in you left at all. You've been like a machine. A quiet, deliberate machine, doing what you have to do day in and day out."

"What's wrong with that?" She sounded so defensive. So pissy.

Damn you, Adrianna.

"What's wrong with that is that you get to a point where you're too shut off. No one can reach you and you don't want them to. You drift too far out to sea where you're on your own with no one close enough to help you."

"I don't need any help." She suddenly didn't want any company either. She was ready for the conversation, as well as the evening, to be over.

"Everyone needs help, Nevaeh. Even if it's just a friend keeping an eye out for you. I've tried my best, but you've drifted so far out, it's beginning to get difficult to see you. It scares me. Because if you need help, I wouldn't be able to get to you in time. Or worse, I may not even see that you need help at all and down under you'll go."

Nev set her glass on the coffee table and ran her hand through her hair. "I think you're being a little melodramatic."

"I don't think I'm being dramatic enough."

Nev looked at her. "Is that why you're doing this with Kinsley? To somehow save me?" Nev shook her head in disbelief. "And here I thought you were wanting me to save her."

"I'm hoping you can help each other."

Nev laughed and stood. "I knew it. I knew there had to be a reason for you letting her stay and I knew it probably had something to do with me." It all made sense now. Adrianna was meddling, trying to force the two of them together. What she hoped to accomplish by doing so, Nev didn't know.

"Like it or not, you two are tied together, Nevaeh. And I had nothing to do with that."

"No, but you're making damn well sure we stay that way, aren't you?"

Adrianna rose. "I'm doing what I feel is right in my heart. Whatever happens between the two of you as a result is out of my hands. I will not ask you to help her and I will not force you two together. I'm going to stay out of it." She started walking toward the front door.

"It's a little late for that, isn't it?" Nev said, storming after her.

She turned at the door and faced Nev. "No, Nevaeh. If it's one thing I've learned about life and love and taking chances…" She reached up and touched her face. "It's that it's never too late."

CHAPTER ELEVEN

K insley tentatively took the brush from Zachery, one of the volunteers, and slowly began running it along Willow's body. Willow's skin twitched at the contact, and Kinsley paused, startled.

"Did I—hurt her?"

"No, no. You're doing fine." He stroked Willow's snout. "She loves being brushed."

Kinsley hesitated for a moment before she continued. Again, Willow's pelt shifted, but this time she flicked her tail along with it.

"I think you're right. I think she likes it."

"Of course she likes it. It feels good."

Kinsley kept brushing the way Zachery showed her. After a short while she began to grow comfortable and she relaxed her arm a little more, no longer worried about Willow rejecting her. Soon her entire body was calm as the warmth from the sun massaged them out in the corral.

A few of the others were in the corral with her, all of them focused on their assigned horse. Matthew and Stephanie were feeding theirs and Kathy and Judy were learning how to saddle Baby while Deena instructed them. Kinsley turned, shading her brow, and took in the whole property.

"She's not here," Zachery said.

"Sorry?"

"Nev."

"What makes you think I was looking for Nev?"

God, am I that obvious?

"Because you've been searching for someone since you arrived. And seeing as how Nev's the one who worked with you before and she's the one missing, it's a safe assumption." He grabbed another brush and started in on Willow's hindquarters.

"I wasn't looking for Nev," she blurted.

Oh, God, I am so obvious.

"No? Just like you weren't last time either?"

She felt her face flush.

"You were looking pretty hard for someone last visit too."

"I'm just curious."

"Got it."

She sighed. "If I was looking for her, which I'm not, I'd have every right to. She'd implied that she was going to help me with Willow. She knows I'm—uncomfortable around horses."

He looked up at her from under his ball cap. "You seem to be doing all right by me."

"Thanks. I think."

"Hey, does my opinion not count?"

Well, you're definitely no Nev.

"Yes, of course it does. Sorry."

He chuckled and they continued to brush, and Willow swished her tail again.

"If you're looking for Nev, chances are you'll find her in her shop."

"Her shop?"

"Yeah, you know, her forge." He motioned toward the smaller of the two barns next to the house. "She's usually in there working when she's not out here with the horses."

"Is she usually out here? For therapy?"

He adjusted his cap. "Yeah, usually. Come to think of it, it's not like her to not be out here. I don't think I've ever actually seen her miss a day. Especially not two. She likes to supervise when people come to work with her horses." He shook his head. "You want info, your best bet is to ask Deena. Deena's her right-hand man. I mean, er, woman."

Kinsley glanced over at the woman who had a build close to her own.

"What's the deal with those two anyway?" Kinsley asked, trying to sound casual.

"Who? Nev and Deena?"

She nodded. "Are they a couple?"

He laughed. "Uh, no. Deena's straight and Nev's…"

"Nev's?"

"I don't know. She's just not into Deena. They're kind of like working buds. Deena's been a real help around here since Arthur got sick. She was once just a volunteer. Like me. Now she's here pretty much full time."

"Arthur?" She'd heard Nev mention him before but knew nothing about him.

"Nev's mentor." He stopped brushing and looked at her. "You know, her best friend and business partner? He's part owner of the ranch."

"Oh, right." She had no clue, but it seemed easier to act like she did.

"Why isn't he around?"

Zachery moved to Willow's other side. "He's around. Just not a whole lot. Not since he got sick."

"He's sick?"

"Yeah. He has Parkinson's."

Oh. God.

"How terrible." How had she missed all this? Did everyone else know all this stuff about Nev and the ranch?

Had Adrianna been holding out on her? Come to think of it, she might have been. She hadn't said a whole lot to her other than pleasantries since their little talk on the front patio the week before. Was she just giving her space? Or was she afraid to approach her because she'd sensed how upset Kinsley had been over her knowing her secret?

I need to talk to her.

Kinsley eyed the barn. She needed to speak to both Nev and Adrianna. But for the moment, her focus was on Nev. She owed her an apology.

She set down the brush.

"Would you excuse me?"

"Yep."

She left Zachery brushing Willow and exited the corral. With a quick glance behind her to make sure no one else was looking, she darted across the grounds to the small barn. She found the door partially ajar and she could hear music playing and something that sounded like hissing.

She eased open the large door and stepped inside. She could smell the scent of hot metal, and the heat in the barn was more significant than it was outside. She expected the barn to be bright, lit up from above, but what she found was quite the opposite. Most of the light was filtering in through a side door that was standing open, while some of the rest filtered through the slats of the barn. What remained was an overhead light toward the back of the barn where Nev stood over a large table, appearing to be working on a piece of gate.

The music, which sounded like old blues, was so loud Kinsley approached without being heard. She stood watching as Nev worked, holding a torch to a rivet, while her left hand held fast to the gate. She was wearing a long black leather apron, safety goggles, and gloves. Her strong arms were grease stained and slick with sweat, which was easily seen in the short sleeved gray T-shirt she wore. Below that she had on tight-fitting jeans and heavy looking black work boots.

Kinsley didn't think she'd ever seen anything hotter.

And then Nev started to sing and she moved her hips a little. The sight caused Kinsley's own temperature to rise.

Nev paused her singing for a moment as she adjusted her goggles. Kinsley chose that moment to make her presence known.

"Nice moves."

Nev jerked and straightened. She wiped the sweat from her brow with her forearm.

"What are you doing in here?"

"Isn't it obvious? I'm looking for you."

Nev set down the torch and tightened the gate in a vise. She seemed to be having trouble getting it tight enough. Then she crossed the room and killed the music.

"You can't be in here," she said upon returning. She removed her gloves and goggles and crossed her arms over her chest. A black streak marked her jaw, and Kinsley had to urge to touch it and trace her fingers down the strong column of her neck.

"Well, I wouldn't be if you were where you're supposed to be."

Nev stared into her eyes, but only after she quickly swept the length of her body. Kinsley briefly wondered how she measured up in her soft jeans and long-sleeved shirt. She felt ridiculous in her sneakers, but she'd yet to go into town to buy anything more suitable. It seemed everyone else was way more prepared for life on the range than she was. Even Kathy had that silly cowboy hat. She probably bought it at a local gas station.

"And just where is it that I'm supposed to be?" Nev asked.

"Working with the group. With the horses."

"You mean with you."

Kinsley almost faltered. "Well, yes."

Nev laughed. "I see." She leaned back against the table. "Where's Adrianna? She send you in here? That woman never wants to do the dirty work herself."

"I don't know. She mentioned something about driving into town. And what do you mean by dirty work?"

"Nothing." She pulled a towel from her back pocket and wiped her face. She looked tired, almost defeated.

"I've never heard you sing before," Kinsley said. "I thought singing was, you know…"

Nev's face clouded. "Viv's thing? It was. And I used to hate it. Drove me nuts."

"Yeah, I remember." She laughed a little. "She was pretty awful, wasn't she?"

"Terrible." Nev shook her head. "I'm not much better."

"You didn't sound so bad to me." She smiled at her, a peace offering.

Nev didn't seem to receive the message. "Doesn't matter." She tucked the towel back into her pocket. "I really need to get back to work, so—"

"Why are you avoiding me?"

Nev didn't respond. Just stared. And for a few long seconds, Kinsley thought she'd blown it.

"Is it because I was such a bitch the other day?" Kinsley asked quickly, trying to make nice before Nev ran her out. "Because I wouldn't blame you if it is. It's just—I don't want things to be like this between us. I'm not here for very much longer, and I want to try to get the most out of this experience. And I'd like to try to make things right with you. Or at the very least make it so we're civil. So you don't have to avoid me and hide away in here every time I come around." It had sounded so much better when she'd rehearsed it on the way to the ranch. She'd hoped she wouldn't have to say a whole lot, but Nev had been absent again and she was worried it was because of her.

"I'm not hiding. I'm working. I have a lot that needs to be done."

"Like that gate." She motioned toward the table behind her.

"Yes."

Kinsley looked around and caught sight of several other large pieces. Some appeared to be gates, two of them with elaborate designs. Some were just amazing even if she didn't know what they were.

"Your work is really something. You're very good."

Nev just continued to stare at her.

Kinsley knew she should be growing uneasy under her gaze, but she wasn't. She wasn't intimidated at all. She did, however, feel bad about the way things obviously still were between them.

"So, what do you think? Think we can call a truce?"

"If I say yes, will you leave?"

Kinsley blinked. "Really? I guess my apology doesn't mean much, does it?"

"I didn't hear an apology."

Kinsley sighed. "Fine. Nev, I'm sincerely sorry for being such a bitch the other day. I hope you can forgive me and we can at least continue being civil." She raised an eyebrow. "How was that?"

"That was good."

She pushed off from the table and slid her gloves and goggles back on. She started messing with the vise and arranging the gate, but again she seemed to be having trouble.

Kinsley rounded the table, found a pair of gloves, an apron, and some goggles on a nearby workbench and suited up. Then she went back to Nev and held on to the gate.

"What are you doing?" Nev's shock was more than apparent. She even looked a little pissed.

"Helping."

"I don't need—"

"I'll hold the gate since your vise seems to be slacking on the job."

"You said you would leave."

"I will. Just as soon as I finish holding this for you."

She didn't seem convinced.

"You were having trouble holding it and hot riveting before, so let me help."

"I—you know what hot riveting is?"

"Yes. Airplanes have rivets, you know."

"Airplanes?" She swallowed as if the word tasted bad, and Kinsley realized that Nev had no idea who she was or what she did for a living. Adrianna must not've said a word.

"I work with planes. Doing everything you can imagine. Professionally and privately." Her voice cracked as she thought about her private ventures and the hobby she and Marty shared.

"What do you mean you work with planes?" She seemed as irritated as she was perplexed.

"I'm an aeronautical engineer, a pilot, and an aviation expert."

"No kidding. Huh. I never would've guessed."

"You're wondering why I went into aviation, aren't you?"

"It's crossing my mind, yes."

"After…Viv I made a vow. I vowed to learn all I could about airplanes so I could help prevent what happened to her from happening to anyone else."

Nev's eyes softened a bit and she glanced away. After a short while she cleared her throat and adjusted the gate. It seemed they were now moving on to other things.

"Hold it tight."

Kinsley nodded and Nev turned on the torch and continued to hot rivet. Kinsley watched her quietly, holding tight to the gate, thinking about what Adrianna had said about Nev having her way with metal. Nev forced her back to reality when she stopped and straightened once again, tugging off her gloves and goggles.

"That should do it. Thanks."

Kinsley removed her own gloves and goggles and untied the apron.

"You're stronger than you look," Nev said as she wiped her hands on her hand towel.

"What I lack in build I make up for in willpower."

"I can see that."

"It's what having two older brothers will do to you."

Nev tossed the towel in a bin next to the workbench. She motioned back behind Kinsley. "Will you hand me those tongs?" Kinsley did and Nev put them away.

"So, you done for the day, then?" Kinsley asked.

"Me? Hell, no."

"But you're cleaning up."

"I'm cleaning up for the time being. So I can go work with you. If I don't, Arthur will come in here and think he needs to do it. And I can't have that."

"Arthur's your friend?"

Nev seemed surprised. "Best friend."

"And it's a problem for him to put away the tools?"

Nev loosened the vise and removed the gate. "At the moment, yes. He's too weak to be in here messing around unsupervised. Last week he dropped a hammer on his foot."

"Oh, no. Is he okay?"

"Thankfully, yes." She set the gate up inside a rack and made sure it was secure.

"He has Parkinson's. Advanced Parkinson's, so I have to keep a close eye on him. He's forgetful."

"I'd love to meet him."

Nev shot her a look and Kinsley briefly worried she'd crossed a line she wasn't supposed to cross.

"Sorry, I just meant—"

"Maybe."

She headed for the forge, which was large and black, and knelt to turn off the gas. Then she moved toward the side door and switched off the overhead lights.

"You said you weren't staying much longer," Nev said. "What does that mean?"

"My reservation will be up soon."

Nev motioned for her to exit and then she followed. "You aren't staying longer?"

Kinsley looked at her as they headed toward the corral. "No. I haven't even thought about it, really."

"You haven't spoken to Adrianna?"

"Not recently." Kinsley stopped her with the press of her hand to her arm. "Why? And what is it with the two of you and me? Is there something I don't know?"

Her phone rang and Kinsley quickly pulled it from her back pocket. She fumbled with it when she saw it was Eric and nearly dropped it.

"I have to take this." She pressed the phone to her ear, walked away from Nev, heard Eric's voice, heard the words he said, and then fell to her knees and cried.

CHAPTER TWELVE

Nev carried the glass of ice water across the living room to Kinsley who was sitting on her couch with red-rimmed eyes and moist cheeks. Her breathing had finally slowed, and she seemed a little more stable than she had moments before when she'd all but collapsed outside the barn.

"Thank you." Kinsley took the glass with shaky hands.

Nev perched on the edge of the coffee table, afraid to get too far away from her for fear she'd fall again.

"Can I get you anything else? Aspirin? A sandwich maybe? Do you need to eat?"

Kinsley had seemed to grow even more slight in the past week, and Nev was now very concerned about those dark circles under her eyes. It seemed they told more of a tale than Nev had originally thought. They hinted at deeper issues.

"No, I'm fine, thank you." She sipped the water.

Nev took the glass gently from her. "Go ahead and lie back and relax."

Kinsley eased backed and closed her eyes. Her breath shook as she exhaled.

"You want to tell me what's going on?" Nev said softly, setting the glass on the coffee table next to her. "And don't tell me it's nothing. I'll do like you and call bullshit if you even try."

Kinsley laughed a little and opened her eyes. "I have no doubt that you would."

"So…what's going on, Kinny?" They both looked away at the use of the nickname Nev had given her all those years before. "Sorry, it just came out."

"It's okay. It was...I like it."

Nev met her gaze and saw those soulful hazel blue eyes, and for a second it felt like she was in the past. And for a second, she felt like all was right again. But the second quickly passed.

"That was Eric on the phone," Kinsley said. Tears filled her eyes again.

"And it was bad news?" Nev recalled the way she'd fallen to her knees and sobbed on the grass. The way she'd rocked back and forth. Whatever she was going to say it couldn't possibly be good.

Kinsley wiped her eyes and shook her head. "No. No, it was great news." She smiled through her tears. "Marty, my cousin, he's—going to be okay." She burst into sobs again, and though confused, Nev moved to sit next to her and wrapped her arm around her. Kinsley responded by clinging to her tightly and crying into her neck. Her entire body seemed to be racked by the sobbing, and Nev held her tightly in return, ensuring her she was safe and free to cry as hard as she needed to and for as long as she needed to.

"Shh, it's okay," she said. "You're okay."

Kinsley drew away and Nev felt her own tears brim as she looked at her. She hadn't seen Kinsley cry in many, many years, and it pained her to see her so distraught now. The young girl had grown into a beautiful, strong woman, but her tears still tore at Nev's heart.

I'll do anything to see that she doesn't cry.

The thought came suddenly, on the coattails of her empathy. She felt protective of Kinsley, just like they were best friends all over again. And she felt like she needed to do what she could to make whatever was wrong better.

"What happened to him?" she asked. "Was he sick or—"

"He was in an accident." Kinsley looked down at her hands. She seemed unsure about saying anything further. Nev's curiosity was piqued.

"What kind of accident?"

Kinsley shifted. "He...uh. He was in a small plane crash."

Nev inhaled sharply and stood. She crossed the room, ran her hand over her head, and stared out one of the large windows that looked out toward the stables.

Kinsley continued as Nev's mind flew in reverse, paralleling Kinsley's words as she spoke.

"He was critically injured, and we weren't sure if he was going to survive. He's been in ICU on a ventilator and…I've been so worried. So sick over the whole thing. I—I'm still worried. Not for his life now, but for the repercussions."

Nev spoke but didn't turn to face her. She swiped angrily at a fallen tear.

"Repercussions?"

"I'm worried about Marty's recovery and the damage he sustained. He has to have facial reconstruction, and he'll have to have rehab for his broken leg. I worry about the long-term effects, about what his life will be like now. And…"

"And?"

"The plane—the plane belongs to me. Marty and me. We were responsible for repairs and upkeep. And it's old. An old Cessna that we were restoring—anyway, it could come about that I'm to be held responsible for what happened."

Nev wanted to scoff but held back. What Kinsley had just told her was terrible, another tragic accident that could've ended so much worse than it had so far. And while Nev felt for her, and now understood the stress she must've been under, she couldn't help but feel a little upset.

"That sounds…"

It took Kinsley a moment before she responded. "Familiar?"

Yes.

Nev turned and pushed out a breath. "Well, that explains the big mystery, then. Explains why Adrianna wouldn't tell me what was going on with you."

"I had assumed that she had. With the way you two have been acting and not so secretly discussing me."

"She didn't. She wouldn't do that. Especially with something like this."

"Something…like a plane crash?"

Nev crossed the room. "Right."

"Because it would upset you?"

Nev made her way into the kitchen and poured herself some brandy. She downed it at once.

"Right again." She considered another but thought better of it and put the bottle away. She crossed back to the living room instead and found Kinsley staring at her, her eyes watery and wide, as if searching for clues to Nev's feelings.

Nev felt for her, saw the vulnerability in her eyes and the racing pulse in her neck. She was seeking comfort, reassurance. While Nev couldn't bring herself to give her any reassurances, she did feel like she could offer more comfort.

"I'm glad your cousin is going to be okay."

She lowered her gaze to her hands and Nev knew she was disappointed. "Thanks. I am too."

Nev walked to the fireplace and studied the photograph she'd been staring at for days. She wasn't the only one who was disappointed. Disappointment was all Nev had ever known. And if she couldn't find comfort after all these years when it came to Viv, then how could she provide any further comfort for Kinsley? Better yet, why should she?

"Unfortunately for some, things don't always turn out so well." She swallowed the ball in her throat, her emotions rising to get the better of her. Why couldn't things have been different for Viv? Did she not deserve a second chance? She was only eleven, for God's sake. An innocent child. Why did Kinsley's cousin get the chance that Viv didn't?

"Nev, I—" Kinsley started.

"Hello, hello," a voice said as the front door swung open. Nev turned and saw Adrianna breeze in with a set of brown paper grocery bags and Arthur not far behind on her heels.

"Hello, hello," he said with a stiff smile, shuffling his way in after closing the door.

"There you are," Nev said to the two of them. She'd found the note Adrianna had left on the kitchen counter, explaining that she'd taken Arthur shopping. "Took you long enough."

"We had fun," Adrianna said. "And we had to get just the right ingredients for the chef there," she said, referring to Arthur.

"I take it you sent Louise home?" Nev asked.

"I thought she'd like to have the evening off."

Nev crossed back to the kitchen, irritated. Kinsley, on the other hand, stood and introduced herself to Arthur. It was a sight that should've warmed her, especially in seeing how kind Kinsley was to him, but things felt too out of control. Kinsley was infiltrating her world and everything was spinning.

She tried to help Adrianna unload the groceries, but Adrianna shooed her away.

"Don't you dare. You go entertain your guest." Her face lit up as she looked at Kinsley.

"She's not my guest," Nev whispered. "And I have work to do this evening, A. I don't have time to watch Arthur."

"I'll keep an eye on him."

"And drive the guests back to the resort?"

She waved her off. "That'll take me fifteen minutes tops. You need to relax."

"Yeah, right. You have no idea." She moved away from her and watched as Kinsley and Arthur interacted.

"Well, aren't you a pretty little thing?" Arthur said, his speech slow and a bit slurred. His words spoke of his smile, yet his face remained masked, which was typical for him now with his Parkinson's. "And where did you come from, Miss Kinsley?"

"I'm a guest at Adrianna's." She held onto his left hand with both of hers, cradling it. Her smile was broad and appeared genuine. Her teary eyes were dissipating, leaving behind a sparkle.

"A guest?" Arthur looked at Nev, knowing damn well Adrianna's guests never came into the house.

"Kinsley's an old friend of Nev's," Adrianna said, putting the lettuce away in the fridge. Nev grimaced at her and she promptly straightened and zipped her lips with her fingers.

"Isn't that nice," Arthur said. He managed a stiff smile, and Nev almost smiled with him, it was so good to see.

"Why didn't you tell me we were going to have company?" He directed his question to Nev.

"I didn't know."

"Nev was just helping me out," Kinsley explained. "I, uh, needed a drink."

"Well, you must stay for dinner," he said. "We're making spaghetti. Homemade." He hesitated as he gathered his strength to continue. "None of that jarred sauce. And I make mine a little spicy."

Kinsley laughed. "I must admit, that does sound appealing."

Nev started to protest, but Kinsley beat her to it.

"But I really need to get back to Willow."

"The horse can wait until you accept my invitation." Arthur raised the pitch of his voice a little, apparently not liking what he'd heard. He held Kinsley's hand. "And I'm very stubborn, so I'm willing to wait here all day for you to accept if need be."

Kinsley glanced at Nev, who threw up her hands in defeat. She wasn't about to argue with Arthur in front of Kinsley. He was just going to get his way. Again.

Kinsley looked back to Arthur. "Okay, I accept. Thank you."

"Great," Adrianna said. "Kinsley, you can help Arthur get us started while I drive the rest of the crew back to the retreat."

"I'd love to," Kinsley said as she carefully led Arthur into the kitchen.

Adrianna folded up the last grocery bag, put it away in the cupboard, and then stood next to Nev with her hand on her arm, beaming at Kinsley. "Nev, why don't you walk me out?"

She led Nev out the back door and nudged her playfully. "This is turning out to be some evening."

"It is and I'm not happy about it, for the record." They crossed the property toward the stables.

"Really? I hadn't noticed."

"Why did he have to invite her for dinner?"

"Because he's a kind old man who's not used to meeting anyone from your past."

"That's just it. She's from my past. A past I'd rather forget. Why can't any of you see that?"

Adrianna stopped her, hand on her upper arm. "First of all, Arthur has no idea what's going on, so this isn't some big conspiracy against you. Secondly, Kinsley is here in the present. Maybe you should focus on that and truly let go of your animosity. Truly do as you want and just forget it. Let it go."

"I can't. I look at her and it's all I see."

"Then you need to talk to her about it. Air it out. Work it out."

"How can I do that when what she just told me nearly killed me? And I'm pretty sure it nearly killed her."

"What did she tell you?"

"She told me about the plane crash. About her cousin."

Adrianna covered her mouth in alarm. "Has something more happened?"

"She got a phone call. It upset her."

"Oh, no."

"It was good news, but I think all the stress she's been under finally did her in. She pretty much collapsed on me, Adrianna. So, how can I bring up the past with her now? You've seen her. She looks awful. What she's dealing with now is eating her up."

"I don't think you're going to have to bring it up. I think with the two of you together it will just work its way out. And when it does—"

"I'm afraid I'm still too angry. I almost lost it in there. Almost lit into her about Viv's death being her fault. Right when she's crying over her cousin's plane crash possibly being her fault." She ran her hand through her hair. "God, Adrianna, what's wrong with me? How can I still resent her so much after all these years and when she's suffering on top of it? I feel like a monster."

Adrianna reached up and touched her face. "You're not a monster, Nevaeh, you're just ridiculous. You're human, remember? Humans have all kinds of feelings. Some rational, others not. It's about time you remembered that."

Nev grabbed her hand and removed it from her face. "I liked my life the way it was. This," she motioned all around her, "I don't like this. I don't want or need it. So, when Kinsley says she's going to leave the retreat, I'd appreciate it if you let her."

Adrianna squeezed her hand. "Nevaeh, I'm going to do what's right and let the rest work itself out. I told you that."

"Regardless of how I feel?"

"Because of how you feel." She gave her hand one last squeeze and walked off ahead of her, leaving Nev all alone, with the weight of the past and the present bearing down on her shoulders.

Chapter Thirteen

K insley chuckled at Arthur as she helped him scoop out some sugar from the tin.

"*This* is your secret ingredient?"

They sprinkled two tablespoons into the pot of boiling tomato sauce.

"Uh-huh. And that's not the only one."

"No?" She stirred the garlic and onions and ground beef sautéing in the pan.

Arthur slowly swung the lazy Susan around on the counter and fumbled with a few containers of spices. Kinsley moved to help him but stopped herself, instinctively knowing when to step in and help and when to let him do it himself. When he found the one he was looking for, he held it up triumphantly.

Kinsley eyed the label. "Red pepper flakes."

"Gives it a kick." He was trying to wiggle his eyebrows, and Kinsley couldn't help but find his whole demeanor endearing and adorable. Arthur was a very jovial man, and she felt an instant kinship with him. She hadn't laughed in what seemed like ages and she was smiling so much her face hurt.

Guess it's been a long time since I've smiled this much.

The realization made her sad, but the mood didn't last long. The phone call from Eric had lifted the world from her shoulders, and Arthur's good nature and the smell of a home cooked meal made her feel all the more lighter.

"Don't overdo it with those pepper flakes, now," Nev said from behind. She settled in at the bar, bottle of wine in her hand. She'd come back inside about fifteen minutes before and had quietly left the room.

Kinsley had wondered where she'd gone, but now she knew. She'd gone to shower.

Kinsley could smell her fresh, clean scent from across the bar, and she looked just as fresh and clean with a crisp white T-shirt on and her short, dirty blond hair combed back away from her face. If she could look any more gorgeous butch, Kinsley would die to see it.

"Miss Kinsley," Arthur said, touching her forearm. He pointed at the garlic, onions, and ground beef, which were beginning to smoke in the pan.

"Oh, right." She stirred them and then, at his instruction, slid them off into the pot of sauce.

"Arthur, please call me Kinsley."

Arthur stirred the sauce and looked at Nev. It was a knowing look, like they'd just communicated without saying a word.

"What?" Kinsley asked. Was this the usual around here? People secretly conversing all the time about someone who was supposed to be clueless. Like her?

Nev lined up two wine glasses and a plastic cup. She raised an eyebrow at Kinsley. "Lambrusco?"

"Please."

Kinsley watched as Nev poured them all a glass and then passed Kinsley hers over the bar. She took a sip and groaned.

"Oh, God, this is good. So nice and cold. Mm. I forgot how much I loved Lambrusco."

Arthur came to stand next to her, and Nev handed him his cup. He took it with his left hand, the one without the tremor, and brought it to his mouth carefully. He took a sip and nodded.

"Good."

And then he turned back to the stove.

Kinsley eyed Nev, watching her drink, waiting for an answer.

"You going to tell me what that look was between you two?"

Nev set down her glass. "Arthur's Cajun. From southern Louisiana. He's calling you Miss Kinsley out of respect. Normally, that's how younger people refer to their elders, but here lately Arthur's been doing it to people younger than him. I don't know why and I haven't asked. It could be his dementia or it could be it just makes him feel good. Either way, he's doing it as a sign of respect. Kind of like referring to every female he meets as ma'am."

"Got it."

"Does it bother you?"

"No, not at all. I was just trying to be polite. I didn't want him to think he had to be so formal with me."

"That's just Arthur. He's polite personified."

"He's very kind," Kinsley said, looking at him over her shoulder. "Funny too."

Nev leaned to her left to sneak a peek at him. "There he goes with the pepper flakes again. He forgets how much he's already put in. Arthur, pepper flakes!"

He waved her off and spoke to Kinsley as he set the container aside.

"Nev's a wuss," he said. "Can't handle the heat."

"I can't handle *your* heat," she said. "You're liable to kill someone with those pepper flakes one day."

He turned. "What a way to go."

They laughed and he returned to his sauce, standing there bent over the stove in his blue button-down shirt, loose fitting Wrangler jeans with a large belt buckle, and his Nike sneakers.

"How's his foot?" Kinsley asked as Arthur stirred the sauce and began to hum.

"Okay. It was sore for a little while."

Kinsley thought for a moment as Nev grew quiet. "Does he still work in the shop?"

Nev stared into her glass. She cleared her throat. "No. And no, he probably shouldn't have been in there either, even though I was with him. I just—turned my back for a second. It won't happen again."

Kinsley blinked at her defensive tone. "I wasn't implying—"

"I take really good care of him, okay? Really good care of him. I just—messed up."

"Nev, I wasn't suggesting you don't."

Arthur faced them again. "I need to get cleaned up for dinner."

Nev pushed off from the bar. "Would you please excuse us for a few minutes?"

"Of course," Kinsley said.

She went to the stove and adjusted the heat on the sauce. Then she sat at the table and took in the large kitchen and adjoining living room. The layout gave the house a very open feel, as did the high vaulted ceilings. She felt like she could breathe easily and yet she felt comfortable and cozy too. The house was decorated in warm browns and had a western theme. Framed paintings of cowboys adorned the walls, and a steer skull was mounted above the fireplace. Some of the furniture was mid century and looked original, as were the books on one of the bookshelves. She smiled as she saw the numerous volumes of Louis L'Amour westerns. Her own grandfather had liked to read those, and she wondered if maybe that was why she liked Arthur so much. Because he reminded her of her late grandfather.

She stood and crossed to the other bookshelf. Dozens of books on philosophy lined the shelves. She ran her fingers across the spines and noticed that many were college textbooks. She wondered who they belonged to. Could they possibly be Nev's? She glanced around the home but struggled to decipher what was hers, and she realized she didn't really know Nev anymore and wouldn't know what to look for to begin with. She was no longer the young girl with a soccer obsession and posters of the Spice Girls. And what was her story with Arthur? How did Nev fit into this picture with him and his home?

The back door opened, and Adrianna stuck her head inside. She looked at Kinsley with wide eyes.

"Nevaeh anywhere around?"

Kinsley shook her head and walked back to the table. "She's helping Arthur clean up for dinner."

Adrianna hurried inside. "Good. She's downright pissed at me." She had a bag of French bread and a bottle of wine in tow.

"Oh, goody, Nev brought out the Lambrusco." She set her goods on the counter and poured herself a glass and turned on the oven before joining Kinsley. "Smells damn good in here."

"It does, doesn't it?"

"That's ol' Arthur for you. That man can cook up a storm."

"Yeah, Nev told me he was Cajun."

"Oh, yes indeed. You stick around here long enough, you'll see. He'll spoil you rotten cooking for you. Food you'd die for."

"Sounds nice." She rested her cheek in her hand. "I could use some spoiling."

Adrianna touched her hand. "I agree."

"So, why is Nev pissed at you?"

Adrianna smiled. Patted her hand. "Never you mind."

"Does it have to do with me?"

Adrianna bit her lower lip. "I'll tell you something that does."

Kinsley perked. "Okay."

"I've got an offer for you."

"An offer?"

"A proposition. You stay as long as you like in your cabin for no charge."

Kinsley drew back and blinked. "What?"

"If you want to stay a while longer, I want you to. And you can stay for free."

"Adrianna, I—"

"Now, hear me out. You'll have to pay for your meals and snacks, and you can still participate in most classes. Your time with Holly, however, will be limited because she will have other clients. But you'll have your cabin, you'll have the creek, and you'll have me."

"What about Nev?" The question was out before she could stop it, and Adrianna seemed to like it because she grinned so hard Kinsley wondered if it was going to break her face.

"You can still do the horse therapy as far as I'm concerned."

"But Nev may object?"

"I'm sure she'll have no problem with you continuing, but she may not have as much time to devote to you once the new clients arrive."

Kinsley sighed. "She's already avoiding me, so I guess that wouldn't be anything new."

"She is?"

"Mm. I had to go searching for her today. Found her in the shop."

"During horse therapy?"

"Yes. Second time in a row."

Adrianna appeared concerned. She patted her hand again and stood to prepare the French bread. She began slicing and buttering it, and then she sprinkled on some garlic and parmesan cheese before sliding it into the warm oven. She set the timer and returned to her seat.

"Just keep showing up," Adrianna said. "She'll come around."

"I'm not so sure. There are things…things we can't seem to get past."

Adrianna sipped her wine, lost in thought. She was surprisingly quiet on the matter, which Kinsley found strange. But then she remembered that Adrianna was Nev's friend first and foremost, and then her silence didn't seem so unusual. Her loyalty was to Nev and she probably didn't want to interfere. And yet Kinsley wished she would. The woman was wise beyond measure, and she could've used some good advice as far as Nev went. But then again, maybe Adrianna had given her all the good advice she really needed.

Just keep showing up. She'll come around.

It was straightforward and simple. No frills or bullshit.

Fitting for Nev.

Just then, Nev and Arthur came out from the hallway. Nev left his side when he swatted her away, and Arthur shuffled into the room with a cane. He'd changed into a darker pair of jeans and a black button-down western style shirt. It looked very nice with his salt-and-pepper hair and lively blue eyes. And when he came closer to sit at the table, Kinsley could smell his Old Spice. He'd spruced up nicely for dinner, and Kinsley wondered if he always did this or if this was a special occasion.

He did his best to give her a smile when he sat and then nervously played with his turquoise bolo tie. Nev busied herself at the stove, preparing the noodles.

"Arthur, I want to ask you something," Kinsley said. "Actually, I need to ask all of you." She placed her hand on top of Arthur's with Adrianna's proposition in mind. "I was wondering if you would like to help me work with Willow?"

Nev cursed from her position at the stove and sucked on her finger. She'd apparently burned herself.

"Uh, I don't know," she said, flicking her hand. "Not sure he's—"

"I would love to."

Nev reddened. "Arthur, I'm not sure you can handle being out there—"

"He'll have me," Kinsley said.

"Yeah, I'll have her."

"I'll stick to him like glue, and he can help me with Willow. Since I'm so clueless and you seem to be so busy."

She wasn't meaning to sound like such a smart-ass, but she realized it was coming across that way. Nev seemed to notice too because she clenched that chiseled jaw of hers and went back to stirring the spaghetti.

"I'm still not sure it's a good idea."

"I think it's a great idea," Adrianna said. "It gets Arthur out of the house, doing something he loves, and it helps Kinsley as well."

Nev shook her head. "I don't like it. It could be—"

"What? Dangerous? It can't be any more dangerous than the shop," she said.

Nev tossed down the wooden spoon. "Fine. Let him do it. Who cares what I think anyway?"

Kinsley smiled and squeezed Arthur's hand.

His eyes seemed to dance, and Kinsley suddenly looked forward to more time on the ranch. And if she was reading Adrianna right, what she'd just done had pleased her as well. Because she was sitting there with a smirk, eyes twinkling.

What Adrianna didn't know, though, what none of them knew, was that her doing this had absolutely nothing to do with Nev. She'd done it on her own accord with nothing but her and Arthur in mind.

She had, right?

CHAPTER FOURTEEN

It makes no sense for me to drive her home," Nev said. "You do it."
Adrianna was seriously pissing her off. First dinner, now this. The whole night had turned into chaos as far as she was concerned.

Relaxing dinner, my ass.

"It makes plenty of sense," Adrianna said. "You were downright rude at dinner and you need to make up for that. Besides, dinner was my idea and I'm not leaving you with the mess. I'll stay here and clean up."

Adrianna was right, Nev had been rude at dinner. She'd been quiet and evasive, upset over the whole Arthur helping Kinsley with the horses thing. And, well, she was just upset in general at her overall presence. And it seemed she wasn't going to get rid of her anytime soon. It seemed, with Kinsley's latest revelation about wanting Arthur to work with her, that she was intent on staying a while.

Great.

Thank you, Adrianna.

"Ha. You sure about that? Because it seems you've left me with a fine mess."

Adrianna smacked her upper arm. "Go on, now. She's waiting."

Nev walked toward the door and Adrianna whispered after her, "And be nice!"

Nev sank her hands in her pockets and met Kinsley outside in the crisp canyon air. She was waiting near Adrianna's car, wearing jeans and a long-sleeved T-shirt. The moonlight was reflecting off her dark hair, and she looked almost angelic standing there hugging herself. Nev thought how incredibly beautiful she'd find her had this been any other circumstance. But it wasn't. So, at the moment, she tried to push her beauty far from her mind.

Kinsley seemed equally surprised by her presence, having expected Adrianna.

"Where's Adrianna?"

"She wants to clean up."

"Oh, well, I can stay and help. I offered—"

"Yeah, she won't let you. Don't even bother trying."

She won't budge because she's too busy trying to force us together. Something she said she wouldn't do.

Nev unlocked her truck and climbed inside as Kinsley did the same from the passenger side. She was rubbing her arms from the chill in the evening air as Nev started the truck. Nev was warm-blooded by nature, and the night air felt good to her. After having grown up in Phoenix in the stifling summer heat, she welcomed crisp, cool air any chance she got. But it seemed Kinsley wasn't such a fan of the lower temperatures.

Nev reached behind her and grabbed her soft flannel shirt, hoping it would suffice and she wouldn't have to turn on the heat. "Here. It's warm."

"No, thank you." She kept rubbing her arms, her body shaking.

Nev couldn't stand to see her so cold. She looked so...fragile. It made Nev want to slide over and hold her lithe body until she warmed up. A longing she didn't appreciate. "Just take it. Please?"

Kinsley looked at her but said nothing. She didn't take the shirt.

Nev tried a different tactic.

"It's not even mine. It's Adrianna's." It was a lie but one she excused. Kinsley was as stubborn as she was cold, and Nev couldn't bear to witness either. She would also do whatever it took to ensure that her yearning to warm her up wouldn't prompt her to action.

"Right."

"No, I'm serious. She wears it all the time around here. Must've left it in my truck." Adrianna had worn it before. Once.

Kinsley hesitantly took the shirt and shrugged it on. Nev fought smiling at her silent victory.

Kinsley hugged herself. "You're right, it is warm. Soft too. Funny, though," she said, smelling the collar. "It's smells like you."

"Me?" Nev laughed, a little unnerved at her perceptibility and a little moved by it at the same time. "And what do I smell like?"

"Good."

Nev looked at her in surprise and Kinsley seemed to panic. She shifted in her seat and seemed to be hurriedly searching for words.

"I mean clean. Fresh. Like you did when you got out of the shower."

"You smelled me when I got out of the shower?" *This is interesting. What else has she noticed about me? More importantly, why has she noticed?*

Her eyes widened and she stared out the windshield. "No. Yes. I mean not on purpose. I just—I have a strong sense of smell."

"Okay."

"No, I really do."

"Uh-huh." Nev shook her head, grinning. It was funny seeing Kinsley squirm. And could it be that she had somewhat of an attraction to her? After all these years? After everything?

Her mind went to Kinsley's sexuality, and she realized she'd never even considered that before. Was she gay? Could she be? The way she'd just all but panicked when Nev teased her would suggest that yes, maybe she was. Or at the very least, had some sort of interest in her that went beyond platonic. Or then again, maybe not. Maybe she was freaking out because she knew Nev was gay and she was worried she might get the wrong idea about her. After all, they both surely remembered that kiss in the limousine all those years ago. The kiss that Kinsley had initiated. This added a whole new layer to the chaos of the evening. Now not only was Kinsley going to be in their lives more, but she was possibly harboring an attraction to Nev too.

What would that mean and why was it causing her heart to thrum and her skin to flush to think about?

Nev pulled out of the drive, her mood glum again. Damn Adrianna for making her drive her home. It was ridiculous and Nev just knew it was a ploy on Adrianna's part. It had to be. Even though she'd sworn she wouldn't interfere. How could she do this to her? Did she know of Kinsley's attraction? Was that it? Was she really trying to throw them together?

They rode in silence for a short while before Kinsley spoke again.

"So, you pissed about the whole Arthur thing?"

Nev nearly ran off the road at her frankness. She cleared her throat. "I don't think it's a good idea, no." *I don't think any of this is a good idea.*

"Why?"

"Because of his condition."

"He'll just be helping me groom and visit with Willow. I won't let him do anything too physical. Besides, I thought you'd be all for it.

Working with the horses, like you say, is very therapeutic. It might be really good for him."

"And it might be really bad."

"How so?"

Nev sighed. "Really? You can't imagine all that could possibly go wrong?"

"No, I really can't. Arthur standing there with me brushing Willow doesn't exactly scream danger-danger to me. Especially knowing that Willow is bombproof."

Nev laughed. "Stop trying to use my own words against me."

"I'm not. I'm trying to get you to see reason."

"Oh, I see all right. I know what this is about."

"And what's that?"

Nev glanced over at her. "Me."

"You?"

"My not helping you. You took offense to it and this is your way of having a little revenge. Of shoving it in my face."

"Excuse me?" Kinsley faced her fully. "You think I'd use Arthur to what, to get to you somehow? To piss you off? Jesus, Nev, what the hell?"

"No? Then maybe you're doing it to get to me another way."

"What other way?"

Like a woman wanting some attention from a potential lover.

Nev shook her head, already having said too much. "Never mind."

"No, not never mind. Say it."

"No."

"Yes."

"No."

"Damn it, Nev, say it! Say what you mean for once in your goddamned life!"

Nev slammed on the brakes and they both jerked in their seat belts.

Kinsley grabbed her head and ran her hands through her hair. They both sat breathing heavily.

"Jesus," Kinsley let out. "I said say it, not kill us."

"You want me to say something?"

Kinsley looked at her. Bored holes into her with her turbulent eyes. They were lit up by the dash, and Nev could see the storm brewing just beneath their surface.

"Yes, I do. I want you to say what you've been dying to say since you've first seen me."

"Which is?"

"That it's my fault Viv is dead."

Nev opened her mouth to protest but stopped. She was right. It was true. That was what she thought. There was no two ways about it.

"That it's my fault because I wanted to go to that volleyball camp."

"You're—" What? Ridiculous? She wasn't. She was spot-on and she seemed to know it.

"No, Nev. I know that's what you think, so why don't you woman up and say it?"

"Because I—" She looked at her and fell silent. She couldn't argue, couldn't protest. It was what she thought. It was what she'd been raised to think, and at some point she'd started to believe it.

"You've resented me since the second you laid eyes on me, and I suspect for years before that."

Nev stared straight ahead. "Yeah, well."

"Yeah, well, I'm right, aren't I?" She shook her head. "Jesus, you still can't say it, can you?"

Nev turned on her, her temper finally getting the better of her. The chaos finally coming to a boiling point inside her.

"You want me to say it? Will that make you happy, Kinny? To hear that I think it's all your fault? Fine. I do. I think it's your fault. I think if you'd never said anything about that goddamned camp my sister would still be here. There. You happy?"

"Oh, I'm ecstatic." She laughed. "You really think this is news to me, Nev? You think I haven't blamed myself for this for the past twenty years? Me, at age eleven, thinking that I'd killed my best friend? Fuck you."

"Fuck me?"

"Yeah, fuck you. Because it's ludicrous and I'm not going to let you or anyone else make me feel this way over Viv's death. Not anymore. I was a child. A young girl who wanted to go to volleyball camp. Nothing more, nothing less. The only thing I did wrong was not get on that plane with her. Had I done that then it would've saved you a whole hell of a lot of hate." She unbuckled her seat belt and threw open the door. Then she crawled out and headed off down the dark road, arms crossed across her chest.

Oh great. Just great. She's out of the car. She's walking down a dark road alone in the middle of nowhere. What the hell does she think she's doing? How can anyone possibly be this stubborn?

Nev pulled up alongside her and lowered the window.

"Kinsley, get back in the car."

"I'm fine, thanks."

"It's cold and Adrianna's is still a ways away."

"I want to walk. Need to walk."

"Kinsley, come on. Will you get in? I promise I won't say another word."

"Really? Not even an apology?"

"An apology?"

"Yeah, you know, for blaming me for something I had absolutely no control over."

"I—" But could she? So many thoughts went through her head. Kinsley was talking sense, that much she knew, but it went against everything that had been ingrained in her. Everything. "Please, Kinsley? Get in? Before the coyotes get you?"

"Let 'em."

Nev sighed and resolved herself to having to follow alongside Kinsley until they reached the retreat. She could already hear Adrianna laying into her over the whole thing. But then Kinsley stopped and stared in at her.

"If I get in, without an apology, will you let Arthur work with me?"

Nev stopped the truck. "Yes, fine."

Kinsley opened the door and climbed back inside. Nev started driving again and Kinsley was quiet. Nev stole a glance at her and saw her massaging the cuff of her shirt with her fingertips, her gaze lost somewhere out the window. It was a long few moments before she spoke again.

"Just so you know, I didn't make that suggestion about Arthur for any other reason than to help him. Well, and maybe for myself." She looked over at her. "I really like him, and I think he really likes me. I'm hoping it will be really good for us both."

Nev rubbed her brow. "Okay." She still didn't like it, but not for the reasons Kinsley thought. She didn't like it because it now meant that her time with Kinsley was officially someone else's. What was worse was that it was Arthur's, the man who'd been like a father to her. Her closest friend and confidant. But she supposed she'd made her own bed by avoiding her and now she had to lie in it. Even so, the sting of jealousy was there. For both Kinsley and Arthur. They would have each other now and she'd be out of the picture. Just what would that lead to?

The jealousy, like her accusation of Kinsley being responsible for Viv's death, seemed irrational and ridiculous.

But yet, there it was, staring her in the face and eating her alive.

Just like Kinsley's presence.

Chapter Fifteen

Nev rang the bell to the house and waited not so patiently for someone to answer the door. She could hear the barks of a small dog and the distant sound of a neighbor's radio as she stood waiting on the front stoop. She looked around, noted the overgrown weeds in the yard, a dying aloe vera plant on the ledge, and a sun scorched decorative thermometer on the wall that had long ago stopped at a hundred and fifteen degrees. Nothing else adorned the front of the house. Just gloom. Which was what she suspected adorned the inside as well.

If that were the case, then she could at least take comfort in the fact that nothing had changed. Not since she was a kid anyway. This house, the one she and her parents had to move to after Viv's death, had always represented sadness and gloom to her, and she'd been so eager to escape, she'd even run away at age fifteen. Her folks had hunted her down and brought her back, of course, but she'd always wondered what would've happened had she been able to stay with her first girlfriend and her family. Would her life be any different? Would she be any different?

She waited for a few moments longer and then rang the bell again, wondering if there was a reason all her texts had gone unanswered, until finally, the door creaked open.

"Nevaeh?"

"Mom?"

She pulled open the door and Nev could see that it was indeed her mother, though she looked like she'd aged twenty years instead of the five since she'd last seen her.

"What are you doing here?" she asked. "Your father, he's at work. He won't be home for a while."

"I just came to see how you're doing. Is that okay? You didn't answer my calls or texts."

Her mother pushed the door open farther and headed back inside, motioning for Nev to follow.

"I don't have much to do with those cell phones. Confusing as hell, if you ask me."

Nev followed her into the small, warm living room where her mother promptly sat in a worn, faded maroon recliner. Nev recognized it, along with the rest of the furniture, as that from her childhood. Her folks had held on to everything. Both out of grief and out of necessity. It hadn't been long after the accident that her father had lost his job working for the Padovanos and they'd been nearly destitute.

"I can get you one that's easier to use," Nev said, stepping carefully around an excitable little white dog.

"Sugar, stop it," her mother said, scolding the dog.

"She's fine." Nev glanced around, the air already encroaching on her, making it difficult to breathe. "Can I turn the air down for you, Mom? Aren't you warm?" It had been in the sixties up in the canyon when she'd left, but here in Phoenix the temperature was in the eighties. And currently, in the house, it felt like the nineties.

"If you want to, I'm fine."

Nev rounded the corner and walked down the dark hallway. Though the hall was dim, she could still make out the dozen or so photos hanging on the walls. Most were of Viv, but a couple had her in them too. She lowered the thermostat just enough to get it to kick on and then returned to the living room. The dog had jumped up in the chair with her mother, but she was still wagging her tail at Nev.

"I see you got a new dog," Nev said as she sat down. She noted more photos of Viv on the end tables and the last family photo they'd taken sitting next to the television. It looked odd sitting there next to images from *Let's Make a Deal*.

"Your father brought her home. Some guy he works with had a dog that had puppies."

"She's cute."

"She's a pain in the ass, but I love her." She kissed the dog and then sipped from a large green cup. Nev wondered what was in it and if it contained the vodka her mother had always seemed so fond of. She hoped not, but again, nothing else appeared to have changed, so why should she have?

With the exception of her appearance, which seemed to have

grown more haggard, the house and everything in it looked exactly the same.

"You didn't turn that air down too low, did you? Your dad will have a fit if that power bill goes up."

"No, Mom, I didn't. And I'll leave you some cash to cover it just in case, okay?"

She nodded and sipped again from her cup. It was rather early in the day for alcohol, but Nev had known her to start drinking some days at sunup. Was that the case today?

"You working, Mom?" She knew the answer but asked anyway.

"No," she scoffed. "I got enough to take care of around here."

"But Dad's working, you say? Where's he at now?" Her father had had some trouble keeping employment, so she figured he had changed jobs again since she'd last spoken to him.

"He's down at the auto part store. Assistant manager."

Her father didn't drink like her mother, but he'd gone downhill in other ways. Just like everything else in their lives had after the accident.

"Are you still living with that old man up in Cypress Creek?" her mother asked with a scowl.

"His name is Arthur, and yes."

She shook her head. "Why in the hell you took up with him is beyond me. The way your career was headed at the university...I'll never understand it."

"You don't have to understand it, Mom. It's what I wanted."

"And to think of the money you could've made and helped your father and me with. But no, you had to go move in with some old man and work for him for free. Dropped school. Dropped everything."

"I was his apprentice, and it was only for a short while. And I did what I wanted with my life, Mom. *My* life."

"What about us? Your father and me? Are we nothing?"

"I can't live for you. I have to do what makes me happy. And blacksmithing makes me happy."

"All that time and money on school, and you just—"

Nev laughed. "Dropped it. Right, Mom? Need I remind you that I did graduate with my PhD and that all the money that was spent was done by me, not you. So you didn't lose out on anything."

"You shouldn't have done it. It was the wrong move. Moving in with that old man—"

Nev snapped at her, unable to help herself. "That old man has a name. It's Arthur. So I would appreciate you referring to him as such."

Her mother looked at her like she had been stricken. She covered herself with a throw like she was freezing. It was no wonder; she was practically skin and bones.

"It's unnatural. You and an old man like him."

"Unnatural? Like my being gay?" Nev was incredulous. "Is there anything about me that's okay with you, Mom? Anything at all? Can you name one thing?"

Her mother looked away, as if she could find nothing. Nev laughed again and buried her face in her hands. It was a few long moments before her mother spoke again.

"I don't like your hair that short. You used to have such pretty hair."

"Yeah, well, I like it like this."

"You look like a man."

"So you've said. Dozens of times."

"Why do you want to look like a man?"

"Because it pisses you off, Mom."

She whipped her head around to stare at her. "Don't you talk to me that way in my own house."

Nev shook her head and ran her hands through her hair. For a few seconds she'd forgotten why she'd come. Then, when she remembered, she was suddenly eager to bring it up so she could get her answer and get the hell out. Forget worrying about hurting her mother's feelings in even mentioning it. Her mother didn't seem to give a damn about her feelings.

"I ran into Kinsley Padovano recently, Mom."

Nev watched her closely, saw the slight flinch to her face, but then, nothing. Just a blank stare.

"Did you hear me?"

"I don't know why you'd bring that name up in my house."

"So, you still feel the same way then? About her and her family?"

Her mother looked at her with steely eyes. "How can you even ask me that?"

"Because it's been twenty years. Twenty long years. Isn't it time we let things go, Mom?"

Her mother gripped the soft looking armrests on her chair. "I can't let it go. I'll never let it go. And I can't believe you're even suggesting it. If your father knew—"

"He'd what? Hate me? Banish me? Just like you did Kinsley's family? All because of your self-righteous judgment? Because you two always have to have someone to blame for everything? Like how it's my fault you have no money because I left my career in academia to follow my heart?"

"You did leave it!"

Nev stood. "Because I wanted to! It had nothing to do with you!"

"Exactly! You didn't even think of us."

"Why would I? You certainly weren't thinking of me and you haven't since Viv died. So, I took care of me. Me, Mom. Someone had to." She motioned around the room. "Look at this place. It's still the same. It's a goddamned monument to Viv. I was nowhere in the picture. And I'm still not."

Her mother released the dog, who was squirming from all the shouting. She ran and hid beneath the kitchen table. She yipped at Nev from her fortress of safety.

"I'm never going to be in the picture, am I, Mom? Because I'm just not good enough. Because I'm just not Viv."

She didn't respond. She just sat and stared. When she finally did speak it was soft and sullen but very sure.

"You need to leave."

Nev nodded. "Yes, I do." She fished her wallet out of her back pocket, pulled out a stack of bills, and set them on the coffee table.

Then she walked out and left her mother without looking back.

Nev was once again standing at a door, waiting for someone to answer. This time, however, she was even more impatient, more nervous than she had been at her folks'. This time, she had something very important to say, and there was no one to shout at or to feel angry at. This time, it would be just her and Kinsley.

Kinsley opened the door to her cabin and didn't even seem to bother to try to hide her surprise.

"Nev."

"Hi."

"Hello."

"I was wondering if I could speak to you for a moment?"

"Uh..." She stepped into the light and Nev saw her wipe away tears.

She's crying.

"I—never mind. I'll come back another time."

"No, it's fine." She eased open the door. "I mean, why not, right?"

Nev walked inside after hesitating for a moment. The cabin was small and cozy, just as she remembered, and it smelled like cinnamon.

"Smells good in here," she said, trying to make nice and ease the obvious tension.

Kinsley stood near the entryway in tight-fitting yoga pants and the flannel Nev had given her the other night on the ride back to the retreat. For some reason, seeing her wearing it, made her face flush and her body heat.

She looks good in it, that's why. She looks good in my shirt.

"It's a new candle I bought in the gift shop. Cinnamon Bun or something like that."

"Smells really good."

Nev stood awkwardly, unsure where to go. Kinsley hovered by the door like she couldn't wait for her to leave. It made Nev all the more nervous.

"Can we—please sit for a moment?" She was going to do this, and she was going to do this right.

"Sure." Kinsley led the way into the tiny living room and offered her a seat on the dark brown couch while she sat in the chair next to the wood burning stove. Nev could see the flames flickering through the door.

"Are you—okay?" Nev asked, staring into her watery eyes.

"I am, actually. I just got more good news. My cousin had his surgery on his face and he's doing well."

"That's great news."

"It is." She sniffled and wiped away the tears.

Nev glanced around and noted that the cabin felt cozier with Kinsley in it. It felt lived in. Truly lived in. And if she weren't so nervous, she knew she'd feel comfortable there, like maybe she could sit down to talk with her over a cup of coffee. It was wishful thinking, though, and a wish she decided to keep for herself.

"You liking staying here?" Nev asked.

"Very much so."

"That's good."

Nev rubbed her hands along her denim clad thighs. The silver and turquoise bracelet she wore rolled along her wrist and she could feel the platinum ring she wore on her middle finger begin to grow warm.

"Nev, you okay?"

Nev looked up. Kinsley was watching her closely, her legs curled up under her on the chair. Beyond her, through the window, the sun was getting ready to set, as if putting a time limit on Nev's intentions. She'd left her mother's hours ago, but it had taken her this long to work up the nerve to come to Kinsley's.

"Yeah, I'm good." She was so not good. Her throat felt dry and tight and her heart was careening. "I, uh—"

Just say it, you moron.

"I'm sorry, Kinsley."

There. I said it.

Kinsley raised her eyebrows. "Pardon?"

Damn it.

"I said I'm sorry."

Kinsley looked at her for a long moment, and then released the breath she'd apparently been holding.

"Okay. Can I ask for what?"

"For, you know, the other night. The thing we talked about in the truck."

"Which was?"

Really? Christ, woman, you're killing me.

"I'm sorry about blaming you for Viv's death."

There. Done.

Settled.

Finished.

She slapped her thighs and stood.

Kinsley spoke.

"Wait, that's it?"

Nev breathed deeply. Relieved. She nodded.

"Nothing else, just the I'm sorry?"

Nev felt her brow furrow. "Is that not enough?"

"Well, I thought maybe a little explanation would be included."

"An explanation?"

"Yeah, you know, why you're apologizing, etcetera, etcetera."

Nev sat back down and started in on her legs again.

Kinsley cocked her head. "This is really hard for you, isn't it?"

Nev clenched her jaw. "No."

"I think it is."

She stood again. "Look, I came to apologize. I did that, so that should be enough."

Kinsley scrambled to a stand. "I see, so I should just be grateful I got that much, should I?"

"Yeah, pretty much."

"What?" She looked at her like she couldn't believe she'd just said those words aloud. Nev was just as surprised as she was.

"I need to go, Arthur's waiting."

"So, that's really it?" Kinsley followed her to the door.

Nev opened it and turned, again overcome by how good she looked in her shirt.

"I'm sorry that's not enough."

She headed outside and left Kinsley just like she'd left her mother. Without another word.

Chapter Sixteen

K insley closed her eyes and tried to concentrate on her pose as the soft instrumental music Holly had chosen for the session played around her. She was in yoga class in the main lodge along with her fellow retreat goers, finishing up their early morning class. One of the windows was open, allowing the fresh morning air to filter in, to help awaken their senses. The gentle breeze brought the earthy smell of the creek in with it, and Kinsley realized that if she tried hard enough, she could even hear the rush of the creek over the music.

It was a beautiful morning, and the setting couldn't be more serene. And despite her yoga poses feeling wonderful as they gently stretched her muscles, which were stiff from hiking, she couldn't totally embrace it. Her mind, which she still was struggling to get control of, kept returning to other things.

Namely, Nev.

Kinsley kept replaying her visit to the cabin the day before, wondering what had prompted her apology. Had it been something Kinsley had said? She'd said a lot, some of it pretty harsh, but Nev had seemed to fight it off well, disinterested in her point of view. Could Nev really have had a change of heart?

Kinsley was wary to think so, seeing as how the three-word apology was all she got. Nev refused to say more or to elaborate further. It was just a simple, straightforward "I'm sorry" and "That's all you're getting."

Who does that?

How could she possibly be sincere when approaching the whole thing like that?

Kinsley had noticed that what little she had gotten from Nev seemed to be very difficult for her to voice, but even so, she should feel some sense of sincerity in the matter, shouldn't she?

Instead she was left with a bad taste in her mouth. A confusing taste, one she couldn't identify or understand.

Could Nev really be so emotionally out of touch that that simple apology was all she was capable of? Was she that far removed? That void of emotion?

It scared Kinsley to even consider. Because if that was the case, then it meant that the damage caused by Viv's death and the subsequent events thereafter were more significant than Kinsley could've imagined.

"Okay," Holly said softly, bringing Kinsley back into focus. "Inhale as you come up, palms together, hands up to the sky, and exhale as you slowly bring your arms down. Very nicely done, guys. Great job."

Kinsley shook out her arms and rolled her shoulders. She felt wonderful, her body relaxed and ready for her day. She began rolling up her yoga mat as she wished her fellow retreat goers a nice day.

"Kinsley, you got a second?" Holly asked. She took a sip of water from her water bottle and switched off the music.

Kinsley took her rolled mat, tucked it into her hip, and walked up to her.

"Sure, what's up?"

"I just wanted to check in with you. Adrianna told me you're going to be staying on for a while."

"I thought I'd stay a bit longer."

She smiled. "That's great, I'm glad to hear it. How's the journaling coming along? It getting any easier?"

"Mm, somewhat. I'm just not used to it, I think."

"Remember, this is different from your gratitude exercises, so no-holds-barred, even if it's negative. Just write whatever comes to mind. Thoughts, feelings, memories, all of it. We're going to have a ceremony where you'll get to purge those thoughts and feelings once and for all. I think it'll really help you."

Kinsley nodded, hoping she was right. She'd confided a lot in Holly the past week or so, told her about the crash, about the guilt and the shame. Holly had listened keenly and tailored her itinerary more so to suit her needs. Increasing the relaxation exercises and the classes on self-esteem and depression. And the journaling, which she was currently referring to, was all about getting things out and letting go.

None of it was easy for Kinsley, but when she thought about Nev and how difficult an apology seemed to be for her to elaborate on, she realized she might be being a little hard on herself. At least she was trying.

Nev tried yesterday too.

I'm trying harder.

"And continue on your self-enlightenment hikes," Holly continued. "Commune with nature, really feel her and take her in. You still have the trail map I gave you?"

"Yes."

"If you get tired of those and want something new, ask Nev. There are some great trails out by her place. Has she taken you on a trail ride yet?"

"No." *Oh, God, a trail ride? I have to ride the horse?*

"Must not be time yet." She winked. "You'll get there."

"What if I don't want to get there?"

"Not a big fan of horses, huh?" She shrugged. "In that case you can just ride with Nev."

Kinsley swallowed so hard she worried Holly had heard it.

"Uh, not so sure about that either."

Holly laughed. "I know a couple of others who would gladly take your place if you're not interested."

"Ugh. Yeah. Judy and Kathy are kind of hard to miss. Nev's all they talk about."

"It wouldn't be the first time a guest has had an interest." She rolled up her mat and crossed to close the window. "Nev's pretty popular around here. Most of the time."

"You don't sound like you approve."

"Me?" Holly glanced back at her. "Nah, Nev's okay, I guess. If you like that strong silent type deal." They reached the door and Holly switched off the lights. "That type is just not for me. Learned that the hard way."

Kinsley burned at her words, an image of Holly and Nev taking precedence in her mind.

"You—were with Nev?"

"With her? No. Never got that far." They headed out into the hallway. "Never got anywhere really. I asked her out for dinner once and she showed up, but then made an excuse and up and left. Never gave me an explanation. And I swear I only got an apology because Adrianna said something to her about it."

Kinsley burned hotter. So that's it. Adrianna gave her a hard time. That's why she came to apologize.

She wasn't sincere.

Kinsley's body tightened, and all the work she'd done that morning in yoga was suddenly pointless. She was wound up again. Tighter than a top.

"That seems to be Adrianna's thing," Kinsley said. "Smoothing the waters for Nev."

"Yeah, they're pretty tight. Especially since Izzy died."

"Who's Izzy?"

Holly glanced at her. "Adrianna's daughter."

"Oh, right."

"I thought you knew. You're staying in her cabin."

"Her cabin?" Come to think of it, Adrianna had mentioned something to her about her daughter.

They came to the dining area and the clamor of voices and silverware on dishes filled the air, along with the scent of freshly baked pastries and muffins.

Holly touched her shoulder and headed off. "I gotta go. I have a class in five. I'll see you later, yeah?"

Kinsley nodded. "Sure. See you later."

She looked around for Adrianna, now more curious than ever, but didn't see her. She'd just have to wait for her appointment with her in an hour.

In the meantime, she decided to grab a muffin and some coffee and sit down to mull over her relationship with the one person she couldn't put off thinking about.

Nev.

❖

Adrianna breezed in and greeted Kinsley in her typical fashion of taking both of her hands in hers.

"You're looking more and more well rested," she said with a warm smile. She turned and motioned Kinsley into the room she'd just emerged from.

She led Kinsley to a cushioned table and encouraged her to lie down. Kinsley did so while noting the numerous lit candles and soft music playing in the background. Beautiful paintings of the red rocks of the canyon hung on the walls, and she thought about asking who had painted them but then changed her mind as Adrianna helped her to recline.

"How are you feeling today?"

"Nervous."

She chuckled. "Because of this?"

"Uh-huh."

"Never had any hands-on healing before?"

"Nuh-uh."

"Well, I promise not to hurt you. Not too much anyway."

"I appreciate that."

"I try my best." She winked at her. "Other than nervous about this, how else are you feeling?"

"Mm, a little confused. A little torn."

"Over?"

Kinsley sighed. "Nev."

Adrianna faced the table against the wall and rearranged the candles. "Do you want to elaborate?"

"I don't know. Should I? I mean right now?"

"It might help me balance your energy if I know what's going on with you."

Kinsley had wanted to discuss this with her, but she hadn't been sure if this session was the proper time in which to do it. Adrianna, though, seemed to want her to.

"She came by my cabin yesterday to apologize. For blaming me for Viv's death."

"Oh. Goodness." She adjusted the music. Lowered the volume.

"Right?"

"And that confused you?"

"It's the way she did it. She literally just walked in, said she was sorry and left. No explanation or elaboration as to why she'd changed her mind. Nothing. And when I pressed her, I got more nothing. She just left."

"So, you are thinking what?" She turned and faced her again.

"That maybe she wasn't sincere. That she didn't really mean it."

"Why would she apologize if she didn't mean it?" She moved again and this time dimmed the lights.

"I don't know. Maybe because someone like you put her up to it."

Adrianna's face clouded as she returned to the table. Kinsley continued.

"I know you two discuss me and I know you've encouraged her to talk to me and to work with me and Willow. I also suspect you had her drive me home the other night so that the two of us could talk. So, it's not out of the realm of possibility that maybe you somehow, for some reason, put her up to coming to apologize to me."

This time Adrianna sighed. "Oh, Kinsley." She backed away from her and rubbed her forehead. "I did no such thing. And even if I had, you should know that Nev probably wouldn't have listened. She can be very strongheaded, and doing what I suggest is usually the very last thing she wants to do."

"So, she came on her own?"

"Sounds like it."

"She was sincere?"

"I think you need to ask her that."

Kinsley fell silent.

Adrianna came back to her and held her hand. "I told Nev I'd stay out of her business when it came to you, and I intend to do that."

"So, you didn't purposely have her drive me home?"

A small smile crept upon her face. "I needed to stay and clean up and I figured you wanted to get home."

"So, you did."

"I did what I felt was right at the moment. You did want to get home, didn't you? Especially after how rude Nev was at dinner?"

"You noticed that too?"

"It took all I had not to kick her under the table."

Kinsley laughed. "But you didn't tell her to apologize?"

"No. I told her to be nice. That was the extent of it. I'm dying to ask you if she was, if she listened, but it's best I not know anymore. You two need to work things out on your own."

"Can I ask you one more question?"

"Of course."

"Did you let me stay because you're hoping I'll work things out with Nev?"

"Why would you think that?"

"Because of the way you two discuss me and because you're letting me stay in your daughter's cabin. And from what I could gather in asking around here today, it sounds like that's a pretty big deal. Not something you'd do for just anybody."

A sadness washed over Adrianna, and for a second it seemed to weight her down. Her body went slightly limp, like her bones had softened. Her eyes, so rich and brown, brimmed with tears.

"Sweetheart, I'm letting you stay in that cabin because you need to. You need to be here. And because that's the right thing to do."

Kinsley squeezed her hand. "Okay. Thank you."

"Whatever happens between you and Nev, that's up to the two of you." She smiled and her tears receded. "Now, let's balance your chakras and do some healing. Sound good?"

"Yes. I think. I'm still nervous."

"Relax and close your eyes. Take some deep breaths."

Kinsley did.

"Now I'm going to do a scan, to see where you need the most work. Other than your headaches and muscle tightness, are you suffering any other maladies?"

"No."

She stepped back to the small table, where the lit candles were, and retrieved a necklace with a small stone on the end.

"This is a pendulum." She returned to Kinsley and stood at her feet. She held the pendulum over her ankles and it began to spin. "This clockwise spin means your chakras are open." She moved up her body, and when the pendulum got to her waist it began to swing back and forth. It continued to do the same all the way up her body to her head. "When it stops the clockwise motion and swings like this it means your chakras are blocked."

"Is that bad?"

"It means you're not balanced. And with what you've told me, it makes sense. Now it's time to fix all that and get you feeling better. Go ahead and close your eyes again."

Kinsley closed her eyes.

"Take some deep breaths and relax. You're going to feel me place my hand on you in some areas, okay?"

"Okay."

She began the healing by starting at Kinsley's head. She placed her hand on her forehead, and Kinsley could sense her other hand hovering above her face.

"What I'm doing is asking for healing and compassion and allowing it to build within myself. Then I allow it to flow through me and into you. So, try to imagine my energy flowing into yours, healing you."

Kinsley took another breath and did as instructed. Adrianna stayed at her head for quite some time, and just before she moved lower, Kinsley swore she felt her hand grow hot. And as she moved lower, to her throat, she felt the same. When she got to her chest, Kinsley really felt something.

"This is your solar plexus chakra, or where the mind is housed. It represents the physical and emotional, so you should be feeling a lot here as I work to open it up."

"I am."

"Good."

"No, I mean I really am."

Tears began to fill her eyes.

"Shh, it's okay, sweetheart. It's okay to feel."

"I'm really feeling something."

"You've got a lot of pain here and we're letting it go."

Kinsley tried to take deep breaths, but the more she did, the more she trembled and more she felt.

"Go ahead and cry, sweetheart. It's okay."

Kinsley cried then, with her eyes closed, as Adrianna lightly pressed her hand on her upper chest while her other hand hovered over her sternum. She couldn't explain what was happening, only that a tidal wave of emotion was coming up out of her, without root or source. She was thinking of nothing in particular. She was just being present.

Maybe that's what was doing it. What Holly had kept encouraging her to understand.

Being present.

She continued to cry as Adrianna moved lower once more. This time to her waist where she rested her hand on her lower stomach.

"This is your sacral chakra. This is where emotion, creativity, and sexuality lie."

Again, Kinsley felt the heat radiate from her hand and more feelings came. Sadness, loneliness, and anxiousness. Again, she had no thoughts of anything specific. Just feelings.

Tears ran down her face as she experienced them. All the while Adrianna was gently soothing her. The process continued as Adrianna moved lower, finally finishing up at her root chakra down near her feet. Kinsley didn't feel as much in her lower extremities as she had up top. But nevertheless, what she had felt was incredibly powerful and she was overwhelmed at how she felt now.

"How do you feel?" Adrianna asked.

Kinsley opened her eyes and watched as Adrianna checked her with the pendulum again. This time it continuously swung in the clockwise direction.

Kinsley wiped her face. "I feel…lighter. Clearer."

"Any pain anywhere?"

"None."

Adrianna patted her leg. "How is everything else going?"

"My cousin had his surgery and he's recovering."

"That's wonderful news, Kinsley."

"It is isn't it?"

"Yes. That should be a ton of bricks off your shoulders."

"It is. Only…"

"Yes?"

"I've still got another ton to contend with. The investigation."

"Which means?"

"It could mean that this accident, unlike Viv's, really is my fault."

Adrianna shook her head.

"No, sweetheart. You didn't do anything wrong. Have faith in that. Have faith in yourself."

"I wish I could, Adrianna. I wish I could."

CHAPTER SEVENTEEN

Nev killed the flame to the blowtorch and whipped off her safety goggles. The gate was too loose in the vise again. She couldn't get it secured good enough for the angle she needed. Not without someone holding it steady.

She tore off her gloves and tried, teeth clenched, to resecure it.

"Come on, you piece of crap. Work with me." But it was to no avail. The gate just wouldn't cooperate. Or was it the vise? Neither, it seemed, was willing to work with her.

"Shit." She let go of the gate and it clattered onto the table and then slid to the floor. Furious, she picked it up and chucked it as hard as she could across the room. It landed in a cacophony of noise, making her flinch, but she didn't care. She didn't care if the whole world heard it. She was pissed.

She ran her hands through her hair and leaned against the table. She could feel the sweat on her brow, and it was stinging her eyes. It was like an oven in the shop. Normally, that wouldn't bother her so much, it was just part of the job. But today it was, and she knew why. One reason was because she had the side door closed so there wasn't the usual open ventilation she normally had. And the other reason was standing just outside that side door, across the lawn in the corral, and it seemed her presence alone was causing every little nuance to bother Nev today.

She's here, so what. You knew she was coming.

She'd expected Kinsley to show up to work with Arthur. She'd even helped him get ready. Her old friend had been up earlier than usual, at the break of dawn, wanting breakfast and insisting on a long shower in his seated shower chair. Louise had found the whole thing amusing and said it was good for him to have something to look forward to. Nev, however, was still unhappy about the arrangement. She'd even frowned when Arthur stepped into the living room, shuffling with his cane, freshly shaved, smelling like Old Spice. It was too much. He was too invested. What if Kinsley changed her mind or disappointed him somehow?

Or what if I unintentionally run her off?

She'd tried to apologize to her. To do as Adrianna always said and do the right thing, but that hadn't seemed to be enough for Kinsley. She wanted more. Well, Nev didn't have anything more. She didn't know what she wanted from her, and even if she did, would she be willing to give it to her?

The side door slid open, and Adrianna peeked her head in.

"Everything okay in here?"

Nev crossed to the forge and killed the gas. She moved toward the radio and then realized it wasn't even on. She stalked to the door and switched off the lights. She secured her cowboy hat on her head.

"Fine."

Adrianna caught sight of the gate on the floor. "Doesn't look fine to me."

"It is. For now."

She followed Adrianna out and then closed the door behind them. The cool fall air felt good on her moist skin and she breathed it in deeply, allowing it to rejuvenate her body. She wiped the sweat from her brow and walked with Adrianna toward the corral.

She wanted to see how Arthur was doing, even if it meant a little pain and jealousy had to be endured on her part.

"Bad day?" Adrianna said more than asked. "Wondered why you had the door closed."

Nev grunted her response and avoided telling her she had the door closed so she wouldn't risk sneaking a peek at Kinsley across the lawn.

"Ah, okay. Got it. I'll just shut up, then."

Nev glanced over at her and then laughed softly. "Shut up."

Adrianna looked at her in surprise. "I am. I said I was."

"No, I mean, shut up. You know it's not you."

"I know no such thing, and when it comes to you, I don't like to take my chances."

"Bullshit."

"Okay, you got me there. But for today, I'm not taking any."

They slowed as they came to the pen, and Nev leaned on the rails, searching for Arthur and Kinsley, who seemed nowhere to be found.

"They're still in the stable," Adrianna said. "Arthur is showing Kinsley how to tack up Willow."

Nev didn't respond, just took in the rest of the group who were busy working with their assigned horses, laughing and chatting. The day was bright and sunny, the breeze cool bordering on cold. Nev shoved up her tight shirtsleeves, wishing she'd gone with a short-sleeved T-shirt despite the chill.

"Nev, hi," a voice said to her left. Nev turned and found Judy and Kathy standing there with Baby in tow.

"Hi." Nev tipped her cowboy hat, inwardly sighing at having to put on a happy, friendly face when she felt anything but.

"How have you been? We haven't seen you much here lately."

"I've been busy with other things."

Kathy smiled shyly.

Judy saw her and added, "We've missed you."

Nev felt herself blush and Adrianna cleared her throat.

"I think I'll go check on Kinsley and Arthur."

Nev moved to go with her, but the two women moved closer to her, standing in her line of sight, insisting she pay attention to them.

"We were wondering if you would help us with mounting Baby. Deena says she needs to be ridden a little today."

"I thought Deena was helping you with that."

"She has been. But she's over there working with Matthew and Juno today, and we're still having trouble. Especially Kathy. And I'm not strong enough to support her. Could you spot her?"

Nev sighed, too tired to hide it. "Sure." She rounded the corral and entered through the gate. She crossed to the women and stood alongside Baby, stroking her neck. She looked at Kathy.

"Go ahead, I'm right here."

Kathy looked at her with her gray eyes, her features fine and almost timid. "Can you…help me up?"

Nev stood closer to her and placed her hand on the small of her back and on her hip as she tucked her foot into the stirrup and tried to climb onto Baby. At the last second, just as she was trying to lift herself, she fell back into Nev. Nev caught her and held her tightly.

"You okay?"

"Yes, thank you."

She held on to Nev's forearm until Nev noticed and pulled away. She didn't know if the whole thing was a ruse just to get close to her or not. But even if it was, she was going to remain professional and polite.

"Come on, let's try again."

Kathy stood alongside her and tried again, with Nev supporting her. This time she was able to pull herself up completely with Nev's help. She smiled from atop Baby and Judy beamed up at her. She handed her her cowboy hat.

"You look like the real thing up there," she said.

Nev squinted up at her. "She's right, you do."

Kathy smiled. "Thanks, Nev."

"Yes, thank you," Judy said.

Nev tugged on Baby's lead and began walking slowly with them around the corral. Then she handed it off to Judy, who seemed to have other intentions written all over her face.

"We were going to go into town tonight for a beer. Care to join us?"

"The retreat is getting old," Kathy said. "We're getting cabin fever."

Nev caught sight of Kinsley leading Willow out into the corral. She had on jeans and a ball cap and...her flannel shirt.

"I don't know, I have a lot of work to do. A lot to catch up on."

"Oh, come on. Everyone needs a break. Besides, we're leaving soon."

Judy touched her arm and Nev saw that Kinsley was watching them. But she couldn't read the expression on her face. Then she saw Arthur trail out behind her, his hand resting on Willow's side.

"Would you excuse me, please?"

"We'll be at the Eagle Eye if you change your mind," Judy called after her.

Nev tipped her hat at them to wish them good day and then crossed to Kinsley and Arthur. Adrianna breezed past her with a grin.

"You get some attention?" she teased her.

"Shut up," Nev said.

Nev walked up to greet Kinsley, but she was avoiding her gaze.

"How's it going?" Nev asked, concerned she was still uncomfortable after their last encounter. Nev was, there was no doubt about that, but she wasn't going to be unfriendly.

"Fine. We're doing fine." She still wouldn't look at her, and Nev tried to decide if she was being genuine. She saw nothing other than truth in her face, however. But she'd definitely heard the slight bite to her tone.

"Arthur's doing okay?" she asked softly.

"I'm right here, you know. I'm not deaf."

Kinsley laughed and Nev sank her hand in her back pocket.

"You're right, I'm sorry. You doing okay, Arthur?"

He was stroking Willow, wearing his old cowboy hat and pinning Nev with a hard stare.

"I told you, I don't need no babysitter."

"Yeah, yeah. Don't worry, I won't hover."

"Damn right you won't."

Kinsley laughed again. "He's got your number."

"He's a pain in my ass and he knows it."

"You two have a special relationship, don't you?"

"How do you mean?"

"You're like father and daughter and best friends all combined into one."

Nev bristled at the mention of the word *father*. "Yeah, I guess you could say that."

"I didn't mean to upset you." Kinsley was finally looking at her, watching her.

"You didn't."

"I call bullshit," Kinsley said.

Nev rubbed Willow's snout and ignored her.

"Listen," Kinsley said. "I need to thank you for your apology the other night."

"Oh, there's no need." Nev didn't want to get into it. She just wanted to forget the whole thing.

"There is, actually. You came and apologized, and I was less than gracious and accepting. So, I apologize for that."

"Kinsley, there's—"

"Please. Just accept it, okay?"

"Okay."

They stood in silence for a while and Arthur shuffled closer. He handed Kinsley a brush and started telling her how to use it on Willow. Nev couldn't help but smile, knowing that Kinsley already knew how, but amused that she was pretending she didn't. She just listened quietly and did as Arthur instructed. It was a moving sight to see, Kinsley graciously working with Arthur, so patient and kind. But nevertheless, that sting of jealousy she'd been dreading began to slowly creep in, and she was beginning to understand why.

Arthur was close enough to her to be her father, and in many instances had been like a father, and now he was suddenly bonding with someone else. She wasn't sure how she felt about it, and the jealousy, while she understood the root cause of it, didn't sit right with her. She knew she shouldn't be jealous over something as wonderful as Arthur finding a new friend. But yet she was.

Arthur had been there when her own father hadn't. He'd taken her under his wing, mentored her, guided her, and loved her unconditionally. He'd been the family that hers had refused to be. And with her recent trip home, it seemed all of those old emotions from the neglect and apathy had come rushing back. Leading her to this moment where she was watching her pseudo father, father another daughter.

Would she get the short end of the stick this time too?

Would she end up alone again?

She didn't know. All she knew was she didn't like thinking about it, and at the moment she couldn't bear to watch the two of them anymore. She pulled on the brim of her hat and turned to stalk back across the corral.

Judy and Kathy were anxiously waiting.

CHAPTER EIGHTEEN

K insley wasn't sure what the heck she was doing. All she knew was that it felt good, really good, and she didn't want to stop anytime soon.

"You ready for another?" Kathy asked over the loud country music, sliding the shot of tequila toward her. They were at a local bar called the Eagle Eye, the last place Kinsley thought she'd find herself. But Judy and Kathy had all but dragged her out the door to come with, insisting that she needed to have a little fun. And who was she to argue? She did need to have some fun. If she could remember how.

The booze, of course, was helpful in that department.

"I better not," Kinsley said, already feeling warm and pleasantly buzzed from the first two.

"Oh, come on. Don't be a stick in the mud," Judy said. She pushed the glass farther toward her as the table behind them burst into loud laughter.

"Yeah, one more. Come on," Kathy said. "Everyone's having a good time. Let's join them."

Kinsley eyed the shot and then watched as Judy downed hers and sucked on the wedge of lime. She shook her head and shouted, "Whoo! Yeah! That's what I'm talking about." She started dancing in her seat as a new, louder, upbeat country song began to play.

"Do it with me," Kathy said, tapping Kinsley's hand to get her attention.

"Oh, all right." They both salted their wrists and then Kathy lifted her glass and Kinsley reluctantly did the same.

"Ready? One, two, three." They licked the salt off their skin and downed the shots. Then they both squinted in agony as they sucked on their lime wedges.

"Ugh, God, that's awful," Kinsley said.

Kathy nodded, drinking from her glass of water as Judy laughed.

"You're such a lightweight, Kinsley," she said.

"I told you I don't drink very often."

"Well, you should, you know. You need to unwind."

"Mm, now that you mention it, and now that I'm feeling really good, I think I might agree with you."

"You're one uptight little woman. We've been wondering if you had this in you."

"I've had a lot going on."

Kathy touched her hand. "We figured." She smiled. "But we're here now, so let's have some fun, okay? Unwind a little."

"I'm trying."

"You're doing a hell of a job," Judy said. "Keep it up and you just might sell us on actually being human."

"Judy," Kathy said.

"What? She's been really distant and unhappy."

"You shouldn't announce it when she's trying to have a good time."

"No, she's right," Kinsley said. "I've been a bear. But here's to tonight." She lifted her water glass in a toast. Judy and Kathy joined her.

"To tonight."

"May we all get laid," Judy said.

Kinsley cracked up. "Aren't you two married?"

"Divorced," Judy said.

"Separated," Kathy said.

"Oh wow, I didn't know."

"Why do you think we're here? We needed to unwind and get away from the jerks we married."

"Ouch," Kinsley said.

"It's true," Kathy said. "No sense mincing words."

They laughed as Matthew sauntered over in his cowboy getup and slunk down into his chair. His hat and western attire were brand new and very obviously citified. But he didn't seem to care. He was embracing his new, rough-and-tumble persona, full-fledged.

"How you doing, cowboy?" Judy asked. "You wrangling them in?"

"One or two." He grinned, sipping his beer. "Lots of pretty ladies here tonight."

"We saw you tearing up that dance floor," Judy said. "Now we just gotta get Kinsley out there."

"Me? Uh, no. No thanks."

"Come on." Kathy tried to tug on her. "Come with me."

Kinsley fought her off. "Isn't it enough that I came with and that I'm drinking with you?"

"No," Judy said. "It's not near enough."

Kinsley sighed but shook her head. "You go ahead. I'll watch."

Kathy frowned but grabbed Matthew's hand and yanked him up to follow her onto the dance floor. He stumbled along after her and Judy smiled after them.

"What do you think? He's cute, huh?"

"Matthew? Sure."

Judy looked at her with disbelief. "You don't really think so."

"I do. He's just not my type."

"Who is?"

"What, you mean here?"

"Sure. There's got to be someone here you fancy."

"I don't think so."

Judy's eyes left Kinsley and shifted over toward the door. A sly grin spread across her face.

"What about her?"

Kinsley turned and found Nev standing just inside the door. Kinsley swallowed at the sight of her in a black V-neck tee and tight dark jeans shredded at the knees. She pulled off her cowboy hat and tousled her short hair. Somehow it looked perfect, purposely messy. She stepped farther inside, and Kinsley saw the dampness to her skin. The lingering clouds must've unleashed since she'd arrived. The glistening of the rain set off the bronze of her skin, and Kinsley swore she looked good enough to eat. And it seemed she wasn't the only one who thought so.

"She is positively yummy," Judy said.

Kinsley faced her again and tried to casually sip her water. "You like Nev."

"Woman, who doesn't?"

Kinsley shrugged, uncomfortable at hearing her lust over Nev so freely. It had been bad enough watching them fawn over her back at the ranch, but hearing it firsthand made her feel like she'd been kicked in the gut.

"You don't? Let me guess, she's not your type either?"

Kinsley shrugged again.

Judy narrowed her eyes and lowered herself to catch Kinsley's gaze. "You're lying."

"I am not."

She grinned again. "Are too. And here I thought the reason for the obvious tension between you two was because you knew each other."

"We do know each other."

"Uh-huh. So I've gathered. So, tell me, just how well do you know each other?"

Kinsley played with her straw, disliking the personal direction the conversation was heading.

"We knew each other as kids, that's all."

"So, why the tension?"

"I don't know."

"Because you're attracted to her."

"I didn't say that."

"You didn't say no, either."

"I don't have to say anything."

Judy leaned back in her chair. "Okay, so if you aren't interested, then you'll have no issue if Kathy or I make a move on her?"

"Do what you want. I can't stop you."

"But you want to."

"I didn't say that."

"No, you're not saying much of anything, and yet you're saying a whole hell of a lot."

"What we'd miss?" Kathy asked breathlessly as she and Matthew returned to the table.

"Drop-dead gorgeous cowgirl over there just walked in, that's what," Judy said.

Kathy turned. "Oh, nice."

Matthew laughed. "You two are so bad."

"Yes, we are. And so is Kinsley, she just won't admit it."

"You like her too?" Kathy asked.

Kinsley sipped her water, wanting to escape. But her skin was so warm and her heart so light from the alcohol, she didn't have the wherewithal to do so. She wished she could just enjoy it and have a good time. Why did Nev have to show up?

"Why is she here?" Kinsley asked before she realized it.

"We invited her," Judy said. "And don't act like you don't appreciate it either."

Kinsley rolled her eyes.

"Just admit it," Judy said. "You like her."

"All right, fine. She's attractive. Happy?"

Judy clapped. "I knew it."

"We all like her?" Kathy asked.

"I don't," Matthew said.

Judy smacked him on the arm. He flinched.

"Well, I get dibs on the first dance," Kathy said. "If I can work up the nerve."

"I'll handle that," Judy said. She stood and walked across the dance floor to Nev who then followed her back to the table. Nev froze when she saw Kinsley.

"Kinsley. Didn't expect to see you," she said. She did not look happy.

"Apparently not." It seemed she'd come at the behest of Judy and Kathy, to have a little fun. Maybe Kinsley had just rained on her party. The kick in the gut returned. "Maybe I should go."

"No," Judy said.

"Yeah, Kinsley, don't go," Matthew said. "We can all have fun. You guys can share Nev."

Nev blushed deeply and appeared uncomfortable.

"Would you mind if we all shared you, Nev?" Judy asked playfully.

"Share me?"

"Yeah, the three of use all want a piece. You okay with that? Three women at once?" She laughed wickedly.

Nev's eyes flashed as she looked at Kinsley. They seemed to be questioning her, searching for confirmation that what she'd just heard was true. Kinsley burned beneath her stare, and she shifted her gaze, concerned over what Nev's feelings would be on the matter once she had that confirmation.

"Kathy's dying for a dance," Judy continued. "So she gets dibs."

"I, uh, don't dance," Nev said.

"Oh, nonsense," Judy said, standing. She grabbed Kathy and the two of them pulled Nev onto the dance floor. They sandwiched her and began to laugh as they danced. The sight was too much for Kinsley to bear, and suddenly she wanted another drink, the three shots not near enough.

"Those two are a pair to be reckoned with," Matthew said.

Kinsley downed her water, trying to douse the jealousy churning inside her. "Mm."

"You really into Nev too? God, I never thought I'd kill to be a butch lesbian before."

"Nev and I know each other from way back."

"You didn't answer the question."

God, what is with everyone? Am I that obvious?

Kinsley shrugged. "I'm not sure how to answer your question. I don't really know her anymore."

"But you like what you see?" He smiled.

"She's...yes. Very attractive."

"Does she know you think so?"

"Oh, God no. She doesn't even know I'm gay, I don't think."

"Well, she'll know now. With Judy and Kathy in her ear."

"I don't think she'll believe it. Not totally."

"No? Why not?"

"We're just...not like that. She would never believe I think of her that way. Just like I wouldn't believe it about her." She wondered though, as she said the words, whether or not she was trying to convince Matthew of that fact or herself. Because the way Nev was looking at her from the dance floor made it feel like the latter.

Matthew straightened in his chair. "Here they come."

Kinsley straightened as well, and Judy and Kathy fell into their seats, sweaty and breathless. Nev appeared flushed but as stoic as ever. And she was still looking right at Kinsley.

"Your turn," Kathy said. "She's all yours."

This time Kinsley blushed. "Oh, that's okay."

"Come on," Nev said, surprising her. She offered her hand. Kinsley was so taken aback she just stared at her.

"I don't really dance."

"I'm not asking you to."

"Oh."

"Come on."

Kinsley hesitated, but then took her hand. It felt unbelievably hot in hers. And both soft and rough at the same time. She rose as Nev gently tugged on her and led her across the dance floor to a side room where three pool tables sat, one of them vacant.

Nev tugged her along and deposited some quarters in the far table and began to rack.

"We're playing pool?" Kinsley said, relief washing through her.

"I figured you'd rather do this than dance."

"You figured right."

Nev chose a cue stick. "And I figured it was a good way to get you away from your group of friends there."

Kinsley laughed, feeling warm and light. "Was my discomfort that obvious?"

"Probably about as obvious as mine."

"Yes, that blush you were sporting was pretty obvious. Though I don't think your fan club picked up on it."

"Either that or they just don't care."

"Mm, very possible. They got it pretty bad for you."

"So, I've just been told." She motioned for Kinsley to break.

Kinsley chose her cue stick, then leaned down and lined up her shot. She hadn't played since that last day Nev had been at her house. After that, pool, along with almost everything else, didn't seem as fun.

"I've also been told you're a part of that fan club too," Nev said.

Kinsley scratched, her cue stick hitting the bottom of the cue ball, causing it to jump and bounce from the table.

Nev scooped it up and returned it to her, holding her gaze.

"I guess I heard correctly."

CHAPTER NINETEEN

K insley blinked at her, dumbfounded. Then Nev did something completely unexpected. She winked at her.

Oh dear God, I'm done for. I'm drunk and I'm done for.

"Don't worry, I told them they were wrong. Told them you couldn't possibly be into me."

Kinsley fought laughing. *Yeah, right. I'm so not into you. You're just way too good-looking and talented for me to have any interest whatsoever.*

Kinsley took the ball. Nev motioned for her to shoot again.

She placed the ball back on the table and lined up her shot as best she could. The alcohol was making her woozy, but it had nothing on what Nev was making her feel. She tried to concentrate, tried to focus only on the ball. She drew back her cue.

"Because a Padovano couldn't possibly be into a Wakefield."

Kinsley scratched again, sending the ball flying from the table. Nev caught it on the first bounce. Kinsley burned from embarrassment, and when Nev brought it back to her she shook her head.

"You better break."

Nev smiled and set the ball on the table.

She kept talking as she lined up her shot. "Unless of course we've finally moved beyond all that Hatfield and McCoy bullshit."

She broke and sent three balls into the corner pockets.

She was still as good as ever.

"Seeing you in my shirt kind of signifies we might be headed in that direction."

Kinsley glanced down and thumbed the flannel shirt. Nev's shirt. She'd been wearing it a lot lately, loving how soft and warm it was and, of course, loving how it smelled like Nev. But Nev didn't know that. As far as she knew, Kinsley thought the shirt belonged to Adrianna.

"I—didn't know it was yours." *Lie. I'm a liar. A drunk liar.*

Nev eyed her. "I call bullshit."

"Well, I didn't know for sure." *Another lie. Oh, God help me.*

"But you suspected."

"I—yes." She was too tipsy to try to hide it anymore. Nev was seeing right through her. What all could she see? What all was there to see? Could she see her desire? See it churning just below her depths? Just waiting to explode?

Nev lined up another shot after calling stripes. Then she called her shot. She made it.

She's still so good. Is there anything she isn't good at? How could someone be so close to perfection?

"So, is it true then, Kinsley? Have we finally moved beyond the past?"

She set up another shot.

"I don't know," Kinsley said. "I'd like to."

I'd like to do a lot more than that. But I'm scared to say it.

Nev took the shot. Missed.

She straightened. "I would too."

Kinsley rounded the table, burning so hot the tips of her ears were on fire. She tried to blame it on the booze, but she knew she'd only be kidding herself. It was Nev. She now had her on fire.

She found a shot, lined it up, called it, and took it.

Somehow she made it.

She bounced a little with excitement.

Nev laughed at her.

"What? I haven't played in twenty years, okay?" It felt good to relax and be herself. It felt good knowing that they both wanted to move on from the past. And it felt good wanting her so badly she could hardly see straight. Booze or no booze.

"Okay," Nev said with a teasing grin.

The waitress came and Nev ordered a beer while Kinsley ordered another glass of water.

"Not drinking tonight?" Nev asked.

"Already have. I'm three shots of tequila in."

"Impressive. I'd be on the floor by now."

"I'm surprised I'm not." Her bones felt like they were slowly melting, and she still had a smile plastered on her face, but she decided not to elaborate anything further for fear she'd start outwardly drooling over Nev.

"No, you're doing well. You haven't even spouted off anything crazy yet. You know, in your all-time-famous 'Kinny the mouth' fashion."

Kinsley scoffed. "'Kinny the mouth'? I haven't heard that in years."

Nev just laughed.

Kinsley laughed too. It felt so good to reminisce about things that didn't upset them. Nev and Viv had been her very best friends and they'd had a lot of really good times. Times she was actually okay with remembering and talking about. Times she wished she could relive. She wondered if Nev felt the same, or if every memory for her was painful. If so, how could she stand being around her at all? Maybe she couldn't, maybe that's what all the sudden distancing had been about. The possibility of that being the case made her feel incredibly guilty, and she almost apologized to Nev. For what though, she wasn't sure. Her mind wasn't functioning at its highest caliber, the tequila making it all a little fuzzy. But one thing she knew for certain, she didn't want Nev to hurt.

She walked around the table and somehow managed to find another shot. It was impossible, but she called it anyway, laughing a little at herself. Then she took the shot and missed.

The waitress returned with their drinks, and Nev sipped her beer.

"So, 'Kinny the mouth,' you gonna tell me whether or not you're really into me?"

Kinsley almost dropped her water. *Holy shit.* "You're being unusually forward."

"Am I?"

"Yes. And I thought the second you heard that from Judy and Kathy you'd take off and run for the hills."

"Why would I do that?"

"Because, you know, our past and the fact that we haven't been getting along all that great." *And the fact that you've been all but avoiding me at the ranch. Not to mention your disdain at my working with Arthur. But hey, who's counting?*

Nev shrugged. "Still, I'd never run for the hills, as you say. And I don't know. Maybe I'm curious."

She stalked the table for a shot. God, she looked good in that outfit. So tall and strong. And wet.

"Why?" Kinsley asked, suddenly feeling a little brazen herself. Why did she care so much if she had no interest in Kinsley? What did it matter? Was she just one of those women who got off on everybody wanting her? Kinsley didn't think so. Nev was too down-to-earth. Too unassuming to be that way. The woman probably had no idea just how gorgeous she really was.

And boy, was she ever.

She shrugged again. "Same reason you're asking why, I guess. I just want to know."

She leaned down, slid her cue stick back and forth, and eyed Kinsley.

"So, are you?" She took the shot. She made it.

"You didn't call it," Kinsley said. She grinned, feeling a little satisfied. Plus, it gave her an excuse to avoid answering the question.

Nev groaned. "That's not fair, I was distracted."

"Not my problem."

"You gonna answer me?"

Damn, she's not letting it go. Reminds me of me when I want to know something.

"Should I? Or should I be as evasive as you always were?" She could recall a time when she'd grilled Nev with similar personal questions and Nev had squirmed and tried to put her off.

"I'm not being evasive now."

"No? Then how about you answer the question first. Are you into me?"

She'd turned the tables and felt satisfied. How was Nev going to get around that one?

Nev slowly sipped her beer and Kinsley watched, fascinated.

"You can't turn the tables on me."

"Why not? You're coming at me like a Mack truck without brakes."

And I'm kind of liking it. Okay, I'm really liking it.

"I always do when I know what I want."

Kinsley stiffened and stared at her. *What?* "You—" She shook her head and swallowed. "This is crazy."

"It is."

"We don't even know each other anymore."

"No, we don't."

"Then what are we doing?"

"I don't know. Flirting? Is that so bad?"

"It seems out of character for you, Nev." It seemed way out of character. And for that matter, if she wanted to flirt, why wasn't she in there doing it with the two women who were dying to flirt with her?

"But you don't know me anymore, remember?"

"Still, from what I do know."

"Like I said, when I know what I want…"

You—want me?

"I'm not buying this." She shook her head again. "Did Judy and Kathy put you up to this?" *That's it. I'm so drunk they're all playing a joke on me.*

Nev's face clouded. "No."

"Yeah, right. You're all going to get some great big laugh out of this later, right?"

Nev studied her. "Is this going to be like the apology all over again? You not taking what I'm saying at face value?"

Kinsley searched for a response. Could she really be telling the truth?

Nev took her silence as an answer and tossed her cue on the table. Then she grabbed her hat and hurried by her to rush across the dance floor. Kinsley followed her, running out into the night after her. Rain was pouring down and lightning flashed overhead.

"Nev, wait!"

But she kept going, making her way to her truck.

Kinsley chased her, reaching her just as she pulled the door open.

"Nev, stop. Wait." An image of her riding away on her bike all those years ago came, and it terrified her. She wasn't going to let her run, not this time.

Nev stared at her, her hat and shirt already soaked, her face reflecting the red light from the neon sign of the bar.

"What?" she said. Her breath came out in a mist of white.

"I'm sorry."

"For what? For not listening to me? For not ever taking me seriously? You always wondered why I was so quiet. It's because when I do speak, no one seems to hear me. No one takes me seriously. Not you, not my family. Only Arthur."

"Nev, I'm sorry."

"You know I don't have a whole lot to say much of the time, but when I do, it's usually important. I've usually thought long and hard about it."

"You've thought long and hard about…this? About me?"

Nev looked away from her. "I haven't been able to get you out of my mind since I first laid eyes on you. And then when I saw you in my shirt…and then with what Judy just said…I don't know, it just sent me over. I don't know. Maybe I'm crazy. I feel like I'm crazy." She looked up at the sky like maybe it had the answers she was seeking. "I should probably just go, forget this ever happened."

"Nev—don't. Please." Kinsley had no more words, only desperation. So when she didn't see the belief in Nev's eyes, she reached up and grabbed her face. She tried to bring her in for a kiss, but Nev resisted and touched her hands.

"Don't," she said softly. She was trembling.

"Why not?"

"Because I'll lose control. And I don't—I can't lose control with you."

Gently, she pulled Kinsley's hands from her face. But she didn't release her. Instead, she tugged on her and encouraged her to climb inside the truck. When Kinsley struggled to do so, Nev gripped her waist and lifted her up onto the seat.

Kinsley scooted over and Nev crawled in.

She started the truck and they sat there for a moment, both breathing hard, wipers slashing at the windshield.

"Where are we going?" Kinsley finally asked, her burning body already shivering from the cold.

"I don't know. I just know I'd like to be alone with you."

CHAPTER TWENTY

Nev pulled into the drive and killed the engine. Kinsley had finally stopped shivering, thanks to the heat, but Nev was sure she'd start again just as soon as they stepped back out into the rain.

"Louise is still here," Nev said. "But hopefully Arthur is already asleep."

"Louise is his nurse?"

Nev nodded. They'd been mostly silent on the ride over, with Kinsley gripping her hand and trembling. Nev had wanted so badly to pull over and hold her, to ensure she would warm up, but she knew if she did, they'd end up making love in the truck, and that was something she didn't want. If anything was going to happen with Kinsley, she wanted it to be special.

She wanted it to mean something. And she wanted to be able to take her time.

"Come on, let's get you out of those wet clothes," Nev said as she opened the door and helped Kinsley slide out into the rain. The droplets were cold and fat, splattering off the truck like a machine gun. Kinsley ducked and ran for cover with Nev not far behind her.

They stood at the front door, rain coming down all around them, their breath coming out in white clouds.

"Will she think it's odd that I'm here?" Kinsley asked.

"Yes, but it's none of her business."

"Okay then." She smiled. "Because I can wait and hide in the truck if you like."

"No. We aren't kids anymore. We have no reason to hide."

She unlocked the door and they stepped inside. The house was warm and smelled of coffee. Louise drank the stuff twenty-four seven, caffeine and all. Nev used to wonder if she ever slept. Now she had settled on the fact that she probably didn't.

Louise met them in the living room, standing next to the couch, thick paperback book in hand. She slid off her reading glasses and tucked them into her light blue scrub top.

"I see you have company," she said.

"Louise, this is Kinsley. Kinsley, this is Arthur's nurse, Louise."

Louise rounded the couch and shook Kinsley's hand. "I'm Arthur's nurse as well as the resident cook and house cleaner. But she always fails to mention that for some reason."

"Yes, Louise does a little of everything. She's invaluable around here."

"Got that right. And don't you forget it." She gathered her purse and shoved her book inside. Then she slipped into her jacket and headed for the door.

"He went down about an hour ago. Not long after you left."

"How was he?"

"He's had better nights."

"Still feisty, huh?"

"Oh, yes."

Nev walked her to the door. "Thanks for staying."

"No problem." She looked at Kinsley and spoke softly to Nev. "You need to get out more often. Nice to meet you, Kinsley."

"You as well."

"Night, Nev." She winked and walked out the door. Nev bolted it shut and turned to find Kinsley slinking out of her wet shirt.

"Let me go grab you something warm to wear."

Nev headed for her wing of the house and hurried down the hallway. She was rummaging through her dresser drawer searching for a pair of pants when Kinsley entered. She stood just inside the door in a yellow top that was clinging to her like a second skin. Her hair was wet and hanging around her shoulders, and Nev had been right, she was shivering again. And yet she looked so beyond beautiful, Nev was nearly speechless.

"I found you a shirt." She brought it to her. "Still trying to find you a pair of pants that will fit."

Kinsley took the shirt. "Thanks." She began taking off the yellow top and Nev turned, giving her some privacy. She returned to her dresser and kept digging for pants.

"All of my sweats and pajama pants will swallow you whole, I'm afraid."

"That's okay. I don't really need them."

"But your jeans are soaked."

"I'm making do." Nev glanced over at her. She was standing there in the new, soft flannel button-down holding her jeans in her hands. Nev swallowed at the sight of her bare legs, at the sight of her nearly nude in another one of her shirts.

"I—uh—you sure?"

"Positive. I just need a pair of warm socks and a cup of that coffee I smell and I'll be right as rain. So to speak."

Nev smiled and opened another drawer for a pair of thick socks. She brought them to her.

"Thank you."

"My pleasure." Nev reached out and touched her face. She brushed her damp bangs away from her eyes. Nev couldn't believe she was there, in her home, looking at her like she meant the absolute world to her. Judy's words had knocked her for a loop, yes. To the point where she almost didn't believe them. But the way Kinsley was looking at her right now caused her whole world to spin, leaving little doubt. "You have the most beautiful eyes, Kinsley Padovano."

Kinsley closed them, as if her words and her touch had completely moved her.

"So do you," she said as she opened them again.

She placed her hands on Nev's arms and started to pull her close but then stopped. "You're still wet."

Nev looked down. "I am, aren't I?"

She kicked out of her boots and began unfastening her belt. She stopped when she realized Kinsley was watching her.

"What?"

"Nothing, I'm just enjoying the view."

"It can't be near as good as mine."

"Mm, it's pretty good."

Nev slinked out of her jeans and tossed them aside. Then she pulled off her shirt and trembled, though not from the chill. From the look in Kinsley's eyes.

A noise sounded from down the hallway. A rustling. Then Arthur called out.

"Shit, he's up." Nev scrambled for clothes and Kinsley found the robe on the back of the door and slid into it. Then she stood in the doorway.

"Nev, let me."

"He won't understand—"

"It'll be okay." She said it so softly, and with such kindness and caring, that Nev stopped in her mad dance to dress and just looked at her. Eventually, she nodded.

"Okay."

Kinsley left her and went to Arthur. Nev strained to hear their conversation as she finished dressing in her flannel sleep pants and a T-shirt but struggled to make out what they were saying. Their voices were soft and calm, so whatever was going on, it must be under control.

She picked up the wet clothes and carried them back through the house to the laundry room. She turned on the washer and grabbed a couple of fresh towels from the laundry basket. She deposited them on the couch and then got busy tending to the fire. After she got that going strong, she crossed to the kitchen and made Kinsley that cup of coffee she was wanting. She also poured one for herself, knowing it was probably going to be a long night.

"That smells so good," Kinsley said as she emerged from the hallway.

Nev waited a moment to see if Arthur was following, and then relaxed and sipped from her own cup.

"It doesn't taste half-bad either."

She handed Kinsley her mug. "You take cream or sugar?"

"Cream, please."

Nev opened the fridge. "Pick your poison. We have several kinds."

"Mm, the pumpkin spice sounds good." She took the creamer and poured some in her coffee. Nev handed her a spoon and returned the creamer to the fridge.

"God, it is good." Kinsley groaned as she took a sip.

"Who knew a simple cup of coffee did it for you?"

Kinsley smacked her playfully on the arm.

"What was that for?"

"I don't like you knowing all my secrets."

"Why not?"

"Because you'll use them to your advantage."

"Would that be so bad?"

"Mm." She cocked her head. "I don't know."

They left the kitchen and settled in on the couch by the fire.

Nev handed Kinsley a towel and she dabbed her hair and face.

"How was Arthur?"

Kinsley lowered the towel. "He had a nightmare."

Nev sighed. "He's been having those a lot here lately. Did he settle down okay with you?"

"He was surprised to see me. But—"

"But what?"

"Not as surprised as I thought."

"Ah."

"He's very intuitive, isn't he?"

"Yes."

"I, of course, explained that we had just come in from the rain and that was why I was in your robe."

"What did he say?"

"Something to the effect of bullshit. That he was old but not stupid."

"Figures."

"But he settled down nicely. Said he was—"

"Yes?"

She shook her head. "Said he was glad I was here. That you needed someone like me in your life."

Nev cleared her throat and fought the tears that were threatening.

"What do you think? Do you agree?" Kinsley asked.

Nev sipped her coffee and avoided her gaze. "He's just an old sentimental guy."

"So, you don't agree."

"I—I don't know what I think."

"Why is that?"

"Because I like my life. I liked it the way it was."

"You mean before I suddenly showed up again."

"I didn't mean it like that."

"No, it's okay. I understand and you feel how you feel."

"You have to understand. My life was simple, relaxed. And it seems so much of that has changed recently. Not just because of you, but with Arthur too. Nothing is as it was."

"And it's scaring you."

Nev stared into her coffee. "A bit, yes."

"That's understandable." She sipped her coffee and stared into the fire. "I actually feel somewhat similar. Once upon a time I liked my life the way it was. But somewhere along the way it all started to go to shit. First the headaches, then the constant traveling, the stress, the loneliness. And then the damn crash and now…you." She looked at her. "It's all a bit scary. More than a bit scary."

"What does it say about us that we scare each other?"

"I don't know. I guess we have to ask ourselves if we'd be scared if all the other stuff wasn't happening at the same time."

Nev considered that for a moment. Kinsley was watching her.

"What do you think? Would you still find the idea of me frightening?"

Nev shifted.

"You would, wouldn't you?"

"Yes."

"Me too." She smiled.

Nev did as well. "What the hell does that mean, then?"

"Beats me. I think that's one for Adrianna."

"Oh, God, no. Please. Don't involve her."

"Why not? She's given me some really good advice."

"Just please, don't. She's given me way too much advice. In fact, I think she lives for it."

Kinsley laughed. "Well, maybe you need it."

Nev narrowed her eyes at her.

"Is that supposed to scare me? Because it doesn't. It's actually turning me on a little."

"Really?"

"Mm-hm. I kind of like you mad. You're cute."

"Cute?"

"Yes."

Nev set down her mug. She looked at her for a long moment. Took in her dark, wet hair, her scarlet cheeks, her full lips. She was so beautiful, so perfect.

"I want to kiss you so badly right now," Nev whispered.

Kinsley set down her mug, scooted closer. "Then why don't you?"

"Because we both just admitted that we scare each other."

"Then why does it feel so right, Nev? I don't understand."

"I don't either."

Kinsley reached out and touched her hand. "I think at this point, I'm more scared of you *not* kissing me. Because if you don't, I don't know where we would go from there."

Nev lifted her hand and kissed it softly. She heard Kinsley inhale, saw her eyes widen and then narrow with desire. She kissed her hand again and rubbed it against her cheek.

"I want it to be right. For both of us to be sure."

"You seemed sure back at the bar."

"I am sure that I want you."

"You're just not so sure what to do about it."

"Something like that."

"Or *if* you should do anything about it."

"I'm worried about that too, yes."

She thought of the last time she'd given herself to someone completely, and she felt her brow furrow. It had been years ago, back when she'd just finished grad school. She'd been seeing an older woman, a friend of one of her professors.

"Hey, what's that look for?"

Nev released her hand. "Nothing. It's nothing."

"It's obviously something, Nev. Is it…me? Are you thinking about the past again?"

"I'm thinking about the past, but it has nothing to do with you."

"What, then? Would you like to talk about it?"

Nev stared into the fire. Kinsley held her hand again, and Nev closed her eyes at how wonderful it felt to be touched again. Kinsley's warm hand in hers warmed her heart, and she wished she could just move past everything and reach out and love this woman. But so many things kept stopping her along the way to this moment. And it seemed one last thing still was.

She opened her eyes and began to speak, wanting Kinsley to understand, hoping she would understand. She needed her to know why she was so afraid.

"She was older than me. By almost twenty years." She swallowed and stared down at their entwined hands. "We saw each other for about a year, and I thought everything was going well. I had just finished grad school and she had hinted at me moving in with her. I told her I loved her. I was…madly in love with her. She was brilliant and beautiful. I'd never met anyone with a mind like hers."

"What happened?"

Nev took in a deep breath. "One day I got finished early with something I was working on and I headed over to her place to surprise her. She was on her front porch with a man. At first, I didn't think anything of it. But then they embraced and they started to kiss. It took me a moment to understand what I was seeing. And then when I did, it killed me. Crushed my insides. I—"

Kinsley squeezed her hand.

"I ran up on the porch and confronted them. And the man…" She paused, laughing. "He looked as shocked as I was. Turns out he was her ex-husband and they had been seeing each other again for weeks." Nev looked up at Kinsley. "Weeks, Kinny. And I didn't know."

"I'm so sorry, Nev."

"How could I not know?"

"She kept it from you."

"She was sleeping with the both of us."

Nev wiped her eyes, upset for being so upset. "I don't understand how I can still be so affected by it. She—it was an affair. I was cheated on. So what?"

"She broke your trust, Nev. Betrayed you. That's a big deal."

"That's what Arthur always said. Only he had some choice words for her when he talked about it. Didn't put it nearly as nicely as you just did."

"Arthur knows?"

"He helped me through it. So did Adrianna."

"Really?"

Nev nodded. "I actually went to Peace of Life to try to lick my wounds. To heal somehow. That's how I met them both."

"No kidding. You at Peace of Life?"

Nev chuckled. "Seems ludicrous, doesn't it? I actually was there, stayed a few weeks before Arthur offered me an apprenticeship with him. Told me I could move in here and work for him, so I jumped at the chance."

"That sounds really fast."

"It does, I know. But if you only knew how much those two helped me…Adrianna with her healing and Arthur with his wise old ways, it makes so much sense. When I first walked into his shop with him and watched him work, my first week at the retreat, I was hooked. So when I wasn't with Adrianna, I was here, watching Arthur. Something about working with my hands at that time really spoke to me. It was so different from academia. So much more visceral. And I could work and sweat and pound and hammer. Work all the shit out that was inside me. It saved me, Kinny. I really think it did. I mean, my own folks pretty much disowned me when they found out I'd given up everything to blacksmith, so I had no one. Arthur knew that and he was there for me.

Loved me like no one ever has. Like a daughter. And I'd never had that before."

She teared up again, and Kinsley wiped her face.

"Now I understand the bond between you. Understand why you love him so."

"I do. I love him so much." More tears came as she thought about his failing health. "I don't want to lose him."

"I know." She moved in closer. "I know, Nev."

CHAPTER TWENTY-ONE

Kinsley woke while it was still dark. She shifted slightly and felt someone warm and firm beneath her and suddenly remembered where she was. She was at Nev's, on the couch, snuggled in her arms. She shifted again, causing Nev to moan. Kinsley wrapped her arms around her and held her tighter and laid her head against her chest again, content to feel the soft curve of her breast and to hear the soft thudding of her heart. They'd talked until the early morning hours, listening for and checking in on Arthur, until Kinsley had finally dozed off, unable to help herself. The last thing she could remember was Nev getting a blanket for her and taking her in her arms.

She snuggled down deeper and inhaled her scent. She hadn't expected to end up there for the night. Hadn't really expected anything that had happened. But it had been wonderful. The best night she'd had in a very long time. She couldn't explain it, but she felt so right there with Nev, so safe. And for the first time in years, her mind wasn't clouded with worry.

She closed her eyes and focused on the present. On Nev's breathing and her heartbeat. She thought about Nev's confessions hours before. About the pain she'd expressed and had to live through. She understood now why Arthur and Adrianna were so important to her. Nev really didn't have anyone else. Not much had seemed to change since Viv's death. Kinsley had known Nev was on her own, but unfortunately, at the time she couldn't do anything about it. At the time, there was very little she could do at all.

Kinsley's mind carried her back to that time, to the very last time she'd seen Nev.

Kinsley rang the doorbell again and bounced on the balls of her feet. She wrung her hands, nervous about who would answer the door. She didn't see Nev's father's truck in the drive so she hoped she'd catch Nev alone. She wasn't yet ready to face her parents, especially knowing how they seemed to be blaming everything on her and her family. Not to mention the kiss. So, she'd waited until a weekday when she was sure Nev's father would be at work. As for her mother, Kinsley had to risk it. She missed Nev like crazy, and she couldn't bear to be away from her any longer.

She went to push the doorbell again but stopped as the door inched open. Nev's face came into view through the crack.

"What are you doing?" she whispered.

"I came to see you."

The door closed, and for a moment Kinsley thought it might not open again. But then Nev pulled it open and motioned for her to hurry inside. Kinsley did so and noticed how dark the house was. All the blinds were closed and she had to wait a few seconds for her eyes to adjust.

"Come on," Nev said, pulling on her hand.

"I can't see."

"Shh." Nev put her finger to her mouth and led them down the hallway.

"Is someone home?"

"My mom." She pulled her harder and they entered her bedroom. Nev was about to close the door when they heard her mother call out.

"Nevaeh!"

Nev flinched and dropped Kinsley's hand. "I'll be right back." She left her and Kinsley stood just inside the door to listen. Nev walked into her mother's bedroom across the hall and disappeared. Kinsley heard voices, one loud, her mother's; and one soft, Nev's. Her mother sounded distraught and strained. Almost hysterical. Kinsley's chest tightened at the sound of it and she felt for Nev, worried for her.

Nev appeared at the doorway and closed her mother's door carefully behind her.

"What's going on?"

Nev put her finger to her mouth again and whispered. "I'll be right back."

She disappeared down the hallway and Kinsley heard her in the kitchen. When she returned, she had a big green cup in her hand and a look of sadness on her face. Her hand was clenched in a tight fist at her side.

"She was thirsty?" She'd sounded like she was dying. All that over a simple glass of water?

Nev shrugged. "Her head hurts." She opened her palm. Three thick, white pills sat in the center. "And she wants a drink."

Kinsley's heart sank to her stomach. "Oh." She knew then what was going on. She watched helplessly as Nev went back into the bedroom and then reemerged a few moments later.

She came back into her room and closed the door behind them.

"She'll sleep now," she said, collapsing onto her bed. Kinsley followed and sat next to her.

"Were those...painkillers?"

Nev swallowed. Then nodded. She looked away from her.

"She's taking a lot," Kinsley said. Her father had taken prescription painkillers after falling off a ladder at work, so she knew how one was supposed to take them. One every four to six hours. Not three at once.

"Is she...drinking too?"

Nev kept staring at the wall before she finally looked down at her hands. "Vodka. It's about all she drinks anymore."

Kinsley took her hand. "I'm sorry, Nev."

Nev pulled away, swallowed again, and wiped a stray tear from her eye.

"It's no big deal. She's just grieving is all."

"So are you. Who's helping you? Who's taking care of you?"

Nev glared at her. "She's doing the best she can, okay? She just lost her daughter."

"And you lost your twin sister."

"Yeah, so?"

"So, you're grieving too."

"I'm fine." She stood and started picking up her room.

"Yeah, you seem real good to me," Kinsley said.

"I am."

Kinsley glanced around the room and noticed her soccer posters were missing. She looked in her closet for the cleats she always seemed to be wearing on and off the field. They were absent too.

"You still playing soccer?" she asked softly.

Nev quickened her movements, tossing things aside.

"Mom and Dad said there isn't time now."

"Isn't time?"

"They—can't take me to all my games and practices. They're grieving."

"Oh."

"So it's just better if I quit for now."

"That doesn't sound fair."

"It doesn't matter. I have to do what's best for my family. I can't think about myself."

Kinsley watched as she picked up a garbage bag and began tossing in her stuffed horses.

"You're throwing away your horses?"

"I'm giving them away."

"Why?"

"I don't need them."

"But you love them."

"I don't. Not anymore. They're childish."

"Nev, you—"

"Don't. Just don't, Kinny. I don't need your shit right now, okay?"

Kinsley blinked. Her heart fell to her feet at her harsh tone. "Okay."

Nev finished and then started in on her other stuffed animals. Every once in a while she'd wipe away a tear.

"Nev, you know I'm here for you, right? I miss you."

"I'm not supposed to see you," she said. "So it doesn't matter who's missing who. It can't happen."

"But why?"

Nev shoved the full bag aside. "Because my parents hate you, that's why. They hate your whole family. They—blame you for Viv. I told you that."

"But it's not true. I had no control over any of that, Nev. The plane—it was an accident. A freak thing."

Nev shook her head. "No, it's your fault. That's what they say. Because you told Viv about the camp. The camp was your idea."

Kinsley wanted to cry. "Nev, please—it wasn't—"

"Just stop," she snapped. "Stop. I don't want to hear it."

"But, Nev—"

A door closed from the front of the house and Nev froze, her face ashen.

"Oh, no."

"What?"

"My dad. He's home early. You have to go."

"But—"

Nev's door opened and her father's eyes widened when he saw Kinsley.

"What's she doing here?" he demanded. His words were slurred, and he stumbled just inside the door as he pointed at her.

"She came to visit, Dad. She was just leaving."

"Visit?" He waved his finger at her. "You're not welcome here anymore, young lady. So get the hell out."

Kinsley stifled back sobs, never having seen him like that before. And never had he spoken to her harshly.

She rose and edged past him.

"And tell your dad to go to hell. Son of a bitch just fired me."

Kinsley shook her head. "No, he wouldn't do that."

"Well, he did, little girl. He did. So I went to the bar and had me a drink. Had me a few drinks to try to drink him away. Did I do it? Nope. Cuz you're here. You're here in my house. Another fucking Padovano. Can't seem to get away from you people."

Kinsley moved past him, throat burning with tears, and hurried down the hallway. She made it to the front door as he kept calling out behind her.

"Go on, get out. And don't come back."

Kinsley threw open the door and glanced back. Nev was standing there hugging herself, tears in her eyes.

"It's probably best if you don't come back," Nev said.

Kinsley bit her lower lip to keep from crying. "Okay."

Then she turned away from her and walked out.

Kinsley opened her eyes as tears threatened to come. Nev truly had been alone and she'd been helpless to do anything about it. How could her parents have been so selfish? How couldn't they have seen what they were doing to their own daughter?

Kinsley wondered if Nev was still in touch with her family at all, or if, when they wrote her off as she said, they did so forever. She held her closer, hurting for the young girl Nev used to be and the woman she now was. Would she ever find happiness?

Or would she be like her, and feel like it just wasn't possible?

Nev stirred beneath her. The gray light of dawn crept in through the windows, kissing her face. She opened her eyes as Kinsley slowly released her and sat up.

"Good morning," Kinsley said.

"Mm, morning." Nev stretched and rubbed her eyes. "What time is it?"

Kinsley checked the large face of her watch.

"Close to six."

Nev studied her a moment, then smiled. "You're here."

"I am."

"I'm glad."

"Me too."

Nev sat up and skimmed her thumb across Kinsley's hand.

"How long have you been awake?"

"Not long."

"I hope you weren't having to listen to me snore."

Kinsley chuckled. "No, I was just thinking."

"Really? About what?"

Kinsley rubbed her forehead, unsure if she should share. Nev grabbed her hand.

"Hey, you gonna tell me or worry yourself to death over it?"

"The old me would just worry."

"And the new you?"

Kinsley sighed. "I was thinking about the last time we saw each other. When we were kids."

Nev's gaze drifted and she pulled her hand away and repositioned herself on the couch, hugging her knees. "What made you think about that?"

"Our conversation last night. You mentioning how your folks disowned you when you started blacksmithing."

"That doesn't have anything to do with the past."

"It does, Nev."

"How so?" She looked at her, her eyes so wide and seeking. She looked like the young Nev again. So innocent and vulnerable. "Kinny?"

"Because you were pretty much on your own after Viv's death. And that day, that last day I saw you, it was really evident. You were alone. Your parents—they were all about themselves."

Nev hugged herself tighter and rocked a little.

"You took care of them, didn't you? For how long? Who took care of you, Nev?"

"No one." The words sounded strained and she looked away again, her eyes brimming with tears.

"That's why I thought of that day." Kinsley rested her hand on her arm. "Nev, I'm so sorry I wasn't there for you. I'm so sorry you were all alone."

"There's was nothing you could've done," she rasped.

"I feel like there was. Like maybe I should've made a bigger fuss over it or something. But my folks—at that point—I think they were upset and a little afraid of your folks."

"Afraid?" Nev said. "Your father fired mine."

Kinsley hesitated, knowing she needed to tell her but worried about how she would take it if she didn't know.

"Nev, your dad kept showing up to work drunk. That endangered everyone else on the site." Her parents had owned a sprinkler installation company, and Nev's father had been a loyal employee for years. It was how the two families had met, and they'd become fast friends, spending a lot of time together. Birthdays, holidays, weekends. That is, until Viv's death.

Nev swallowed and rocked more. "No, my dad didn't drink. Not like my mom."

"I think maybe he did, Nev. For a time anyway. Maybe not around you so much."

"We were nearly destitute after he lost that job," Nev said. "We had to move. Had to—we lost almost everything. I worked two paper routes, rode my bike to the food bank sometimes to get food."

"I'm sorry," Kinsley said, squeezing her arm. "I'm so sorry for all you've gone through."

Nev pulled away and stood. She walked to the fireplace and ran her fingers over a framed photo.

Then she turned. "I'll get your clothes from the dryer so you can change. Then I'll drive you back to the retreat."

"Nev, I—"

"I really need to be alone right now, Kinsley. Please."

Kinsley quietly nodded, knowing it was useless to argue.

Chapter Twenty-Two

Nev pulled up alongside the curb in front of the house. She killed the engine and looked out at the neighborhood. It was quiet for a Sunday, the street empty, no kids riding bikes or playing out front. The only person she saw was her father, who'd been under the hood of his truck when she pulled up. But now he'd turned and was looking at her.

She grabbed her cowboy hat and slid from the truck, closing the door behind her. Securing the hat on her head, she rounded her vehicle and walked through the overgrown lawn to him.

"Dad," she said by way of greeting.

"Nevaeh," he said in return. He tugged on the bill of his ball cap and turned back to his engine. Nev joined him.

"Got engine trouble?"

"Nah, just replacing some old spark plugs."

He leaned forward, his ample waistline pressing against the truck. Sweat trickled down his temple, escaping his gray hair. He, like her mother, hadn't aged very well. His once tall frame now stooped a little, and his once muscular body had softened.

"What brings you by, Nevaeh? Your last visit had your mother all upset. So, I'd appreciate it if you called first before you stop by."

"I did call, Dad. Numerous times."

"You did?"

"Yes. Both your phones."

He grunted some as he removed the spark plug and drew back. "Well, I didn't get no call. And your mother—she doesn't use her phone all that much."

"So she said."

Nev didn't bother mentioning that she'd also texted both phones. She figured he would just deny getting those too. And, if she was right, there would soon be enough denial to last her the rest of her life.

He tossed the old plug to the ground and then knelt and dug the new ones out of a bag. She assumed he'd brought them home from his job at the auto part store. She wondered how long he'd been able to hold that job.

"Well then, just come by when I say it's okay, all right?"

"I don't think you're going to have to worry about that, Dad."

"No?"

"No."

"How's that?" He opened the new package and retrieved a plug. His fingers were stained black, the nail beds outlined in it. She wondered why he didn't wear gloves like she did to protect his hands. But maybe that, like everything else in his life, wasn't something he gave a damn about.

"I'm not going to be coming around anymore."

He looked up at her.

"Ever."

"You come all this way to tell me that?"

"Yes."

He made a noise that sounded like a laugh. Then he leaned over his engine again. "Wasted your time, you ask me."

"I didn't ask and I don't care."

He grunted as he worked.

She waited until he was finished before she continued.

"Dad, I need you to hear me."

He fumbled with the package, trying to retrieve the other plug.

"I'm listening."

Nev reached out and closed her fingers around the stupid spark plug packaging in order to get his attention. "Dad, did you show up to work drunk when you worked for the Padovanos?"

He dropped his hand and his eyes flashed. "What?"

"You heard me. Did you?"

"You got no right coming here asking me that. No right."

"Oh, but I do, Dad. Because all I heard growing up was how we were poor because Mr. Padovano fired you. You said he did it because you were fighting over Viv's accident. But that wasn't true, was it? He fired you because you were showing up to work drunk."

"You got no right, Nevaeh. No right." He poked her chest with his finger.

She grabbed it, held it tightly. Held it so tight he winced.

"I do, Dad. And don't even try to deny it. I remember you coming home drunk that day. Coming home bitching about how he fired you. Bitching about the Padovanos and how you wanted Kinsley out of your house. *My* best friend. The only person in the world I had left."

"You had us," he said. "We didn't need them. They—"

"I had you? More like you had me." She shoved his hand away. "I was the one who took care of you two. You guys didn't give a shit about me. The only time you thought of me was when you needed something. And as for the Padovanos, they didn't do anything wrong, Dad. None of them. They were our friends. Our closest friends, and they lost Viv too. And had Kinsley gone with Viv, they would've lost her too. And that's what really bothered you, wasn't it? That they still had their daughter and you didn't."

She stopped, her voice hitching. "Well, you had me, Dad. You still had me. Why didn't I count? Huh? Why? Why wasn't I worth anything anymore?"

He shook his head, went back to the truck, and leaned over the engine again.

"I don't know what you're talking about. We took care of you." But his voice had lost conviction. He knew he hadn't. He knew. She could hear it in him. He was just too cowardly to admit it.

"I didn't come here expecting you to admit to anything. I came here to say my piece."

He struggled with the new spark plug. "Well, you've said it."

Nev waited for him to finish, wanting to look him in the eye, but he kept fumbling and she realized he was doing it on purpose, to avoid her. She dug in her back pocket for the envelope full of bills she brought. It wasn't a whole lot, but it was enough to help them for a few weeks. She tossed it on the ground next to the old spark plug.

"Yeah, Dad, I have. I've said all I need to say." She turned and walked away. As she climbed in her truck and started the engine, she glanced over at him. He was bending down for the envelope. When he straightened he took a peek inside and shoved it in his pocket. Then he refocused on his truck without giving Nev a second look.

❖

Nev stood as Adrianna opened the door to her healing room and escorted a client out. She wished them a good day and then startled a little when she turned and saw Nev.

"Nevaeh. I didn't expect to see you."

Nev struggled to speak. "I know. I was hoping you had a moment."

Adrianna's brow creased in obvious concern as Nev stood clinging to her cowboy hat, nearly wringing it in her hands.

"You look like you could use a walk." She closed the door to her healing room and then linked her arm with Nev's. "Some fresh air will do us both some good."

They headed down the hall and into the main lobby, a few people passing them along the way. Nev nodded her hellos, welcoming some of the new batch of clients. Judy and Kathy were finally gone, having come to an end of their stay, and Nev was grateful. She wasn't up for any awkwardness, and she wondered how Kinsley had handled things with them when she'd returned to the retreat. Nev hadn't seen her again all weekend, and she was somewhat grateful for that too, simply because she didn't know what to say. Not yet anyhow. But as they walked past the front counter to head for the back door, Kinsley rounded the corner and nearly ran into them.

"Oh, sorry," she said. She had a travel bag thrown over her shoulder and she was dragging a suitcase. Nev's heart plummeted to her stomach.

"You're leaving?" she let out.

Kinsley appeared to be just as shocked as she was. "For a few days."

"Whatever for, Kinsley?" Adrianna asked.

"I need to go see my cousin and try to tie up some loose ends with the NTSB."

Nev watched her closely and saw the color rise to her cheekbones as she spoke. She was nervous, and Nev wondered if she was telling them the whole truth.

"You're coming back, though, right?" Adrianna asked. Nev was almost afraid to hear the answer.

"Yes. Like I said, it's just for a few days."

She gave them a smile, hesitated, and then wove her way around them. "Bye."

She'd held Nev's gaze for all of two seconds.

Nev wanted to chase her down, try to explain what was going on with her, but she wasn't even sure herself. So how could she explain it?

Instead she and Adrianna told her good-bye and continued walking out through the back door and down the patio steps.

They stepped into the fall sunshine and onto the foot path that ran along the creek. They followed it quietly, leading away from the retreat. Nev stared up at the sun as it broke through the leaves on the trees. She listened to the creek water as it flowed quickly over the stones. These things usually comforted her, for they represented home. But at the moment, she was finding very little in the way of comfort.

Her mind kept returning to Kinsley and whether or not she'd just lost her forever. Lost her before she'd ever even had her.

Adrianna pulled her closer, and her stack of silver bracelets pressed into Nev's arm.

"What you got going on, love?"

Nev sank a hand into her pocket and bowed her head. She kicked a pebble, searching for the strength to speak. With Kinsley's leaving now added to the mix, she knew it would be a miracle if she could speak at all. She had so much going on inside her.

"I haven't seen you this distraught since you first came to see me all those years ago. You looked like you were going to up and crumble on me then."

"I did up and crumble."

"Yes, you did. But it took a little probing on my part, didn't it?"

"I suppose."

"So, do I need to probe some now? Or are you able to tell me?"

Nev swallowed against the tightness in her throat. "You know this isn't easy for me."

"No, you've never been good with sharing your feelings, have you? But I suspect this is something serious by the looks of you. And you came to see me, so I know you want to get whatever it is off your chest."

"I'm not sure what I want. Not anymore." She'd come to her to talk, but now...

"You want the pain to ease."

Nev sighed. "Yes, that I do."

"Then talk to me, love. I'm right here, and it's just you and me and this old ambling creek."

Nev angled her face to the sky and took a deep breath. She did need to talk to somebody. And she didn't want to burden Arthur with all he had going on. So, she decided to just get it out. "I went to see my father today."

Adrianna looked at her with a raised brow. "Really? How did that go?"

"Not well. He—I—I didn't expect it to go well. I went there to tell him good-bye."

"Good-bye?"

"I can't do it anymore, Adrianna. They only contact me if they want money, and when I do go and see them on my own they aren't interested. All they do is bitch. Either about me or about their finances or about the Padovanos."

"Kinsley's family? They still bring that up?"

"They'll never move past it, Adrianna. I've finally realized that. And I realized that they've been holding me captive all these years in their prison of accusation and blame. I don't want to be like them. I— want to be free. From them and their beliefs."

"It sounds like you've just set yourself free, love."

"Then why don't I feel better? Why do I still—"

"Hurt?"

"Yeah," Nev rasped.

"Because you've finally faced the fact that they don't care."

Nev's breath hitched at the words and Adrianna pulled her closer.

"That has to hurt, darlin'. I don't care who you are or how tough you try to be. That just downright hurts."

"It does," Nev said through tears. "He didn't even try to talk me out of it. He didn't object or try to make things right. He just—didn't care." She broke down and sobbed. She bent over, crying hard for the first time in years. Adrianna rubbed her back, soothing her, telling her it was going to be all right, to just get it all out. But Nev could barely hear her, her sobs were so all-consuming and body-racking. She cried for Viv, she cried for her parents, and she cried for all the loss she'd suffered with her family throughout her lifetime.

And when she struggled to garner breath, Adrianna embraced her and let her cry some more, this time on her shoulder. She continued to soothe and comfort her, praising her for letting it out, for letting it go. Nev's hat fell to the ground as the tears fell from her eyes. And when she finally finished, the last of the sobs leaving her body, she fell limp against Adrianna and her longtime friend supported her, just like she'd done for as long as Nev had known her.

"There," Adrianna said as Nev drew away. She wiped Nev's face and palmed her cheeks to look up into her eyes.

"Clear as day now," she said. "Those pretty green eyes of yours." She smiled. "Got all those icky clouds out."

"Icky clouds?"

"Don't make fun."

Nev smiled. "I can't help it. You're so silly sometimes."

"Silly but effective."

"Okay, yeah, I'll give you that."

Adrianna patted her cheek at the phrase she typically used, and Nev knelt to retrieve her hat. She placed it on her head and they continued to walk, arm in arm.

"Feel better?"

"Much."

"Good."

They walked a little farther before Adrianna spoke again.

"May I ask what prompted you to do all this, Nevaeh? To go and face your father?" She knelt and picked up a giant orange leaf. She smiled as she studied it. She kept it as they walked once again, Adrianna spinning the leaf by the stem. "It just seems a little out of the ordinary for you."

Nev thought long and hard about how to answer. She knew what the answer was, but she was hesitant to say, knowing it would only open a whole other can of worms with Adrianna.

But she decided she didn't care. She'd just purged a lot of pain, and she had one person to thank for being able to do that. One person who sparked the life back into her and made her take a closer, harder look at herself and her family. One person who was making her feel all kinds of things again.

"What was it, love?" Adrianna asked.

Nev stared at the sunlight reflecting off the surface of the creek, shattering it into thousands of crystals.

"It was Kinsley."

CHAPTER TWENTY-THREE

Kinsley straightened in her chair as Marty opened his eyes. She was in his hospital room in Flagstaff, the afternoon sun slanting through the blinds, marking his bed with horizontal bars. He'd been asleep for the duration of her visit. Over an hour now. She just hadn't had the heart to wake him.

"Hi," she said softly.

He blinked and tried to smile, but it was obviously painful. His entire head seemed to be wrapped up, and what little she could see of his face was yellow and purple from bruising. He'd had his surgery days before, but he still looked a little worse for wear. But he was off the ventilator, his lungs having fully recovered, and his leg was elevated and in a cast.

"Hey, stranger," he managed with a raspy voice.

Kinsley scooted her chair closer and reached out for his hand. She gently squeezed it, careful of his IV. His hand felt cool and pliable in hers, and for a second, her mind shot to her not being able to hold his hand at all. To him having been lost in the crash. It terrified her and her stomach dropped and she forced the thought from her mind.

"How are you feeling?"

"Like a million bucks. Can't you tell?"

She laughed a little and then teared up. It was so good to hear his voice. To hear his crazy sense of humor. She'd been so afraid he'd reject her or that he'd be upset with her. She knew it was a bit irrational, but she felt so guilty over the crash, she felt responsible for every little thing.

"Hey," he said, squeezing her hand in return. "No tears. Not on my account."

She smiled and wiped her cheeks. "I can't help it. I love you, you silly little man."

"If I weren't beat and battered to hell I'd take offense to that."

She chuckled. "Sorry."

He was watching her closely. "Where's the warden?"

Kinsley cracked up and covered her mouth. "You mean your wife? She went for something to eat."

"I wondered how you got in here." She thought about telling him how she about had to wrestle Diane just so she could remain in the room, but decided against it. He knew his wife was a bear, he didn't need Kinsley reminding him. So she put it nicely.

"Yeah, she's not my biggest fan, is she?"

"It's not just you. She's been keeping everyone away."

"She's just worried."

"What for? I'm out of the woods now. Just gotta heal this ugly mug of mine and I'm good to go."

Kinsley knew he was leaving out the rehab he'd need for his badly broken leg and the long road he still had ahead of him in general. But she suspected he was doing that for her benefit. He always was a selfless guy, very kind and caring. She always wondered what he saw in Diane.

She offered him a smile, trying not to think about how rude Diane was still being to her. She hadn't been at all thrilled to see her when she'd come in, but Kinsley had insisted on staying until Marty woke up. So, Diane had made herself scarce. Which was just fine with Kinsley and apparently with Marty as well.

"Don't listen to her," he said. "She doesn't know anything about planes."

Kinsley stared down at their hands. "She thinks it's my fault." She raised her eyes to look at him. "I even think it's my fault."

"It's not. It wasn't. It was engine failure. Damn thing just quit on me."

"You're sure?"

"Hell yes. I tried to restart. Nothing. Called the tower, told them, and then turned around and tried to find somewhere to put her down. But I didn't have enough time. I knew I wasn't going to make it anywhere safe, so I tried for a lone bank of trees to shear the wings rather than hit those cabin homes in Kachina Village. And that's the last thing I remember."

"You did good, Marty. Probably saved a lot of lives."

"It wasn't good enough. I should've tried for the road. But there were so many cars—" He choked up. "I hate that this happened. Hate what it's doing to Diane and my family."

"I know. But they say you're going to be okay." *Thank God you're going to be okay. It would've killed me to have lost you.*

"What's okay? Months of rehabilitation? Learning how to do shit all over again? Christ, I know I shouldn't complain, but I'm worried I'm not even going to look the same once all these bandages come off."

She searched for a way to reassure him but struggled. "You never know, Marty. Maybe they'll come off and you'll be better looking."

That made him laugh. Made him laugh so hard it hurt. He had to stop himself, but he patted her hand in appreciation.

"Thanks," he said. "I needed that." But then he grew serious again and stared out the window. He cleared his throat. "NTSB been on your ass?"

"They interviewed me pretty quickly afterward, yes. Took a couple of hours."

"They ask for maintenance records and the like?"

"I gave them what I could find in the hangar."

"That's what I told them. Said it was all in the hangar."

"You don't have any at home?"

"No. I'm pretty sure everything was in that filing cabinet in the hangar."

"Okay then. I'll let them know."

"I can't figure out what went wrong. I mean, we did everything by the book. Always have."

"I know, I'm wondering the same."

"Pre-flight check was fine, she was running fine last time out. I don't get it. Just sudden engine failure?"

"I don't know."

"All I know is, we didn't do anything wrong. There's absolutely nothing I can think of."

"We'll just have to wait and see what they find."

"Which could take a year at least."

"Sometimes."

"God, I can't wait that long."

"Me neither. It's been killing me not knowing. It's been killing me not knowing if you're going to be okay."

"Kinsley. You did nothing wrong. You hear me? I've been the one doing most of the work and the flying here recently. So if anything is wrong, it's on me."

She shook her head. "We are both responsible for that plane, Marty."

"Don't argue with me, Kinsley, or I'll sic Diane on you."

She laughed. "Okay, okay. Anything but that."

He lifted his hand, trying to reach his cup of water. Kinsley stood and handed it to him. He sipped and then stared at the muted television.

"Eric told me you've been holed up in some cabin somewhere."

"A spiritual retreat."

"No shit? Wow, never pegged you for that."

"Me neither. But desperate times."

"Yeah, I know the press has been a pain. Guess it's big news when a plane owned by an aviation expert goes down. Especially if that expert is at the top of her field."

"Apparently."

"Diane says there hasn't been anything recently. Not since they updated my condition. It'll go away now. Until they have their answers." He chuckled. "So, it's probably safe for you to go home."

Kinsley poured him some more water. "I don't think I'm going to. Not yet."

"You're kidding? Why?"

She shrugged. "I like where I'm at. And I think it's really helping me."

"Helping you with what? This? Kinsley—"

"It's helping me with everything, Marty. I've been overly stressed for a very long time now. I've been—unhappy."

He grew quiet. "I didn't know."

"No one did. Not even me. Not for a long time. I just blamed it all on the traveling and my breakup. But now I know it was so much more than that."

"Gabby was a witch," he said.

She laughed. "Thank you for that."

"I thought Diane was bad, but that one had her beat."

"Yeah, she did, didn't she?"

"What did you see in her?"

"I could ask you the same."

"Don't. Just tell me what you saw in her. Name one thing."

"She was beautiful. Feminine. Free-spirited."

"Yeah, yeah, yeah. Same old shit. That's what you say about all of them. You realize that, don't you?"

"No. I do not."

"Kinsley, you're like a broken record. You date the same type. Again and again."

She thought back to her last couple of girlfriends and realized he was right. They were all the same. One right after the other. Why had she thought that she'd get a different answer when using the exact same equation?

"Oh, my God."

"Uh-huh. I told ya."

Why had she continuously gone for the same type when none of them had ever worked out?

"It's like you have a formula for your ideal woman. And if someone doesn't meet that formula, you don't even consider them."

"Beautiful. Feminine. Free-spirited," Kinsley whispered, almost to herself.

"Snotty. Rude. Self-righteous."

"Okay, okay. I get it."

"You sure? Because I don't want you going out and bringing home another one."

Kinsley sat back and thought of Nev and her strong androgynous looks. She definitely didn't fit her formula. She was deep and thoughtful. Quiet and introspective. She was incredibly beautiful, though. She wondered what Marty would think of her. He would probably approve. She couldn't think of a reason why he wouldn't.

"What are you thinking about?"

"Hm? Nothing. Just someone I know." She couldn't stop smiling.

"Someone new?"

"Kind of."

"Kind of?"

"Do you remember my two best friends from childhood? Viv and Nev Wakefield?"

"And one died in a plane crash? Sure. It was all anyone could talk about for a long time. And you were never the same after that."

"I—I ran into Nev a couple of weeks ago. She lives on a ranch next to the retreat."

"You serious?"

"Yes."

"And she's why you're smiling?"

Kinsley nodded. "Yes, she is."

"Is she...girlfriend material?"

Kinsley stopped smiling. "I don't know how to answer that."

"Well, do you want her to be?"

Kinsley thought about kissing her, wondered what that would be like. Just holding her hand had been wonderful. Kissing would surely be...

"You don't have to answer. I can see it all over your face."

Kinsley looked out the window, feeling wistful.

What would it be like to be with Nev?

"She must be something. The way you look right now..."

"She is."

"Why do I sense a but coming on?"

She didn't answer.

"Kinsley?"

"She's different. Different from all the other women I've ever been with."

"Sounds good so far."

"I—I don't know. I've never been drawn to anyone like her before. Everything that would normally turn me away from her is drawing me in."

"Such as?"

Kinsley smiled. "Well, she's a cowgirl and a blacksmith, for starters."

"Wow, that is different."

"She's very down-to-earth, easygoing. Sort of stoic when you first meet her. But underneath all that she's very sensitive, very kind, very intelligent. She cares so much for the people in her life. And her horses. She absolutely loves her horses."

"And you like her, don't you? Like really like her."

"I do, Marty."

"So, what's the but? I haven't heard a legitimate one so far."

"Our past. Mutual and individual."

Marty seemed to take that into consideration, and they both stared out the window for a while.

"I guess you gotta ask yourself one question, then," he said.

"What's that?"

"Is she worth it?"

Kinsley cocked her head at him.

He explained. "Is she worth mulling through all that shit again?"

Kinsley thought about their recent conversations and how much she'd learned about Nev in the process. She thought about the tears she'd shed and the way she looked when she cried. She thought about waking up in her arms and feeling her body against hers. Hearing her heart thud gently against her ear. She thought about the way she smelled and the dimple in her cheek when she smiled. But most of all she thought about the way she loved. The way she loved Arthur and Adrianna and her horses.

"Yes, Marty. I think she may be."

Chapter Twenty-Four

Nev tossed down her hammer and crossed to the stereo to switch it off. The music, which was usually a friendly companion, felt like more of an annoyance today. She returned to the anvil, wiped her brow, and started in again on the decorative fire poker she was making for Stephanie, one of Adrianna's clients. Stephanie had ordered one poker and four snakes for her young boys. Nev enjoyed making them all and had even suggested the snakes when Stephanie had asked if there was anything she could make for her boys. Nev had plenty of small scraps to make those, and she should've been looking forward to the process. But currently her work, much like the music, did little to hold her interest.

She sighed as she realized the poker had already cooled too much to work with. So she crossed to the fire and reheated. As she waited, she heard someone enter. The quiet shuffling of feet told her it was Arthur. Louise had called her minutes before, letting her know Arthur was heading over.

"Hey," she said as she turned, orange glowing poker in hand.

"Hey, yourself." He met her at the anvil and watched as she set to work.

"What's that? A fire poker?"

"Uh-huh."

"How much you getting for that?"

"Do you really want to know?"

"If you want to tell me."

"A hundred and fifty bucks."

He attempted to whistle but failed. "Not bad."

"No, it's not."

He moved over to the tool bench and started rearranging things. Nev saw him but hesitated in chastising him for it. He wasn't holding anything for long, just sliding things into different positions. It looked harmless enough, even if it did screw up her organization. Arthur just wasn't used to things being different from the way he always had them. She could understand that. It must be a real struggle for him to come in and see everything change and move on without him.

"How much of that artsy-fartsy stuff you doing now?"

She glanced up at him, wondering why he was asking. "Quite a bit actually."

"You making that kind of good money on all the stuff you make?"

"Pretty much, yeah. But that's not why I do it. I mean, it helps, but it's not the main reason why I do it."

"Why do you do it, then?"

Nev paused her hammering. "Because I like doing it."

"You like doing it."

"No, actually, Arthur, I love doing it."

He turned and looked at her. She wondered what he would say, if he'd warn her against it. She knew he didn't care for it, but she wasn't sure if he'd outright tell her not to do it.

"Well, then I guess that's all there is to say, then."

She blinked at him. "Come again?" She couldn't believe her ears.

"As long as you get the other work done, then there's nothing wrong with it, is there?"

She clenched her jaw, thinking. She decided to push her luck a little with him.

"What if I stopped doing the other work altogether and just focused on the creative stuff. Would there be something wrong with that?"

His eyes shifted away from hers as he thought. "It's not my cup of tea," he said. "But if it's what makes you happy."

She smiled, tears threatening. "Really, Arthur?"

He met her gaze again. "It's not my cup of tea, though."

"I know. I get it. But it's mine. And it means the world that you're okay with that."

"Just take it slow, okay? Don't turn our business into some artsy-fartsy Renaissance fair type deal just yet, okay? I'm not sure I can handle seeing that."

She laughed. "I'll try to hold back."

"That poker with the dragon head there is weird enough for now."

"Okay, Arthur. You got it. Nothing too weird for now."

"You finish that gate the Wilsons ordered?"

"Yes, sir. It was shipped out yesterday."

"Good, good."

He turned back to the countertop and began rearranging things again.

"What are you up to today?" she asked, hoping to distract him from rearranging the entire shop.

"I'm going to work with Kinsley. We're going to bathe Willow today."

She swallowed down the rising jealousy in her throat and focused on how it would help Arthur and Willow both instead.

"That'll be nice. Willow will surely appreciate that."

There was a therapy group arriving soon. Some of them novices and some of them now old hats. She and Zachery were going to take the old hats out on a short trail ride. They felt they were ready to ride, and she had to agree. Matthew and Stephanie both had come a long way in a short time, and they'd been chomping at the bit to get her to let them ride. So she figured the short trail ride up into the canyon was the perfect opportunity for them to put their newly learned skills to the test, while Deena remained back at the stables to keep an eye on the newbies.

As for seeing Kinsley, Nev was a bit ambivalent. She hadn't seen her since her return, and she wasn't sure how Kinsley was feeling about things, if anything at all. She was, however, relieved to know that she'd come back. A part of her had feared Kinsley would get home and get comfortable and decide to stay, the retreat and her be damned. She wouldn't blame her. The way they'd left things was not good, and Nev wouldn't be surprised if Kinsley shut her out completely now. Considering how she'd hardly looked at her when she'd left, the fear wasn't as irrational as she would like it to be.

Regardless of how Kinsley behaved toward her, though, she needed to try to talk to her. To explain why she'd needed to be alone, to explain the mixed emotions she was having over her family. Kinsley had been very understanding thus far; hopefully, she would continue to be. Hopefully, she would be able to forgive her.

She wasn't sure when she would have the time to talk to her, though. She had to get things ready for the trail ride, and Matthew and Stephanie would probably be raring to go. She had to figure out something, figure out a way to get Kinsley alone for a few minutes so they could talk. Then again, maybe the ranch wasn't the best place to have that conversation. Maybe she should save it and wait for a more opportune moment.

Nev continued to hammer away at the decorative fire poker, returning to the fire again and again. And Arthur continued to rearrange, like a little kid lining up his treasured toy trains. It was good to see him in the shop again. He hadn't come in since he'd hurt his foot, and his presence had been missed. She suspected she wasn't the only reason why he'd come, though. She'd told him about Kinsley coming into the shop previously and helping her out by holding the gate for her. Arthur had been impressed, and she'd known by the look in his eye what was coming next. He'd wanted to know why she'd returned to Phoenix, disbelieving it was just a family matter like she'd told him. Nev had tried to smooth her way over the topic by telling him all about the plane crash, but the old man had steely eyes and they'd sussed her out. He'd known it was more than that. He'd somehow known it probably had something to do with her. And now he was back in the shop, and she just knew he was there in case Kinsley walked in. He didn't want Nev screwing things up with her. He didn't want Nev chasing her away. And he'd said as much the days before during their discussion. In fact, his exact words were, "Don't you do it, now. Don't you screw this up. This one, she's special."

Nev couldn't argue—Kinsley was special. All she could do was try to reassure him that she wouldn't mess anything up, but they both knew her reassurances were no guarantee. Nev's track record with Kinsley wasn't exactly great. Arthur was aware, having witnessed Nev's attitude during the dinner they'd had with Kinsley, and what he hadn't witnessed, he'd somehow figured out. The man might have dementia, but in some areas he was still as sharp as a tack.

Nev turned back to the fire, deep in thought, and heard a loud crash. She whipped around and saw Arthur on the ground, one of the small rolling tool carts on the ground next to him, tools sprawled everywhere.

"Arthur!" She rushed to him, tearing off her goggles and apron before kneeling in front of him. "Are you okay?"

He had his arms out in front of him, like he was trying to grab hold of something, anything. She helped him sit up, felt him trembling. His eyes were wide, and he seemed frazzled and confused.

"What happened? Are you okay?" She frantically searched his body for any signs of injury. She found none.

He looked at her like he was totally lost.

"Where are we?"

"We're in the shop."

He looked around. "Oh." His gaze traveled down next to him

to the turned-over cart and mess of tools. "I—turned around and— must've lost my balance."

"Are you okay?" She again scanned him for injury. He lightly touched his head, but there was no mark, no cut or bruise.

"I just lost my balance."

"Are you sure? Nothing fell on you, did it?"

"No, no nothing like that. I must've tried to lean on that cart. Forgot it moved."

"Yes, it has wheels."

He stared at the cart like he'd never seen it before. Like the idea that it might have wheels was completely foreign to him.

"Come on, let's get you up. Are you all right to stand?"

"Yeah, I'm not crippled." He gripped her hand and allowed her to lift him up. He staggered for a few seconds, but then righted himself. She stuck to him like glue.

"Come on," she said. "Let's get you back inside and let Louise check you out."

"No, no, I'm all right. I got Kinsley in a few minutes."

"Louise first."

"No, I—"

"Arthur, don't fight me on this," she said firmly.

They walked back to the house slowly. Louise was noticeably concerned when she heard.

"My goodness, Arthur, what happened? Did you try and bite off more than you can chew again? I oughta tan your hide."

"Calm down, woman, I did no such thing." They helped him into his recliner, and Louise went to get her medical bag. When she came back, she took his vitals and examined him. His eyes started to fall closed before she even finished.

"I'm okay," he said before leaning back and closing his eyes for good.

"I think he lost his balance," Nev said softly. "Tried to lean against a moveable cart and down he went."

Louise stood and sighed. "He's lucky."

"Yeah, no kidding."

"Now will you please agree with me that he shouldn't be in there?"

Nev looked at Arthur sleeping peacefully and nodded. "Yeah." It pained her to say so, but Louise was right. It just wasn't safe to have him in the shop anymore. And seeing firsthand how scared he'd been after that fall, she hoped he would agree with them as well.

"It scared him," Nev said.

"I'd say so. Wore him plumb out too."

Arthur was fatiguing quickly these days, something they'd both noticed. He would be disappointed about missing his date with Kinsley, but Nev wasn't about to wake him. He needed to rest now, and Louise needed to keep an eye on him just in case he had any underlying injuries.

"Can you keep him inside for the next couple of hours while the therapy group is here? I'm taking a few out on a trail ride and I won't be out there to watch him."

"I'll do my best."

"Hopefully, he'll sleep the whole time."

"Mm, if he doesn't, I'll find something to distract him. But if you want my advice, I'd hide that little lady friend of his. Because if he happens to see her out there, there'll be no holding him back."

Nev stared out at the stables. The van had just pulled in.

"I'll take care of it."

She wasn't sure how she was going to take care of it, but she knew she had to.

Kinsley would just have to understand.

CHAPTER TWENTY-FIVE

Kinsley was standing in the pen petting Willow when Nev walked out of the stables carrying a large saddle. She smiled softly at Kinsley as she walked up and placed the saddle on Willow's back.

"What are you doing? I thought Arthur and I were going to bathe her today."

Nev busied herself positioning and fastening the saddle. "Arthur's a bit under the weather today," Nev said. "So I was going to take Willow out with me on that trail ride."

Kinsley bristled and stumbled over her words. "What—Arthur—he—" She shook her head, disbelieving what she'd heard. "Is he okay? Should I go check on him?"

Nev tightened the saddle. "He's okay. He's sleeping peacefully and Louise is with him. So, you're fine out here." Nev turned to face her. She adjusted her hat.

"I am? What am I supposed to do?"

Nev looked up at the saddle. Kinsley did too and then took a step back.

"Oh, no. No, I don't think so. Nuh-uh."

"I'll be right behind you, holding you tight."

Kinsley opened her mouth to argue but stopped.

Holding me tight? What would that feel like? Being in Nev's arms, being so close to her once again? Would it feel as good as it did the other night? She'd thought of little else since.

But her gaze traveled to Willow once again, and just the mere size of her made her uneasy.

"I can't. I'm too scared."

Nev came closer. She spoke softly. "It's Willow. You know her, she knows you. She's as gentle as a lamb and big enough and strong enough to carry us both. Come on. At least give it a try. Let me help you up." She held out her hand.

Kinsley faltered, looking from Nev to Willow and back again.

"I don't know."

"Yes, you do. You know you want to. You know you want to go on this ride and see more of the canyon."

"I would like to see more of the canyon," she nearly whispered.

Nev smiled. "See? It'll be fun." She nodded toward Willow. "Come on. Let me help you up."

Kinsley took a step toward her and hesitated, but once her hand was in Nev's, she was pulled gently toward her and nearly in her arms within seconds. Kinsley looked up into her eyes, and her heart started pounding. She blamed it on nerves from having to mount Willow, but she knew it was Nev and her close proximity. In the short few days she'd been gone, she'd forgotten just how captivating her light green eyes were. How beautiful her chiseled face was. How sexy she looked with that cowboy hat angled over her face.

She struggled to breathe. "Okay."

Nev showed her where to put her foot and showed her where to hold on. Surprisingly, Kinsley was able to mount her on the first try.

"Oh, God," she said, glancing down. "Nev."

"Just hold tight, I'm coming." Nev climbed on swiftly behind her and settled in the double saddle. Willow took a couple of steps and Kinsley clenched her eyes.

"Nev," she said. "Oh, God."

"Shh," Nev said into her ear. "I'm right here. I got you." She wrapped her arm around her waist and held her tight. "You're okay. Just try to relax."

"I can't. She's too big. I'm too high."

"Shh." Her breath tickled her ear, and Kinsley's body broke out in gooseflesh. She trembled, but not from fear. And suddenly, she was okay, more than okay. As long as Nev kept doing that.

"I'm scared," she said, though her voice had lost conviction.

Nev showed her how to hold on and gave her some basic instruction, all the while speaking softly in her ear, her strong hand holding her tight, so that they were pressed together. She smelled like heaven, felt like a goddess, so firm and strong sitting behind her. Kinsley closed her eyes again, relishing her embrace.

"We're going to tell Willow to take a few steps now," she said.

Kinsley breathed. "Okay."

She opened her eyes and Willow took a few steps. Then a few more. Until they were walking around the pen.

"See, nice and easy," Nev said. "You're okay."

Kinsley tried to steady her breathing as she held on to the saddle horn. Willow was calm, walking slowly. And by the time the others had mounted their horses and were ready to go, Kinsley had relaxed a great deal more.

"Are you ready?" Nev said to her, after giving instructions to the group.

"Um." Kinsley clenched her eyes, taking a huge leap of faith in Nev and in Willow. "Sure, let's go."

"All right," Nev said, chuckling.

The group headed out, and Nev and Zachary kept the pace relatively slow since the other two riders were new as well. Matthew and Stephanie were all smiles, not seeming to be the least bit afraid. Kinsley envied them because even though she'd relaxed some with Nev's reassurances, she still had a death grip on the saddle horn.

They headed away from the stables, back toward the rear of the property. Soon they were on a dirt trail that led back through the woods. Gorgeous trees blew their colorful fall leaves in welcome, and a few even fell across their path. Nev filled them in on the surrounding vegetation, telling them all about the trees and plants and wildlife they might encounter. The ride was beautiful, Nev hadn't exaggerated, and Kinsley, though still a little nervous, was glad she'd come.

"How are you doing, Kinsley?" Matthew asked from his position on Juno, a large gray mare. She was just as gentle as Willow, and Kinsley had even ventured over to pet her a few times at Matthew's encouragement.

"I'm hanging in there," she said, smiling over at him. He looked so proud, sitting up ramrod straight, black cowboy hat on. His brand-new boots were dusty, but his Wranglers and western style shirt looked new and spotless, giving him away as a city slicker.

"You look like you might actually be liking this," Stephanie said. Her short bob style haircut bounced as her horse, Daredreamer, walked. She'd never donned a hat, or any cowgirl gear for that matter. Yet she'd taken to Daredreamer like an old pro, claiming that dealing with him was a pleasure compared to her four rambunctious children.

"I am," Kinsley said. "A little."

Nev laughed behind her. "You're doing really well. Do you feel okay?"

"Yes, just a little nervous still."

"Understandable." She held her tighter, pulling them closer together. "How about now? Any better?"

Kinsley could feel the rise and fall of her chest against her back. "Mm, yes, thanks."

"Let me know if you need to stop and we will. We can take a break."

"No, I'm good for now."

As long as I'm in your arms.

Kinsley wished she could fully relax and fall back into Nev's arms completely, recalling how it had felt to lie in her arms those few nights ago. She longed to do it again but knew it might be wishful thinking. They hadn't spoken since then, and she wasn't quite sure what to say about that last encounter, if anything. Nev had needed space and she'd left. It sounded pretty straightforward and simple, but it was anything but. She'd divulged something to Nev she'd obviously not been aware of about her father, and she felt terrible about it. It had bothered Nev, even seeming to maybe have hurt her. Knowing that had really upset her, to the point where she'd convinced herself that maybe she'd really needed to give Nev some space by leaving to return home for a while. That way Nev could have some time to think without worrying about having to deal with her when she came to work with Arthur.

Arthur, of course, hadn't been happy about it, but she hadn't given him a lot of detail. It was something that was between Nev and her, and if Nev wanted him to know, she'd tell him. Kinsley wondered if she had told him and maybe that's why he didn't come out today to work with her.

Could he be upset with her and what she'd told Nev?

She shook the thought away, feeling responsible again.

Why did she always feel responsible for everything?

Did it stem from her childhood? She was the youngest of three, but her brothers had pretty much been in their own little world. The two of them together before she was adopted at age three. And being boys, they'd played a lot together before she grew old enough to join in on the fun. And then she'd always been the one to tattle when one of them did something wrong. She'd always been the first to confess when she'd done wrong too. So much so, that her parents immediately came to her whenever anything went down, because they knew she'd readily tell them what happened.

Was that because she'd been afraid to disappoint them? Afraid they'd send her back to foster care if she did? Her parents had never even suggested such a thing, but it had, if she had to admit, always been in the back of her mind. She'd always thought she'd needed to be perfect.

"You still doing okay?" Nev asked as the red rocks of the canyon came into view.

"I'm good."

She noticed that Zachery had pulled ahead with Matthew and Stephanie, leaving Nev and her to bring up the rear.

"This is really beautiful," Kinsley said.

"It is," Nev said. "I hope you can relax and fully enjoy it. You deserve it, you know."

Kinsley pressed her lips together, moved by the statement. "Thanks."

They rode in silence for a while before Nev spoke again.

"Are you still afraid of horses?" she asked, teasing.

Kinsley humored her with a truthful answer. "Not like I was before Willow. I'm coming around, I think."

"What happened? If you don't mind my asking."

"I was thrown," she said. "When I was five. Mom and Dad took us horseback riding. Thought it would be fun. I was scared to begin with. And they put me on this horse that seemed huge. I started to cry and protest, and I guess the horse got spooked. She reared back and threw me off and I went flying through the air. I still can remember hitting the ground."

"Yikes, no wonder you're so afraid. That would scare anyone and probably scar them for life."

"It has. Being able to remember the impact is the worst. I broke my collarbone."

"Ouch," she said. "I'm so sorry, Kinsley."

Kinsley chuckled. "It's okay. I think I'm finally putting it behind me."

"I hope so." Nev leaned into her and touched her hand. "For the saddle horn's sake."

Kinsley laughed. "I'm not letting go."

"You don't have to," she said gently. "Just relax your grip a little if you can." She lightly stroked her hand. "I've got you."

Kinsley carefully loosened her grip. She exhaled, not realizing she'd been holding her breath.

"There," Nev said. "Does that feel better?"

"Somewhat," Kinsley said, causing Nev to laugh.

Nev held her around her waist again and handed her the rein with her other hand. "How about you steer for a while?"

Kinsley turned her head. "What? No. I really shouldn't."

"It's easy. Just hold the rein. Just like this. Here, I'll hold it with you."

Kinsley took the rein carefully in her hand, and they continued following the others. And before long, they were at their destination, a beautiful spot that looked out onto the vast canyon. The colorful trees seemed to pop against the red canyon, and the creek looked like honey snaking through it in the sunlight.

"Oh, my God," Kinsley let out. "Nev, it's incredible."

"Yes, it is."

"I fully get why you live here now. I wish…" She let her words fall, not quite sure where she was headed with them.

Nev seemed to wait for her to finish, but when she didn't she patted her hand.

"Why don't you go ahead and climb down? And we'll rest a moment with the others."

Matthew and Stephanie had already climbed off their horses and were now taking photos with their phones.

Kinsley looked down at Nev and found her doing the same, only she was taking a picture of her.

"Smile," she said, positioning her phone for the best angle.

"Nev, come on, no."

"Yes, come on now. I've already taken two, so you might as well smile."

Kinsley laughed and Nev snapped the picture.

"Gotcha."

"Not fair," Kinsley said.

Nev laughed. "Who said I play fair?"

Kinsley watched as she took another and then tucked the phone in her back pocket to help her off Willow.

Kinsley landed in her arms and got lost again in her eyes.

"Thanks," she breathed.

Nev smiled and brushed her hair from her face with gentle fingers. "No problem."

"Hey, you two," Stephanie said. They turned and she took a picture. "Come on, come look at this view."

Nev released her. "You really should go take it in. It's magnificent."

Kinsley studied her for a long moment, and then smiled. "Yes, it is." And she headed off after Stephanie, leaving the most magnificent of sights behind her standing next to Willow.

CHAPTER TWENTY-SIX

Kinsley slung her legs over the armrest of the chair, sock-covered feet close to the wood stove for warmth. She held her journal up for inspection, rereading what she'd just written. Pleased with the entry, she set it aside on the floor and stared up at the ceiling. The evening was crisp, with a noticeable chill in the air, a hint of what the oncoming winter season would be. She wondered what Cypress Creek looked like blanketed in snow, how incredibly beautiful it must look against the red of the rocks. She wished she could see that someday, and her thoughts went to her future, a place they'd been going a lot lately.

She turned on her side and studied her journal on the rug. She'd written about her unforeseen future quite a bit, but no answers had been forthcoming. Did she want to return to her job, keep up the mad traveling, living out of a suitcase? Or did she want something different, something more?

Adrianna had suggested she relax and focus on the things she'd always enjoyed as a means of opening up her mind and stirring some creativity. She'd done that recently, beginning with some artwork. Her latest was an enlarged thumbprint, consisting of words she'd used to describe herself. The idea had been Adrianna's in a class on self-esteem, but she'd thoroughly enjoyed making it, enjoyed the creative aspect to it. She'd done hers on a round piece of wood and painstakingly hand painted each small word. It had turned out really well and she was looking forward to doing other things she enjoyed, like flying. The Cypress Creek airport wasn't far from the retreat, and she'd thought more than once about going over there to rent a plane for a short flight. She hadn't piloted a plane in months, and she missed it terribly. Flying had always made her feel so free and yet so in control at the same time. It was a rush she didn't think she could ever live without.

She reached down and ran her fingers over her journal. Its cover was well-worn, and it was almost time for a new one. She'd almost completely filled this one up. Not bad for someone who'd initially resisted the writing, saying she couldn't ever express herself that way. She picked it up and began thumbing through it, rereading some of her previous entries. She came to the recent one about Nev and paused, staring back up at the ceiling.

The day had been glorious, the trail ride amazing. She didn't think she'd ever seen a more beautiful landscape. And Nev, Nev had only added to its beauty. Standing there next to Willow in her cowboy hat, watching as Kinsley walked away from her to go take in the view. She was unforgettable, and Kinsley was glad she'd snapped a few photos of her as well, despite her objections. They'd had a great time, and Kinsley had been surprised at the lack of awkwardness between them. They'd both relaxed and just enjoyed the ride and each other's company, choosing not to discuss anything too heavy. Kinsley had appreciated that and Nev seemed to also, both of them laughing and having a good time over cups of fresh apple cider that Zachery had brought with them before heading back.

Kinsley hadn't wanted it to come to an end.

She rose and searched for her phone, wanting to look at the pictures of Nev. But a knock on her door interrupted her. Thinking it must be Adrianna, she hurried to the door and pulled it open. To her great surprise and astonishment, she found Nev standing on her front porch.

"Hi."

"Hi," Kinsley said.

Nev pulled off her hat. "I hope you don't mind my dropping by. I just thought you might be needing something."

Kinsley searched her face, clueless.

"What's that?"

Nev held out her soft flannel shirt. The one Kinsley had worn for days and left at Nev's house the night she'd stayed.

"Oh." She was so taken aback she was at a loss for words.

"It's quite cold now, and I know how much you liked wearing it."

Kinsley slowly took the shirt, unsure what else to do. Nev was standing there looking at her with such vulnerability in her eyes, wearing nothing but jeans and a gray sweater, her breath coming out in white puffs.

Kinsley blinked back into focus and remembered her manners.

"Would you like to come in?"

Nev surprised her again by agreeing. "Thank you," she said as she entered.

Kinsley closed the door behind them and crossed into the living room.

"Can I get you anything? Coffee, tea, cider?" Kinsley grinned, recalling how she'd made a fuss over the apple cider on the trail ride. Nev had insisted she take some back to the retreat with her.

"No, thank you."

"You sure? I can heat some up. You've got to be cold."

"I'm good, thanks. It's plenty warm in here."

"Is it—too warm? I can—"

"Kinsley, I'm fine. Please, sit."

Kinsley sat in the chair and let Nev have the couch. Kinsley immediately shrugged into the warm shirt and snuggled into it. Despite Nev's comfort with the temperature, Kinsley was still a bit cold. She was so grateful to have the shirt back.

"It's so warm, thank you," she said.

"It looks good on you," Nev said, openly taking her in. "I like seeing you in it."

Kinsley felt herself blush. She wasn't expecting such frankness, and she wondered if she'd ever be able to predict when Nev would choose to be so forthcoming. She cleared her throat. "It, uh, doesn't smell like you anymore, though." She wasn't sure why she'd said that, suddenly feeling rather vulnerable herself. Maybe her confession would help put Nev more at ease, now that she'd also confessed something rather personal.

"I'm not sure how to remedy that." She sounded so serious, like she was really trying to come up with a way to fix it.

"Well, I would suggest you wear it for a couple of days, but seeing as how I'm already in it again and loving its warmth and comfort, I'd say there's no chance in hell you're getting it off me."

Nev smiled but glanced away, as if she were a little embarrassed.

"I really came by for another reason," she eventually said.

"Oh?"

"I'm afraid I owe you another apology."

"No, Nev, you don't." Nev didn't owe her anything. If anyone should apologize, it should be her. She was the one who told Nev something upsetting. Something she obviously wasn't aware of. Kinsley had yet to forgive herself for that.

"Please." She held up her palm. "Let me finish." She paused. "What you said the other day really upset me."

"I know, and I—"

Nev held up her hand again and Kinsley stopped.

"But I needed to hear it. Because I honestly had no idea. I knew my dad drank, but I thought he only did it on rare occasions and only right after the accident. I had no idea he was showing up to work drunk. If you knew my dad, knew him like he was, then you would know how out of character that was for him."

"I did know him," Kinsley said softly. "So, yes, I understand."

"Right," Nev said. "Anyway, it got me thinking, and I recalled all the terrible things my folks had said about yours, how they blamed everything on you guys, and I realized something. They do the same thing with everything and everyone in their lives. They even do it to me. They especially do it to me. They blame me for their current financial situation, complaining about how I left them with nothing when I decided to leave academia and come work with Arthur. It's like everything is my fault. And what's not my fault is someone else's. It's never theirs."

She rubbed her thighs and sighed.

"I'm sorry, Nev," Kinsley said, sensing her pain and sadness.

"No, I'm sorry. I never should've shut you out. Not like that. I should've just explained that it was news to me and told you how upset I was."

"You were shocked, cut yourself some slack."

"I know it hurt you," she said. "You left soon after. And I know it was partly because of me." She looked up at her. "It was wasn't it?"

"I thought it might be better for you if I wasn't around for a little while."

Nev closed her eyes. "No. So not true. I was devastated when you said you were going to leave, Kinny. I was terrified that you wouldn't come back."

"But I did come back."

"Yes, you did. And I'm so glad."

"Me too."

Kinsley gave her a soft smile. "And I'm glad you're here. Right now."

"You are?"

"Yes." She rose and crossed to the couch. She sat next to her and took her hand. "I'm very glad you're here." They faced each other and Kinsley touched her cheek. "And I accept your apology."

Nev closed her eyes against her touch and trembled. "Thank you."

"Nev," Kinsley said, wanting her to open her eyes.

She did. "Yes?"

"I want to kiss you."

Again, she trembled. Tears filled her eyes, but she nodded. "I want to kiss you too. More than anything."

Kinsley cupped her jaw and leaned in. Nev's gaze held hers the entire way, burning her soulful desire right into her.

"Oh, Nev," Kinsley whispered just before their lips connected.

Nev made a small noise of helplessness as their lips touched for the first time in twenty years. Kinsley felt the heat of Nev's mouth against hers and she pulled her closer, needing more. She pulled her in and tasted her, took her time and relished her sweet lips, doing what she'd been wanting to do since that very first kiss in the limousine all those years ago.

And taste sweet she did. Nev was like a nectar she'd never even known existed, and she simply could not get enough. She clung to her and framed her lips with hers, gently tugging her in to taste more of her, to consume her.

Nev kept trembling beneath her, allowing Kinsley to take control, to take her by the hand and lead her toward their destiny.

"Nev," she breathed as they pulled apart.

"Yes?" Her eyes were still brimming with tears and some spilled down her face. Kinsley brushed them away, her heart yearning for her and breaking for her at the same time.

"Are you okay?"

She nodded. "I am."

"Are you sure?"

"It's just—been a long time."

Kinsley inclined her head. "But I thought—"

Nev shook her head. "No. Not with anyone I really care about. Not with anyone I—love."

Kinsley inhaled. "Love?"

Nev wiped a tear and laughed. "Yes. Love."

Kinsley held her face and dove into her eyes. Nev spoke.

"It's okay if you don't feel the same," she said. "I just—can't help how I feel, and I'll take you whatever way I can get you."

"I—oh, Nev." She pulled her in again and tasted her, so moved by the sincerity she saw in her eyes. God, how she felt for this woman. How she—

She stopped and drew back. "I love you, Nev Wakefield."

Nev blinked at her.

"I always have."

Kinsley smiled and skimmed her thumb across her moist lips. "And I think you know that. I think you knew it even then. And that's why you were so nervous and avoided answering my questions."

The corner of Nev's mouth lifted. "Maybe."

"There's no maybe about it. You knew."

"I suspected."

Kinsley laughed and eased her back a little so she could crawl onto her lap.

"But who knew you'd be the first to say it?" She straddled her while up on her knees and ran her fingers through her short hair as she looked down at her. "Certainly not me."

"Me neither."

Kinsley brushed more tears away. "Are you sure you're okay?"

Nev reached up, grabbed her hand, stopping her. "God, yes, I'm more than okay."

And she edged to the end of the cushion and hoisted them up, Kinsley wrapped around her and in her arms.

"Oh, okay," Kinsley said. "I guess you really are okay."

Nev looked into her eyes, holding her safely and securely in her arms.

"I really am, Kinny. And I'm about to show you just how okay I am."

CHAPTER TWENTY-SEVEN

Nev carried Kinsley to the bedroom and set her on the bed. She stood before her, holding her face, staring down into her hazel eyes. Never before had a woman looked back at her like this, reflecting the way Nev was feeling. Never before had she felt for someone so much. She'd been in love, yes, but she'd never truly experienced this kind of love. It went so far beyond lust and desire and the want of another. It was deeper, more visceral, and profound, and she knew without a doubt she'd do anything in the world to make sure Kinsley was happy. Even if Kinsley decided to walk away. Her happiness was all that mattered.

"I love you," she said, truly, deeply meaning it. She dipped her head and kissed her before Kinsley could answer.

They kissed hungrily, both of them tasting and consuming. Tongues seeking and finding. Nev eased her back onto the bed and stretched out atop her, lost in their languid kiss, wishing she could take her in and hold her inside for all eternity. Kinsley moaned beneath her, seemingly torn between hurriedly devouring her and taking her sweet time. One second, she was clawing at her back, the next, she was lightly grazing her nails up her side, just inside her sweater. Both sensations sent Nev into near frenzies, and she had to pull away to garner breath and control.

"You're driving me crazy," she rasped.

"Is that so bad?" Kinsley asked, palming her jaw.

"I want us to take our time. I want it to be special."

"It is special, Nev. It's you and me."

"I want it to be really special, because it's you and me."

Kinsley seemed to think a moment. Then she slid out from beneath her. "I'll be right back."

She disappeared into the living room, and when she returned she had a single jar candle with her and a lighter. She placed the candle on the nightstand and lit it. Then she extinguished the light.

"Better?" she asked.

"Yes."

Nev watched her from her position on the bed as she dug through the dresser and then disappeared into the bathroom. "Don't go anywhere," she said from behind the door. "I'll be right out."

Nev slid from the bed and pulled back the covers. Then she sat and pulled off her boots and socks. She was sitting back against the pillows when Kinsley emerged, wearing nothing but a lacy, dark blue bra and matching panties.

The sight of her small, lithe body in the lingerie took Nev's breath away.

"My God, you are beautiful." The candlelight seemed to kiss her, tease her with its touch, flickering against her alabaster skin.

Kinsley moved toward the bed. She didn't speak, just crossed to Nev like a silent seductress. When she reached her, she held out her hand. Nev took it and stood and Kinsley locked eyes with her and slowly began to undress her. She started with her sweater, which she swiftly pulled up over her head and quietly tossed aside. Then she unbuckled her belt, biting her lower lip as she did so, as if she were anticipating what she'd find underneath. She unfastened her jeans and slowly but firmly slid them down her body for Nev to step out of. Then she came back up and hungrily eyed Nev in her black bra and black boxer briefs.

"You look so good in these I almost don't want to take them off you," Kinsley said, skimming her fingers along her bra and then down her abdomen to her briefs. "But I know, as good as these look, what lies beneath will be so much better."

Nev swallowed hard as Kinsley burned a stare into her, the blue depths of her eyes stormy with desire, a dark blue hurricane of want.

She grazed her nails up and down her sides again, eliciting a gasp and sigh from Nev.

"Is it okay with you if I take these off now?" she asked, seemingly doing her best to respect Nev's wishes and take things slow.

"Yes," Nev said. Her skin was alive with gooseflesh, her nipples tight and erect beneath her bra. "Please."

Kinsley laughed softly, as if she were thoroughly enjoying the tease. Then she leaned in and placed kisses along her chest as her fingers wrapped around her and freed her from her bra. Kinsley dropped the bra on the floor and unabashedly took her in. Her eyes seemed to widen as she slowly brought her hands to Nev's breasts.

Nev sighed again as she touched her. So light and deft, it was like the tease of a breath. Her skin bunched and tightened, and she was dying for more pressure.

"Please," Nev said as Kinsley skimmed her flesh, around and around the centers. "Touch me."

"Where?" Kinsley asked, as if she didn't know. "Here?" She brushed her hard nipple and Nev about came out of her skin.

"Yes," she cried. "Please."

"You like to be touched right here?"

"Yes," she cried again as Kinsley continued to tease her, flicking her nipple every so often as she moved her fingers along her breasts.

"Okay," Kinsley said as she finally ran the backs of her fingers against her firm buds. Nev went up to her tiptoes and gripped her wrists, clenching her eyes.

"Oh, Jesus, yes."

"Shh, it's okay," Kinsley said, slowing her pace. "Breathe." She lowered her hands to her abdomen, and Nev took in several lungfuls of air. Kinsley leaned in again and lightly kissed her chest, carefully trailing her mouth around the edges of her breasts. Then she came to the centers and purposely breathed her hot breath upon them, sending Nev beyond reason.

"Oh, God." She held her head, clung to her, begged for her to do more. "Please, Kinsley, please."

"Shh, not yet, my love." She moved her mouth lower as she dropped to her knees. Nev watched breathlessly as she removed her briefs and freed them from her feet. Then she held her legs and breathed into her inner thighs.

"Mm, you are so muscular," she said. "So strong. I could worship these legs forever." She kissed her sensitive skin, causing Nev to shudder and grip her head once again.

"Kinsley," she rasped, as Kinsley moved upward toward her nestled flesh.

"Not yet, love," she said as she slowly stood. She took Nev's hands and placed them on her hips. "Undress me."

Nev undressed her in much the same manner that Kinsley had undressed her. Carefully tracing her fingers along her smooth, soft skin, removing first her bra to reveal her luscious breasts, and then her panties to reveal the light brown curls at her center.

Kinsley came closer. She wrapped her arms around her, their warm bodies touching, caressing.

"Mm, you feel so good, Nev." She kissed her shoulders, her chest, and once again breathed upon her nipples.

Nev tensed and gripped her hips.

"Kinsley," she breathed.

"No," she said. "Call me Kinny. I want you to call me Kinny."

"Kinny," Nev said. "I can't control myself much longer."

"I know, love, but it will be worth it, I promise."

She took Nev's hands and placed them on her sides. "Let's touch each other together." She ran her hands up Nev's sides, and Nev did the same, mirroring her touch. Nev struggled for breath and stared into her eyes as Kinsley ran her fingers lightly, deftly, over awakening skin. Nev burned beneath her fingertips, as if her every touch were a flame held against her skin, sparking her to life, nourishing her now raging desire.

Soon Nev was touching her everywhere as well. Along her sides, up and down her back, along her inner and outer thighs. All the while Kinsley was doing the same to her, seemingly feeding off the widening of her eyes and then the narrowing of her gaze.

Then Kinsley moved her hand to Nev's center and circled her aching flesh.

"Are you ready, love?" she said.

Nev mirrored her, desperately wanting to delve into her curls. "Yes."

Kinsley grinned and breathed upon Nev's nipple again. "Good. Now let's see how wet you are." She dipped her fingers into Nev's folds just as she closed her mouth around her bunched nipple. Nev arched and cried out, her own hand easing into Kinsley's flesh, finding her hot and slick and seemingly hungry for her touch. Kinsley cried out as well, tearing her mouth from Nev to do so as they both slipped and slid. Nev struggled to stand, the sensation almost too much, Kinsley's fingers like all-knowing pleasure seekers, sent on a mission to conquer her. She trembled beneath her, moaned in response to her magical touch, and then set to evoking her own moans from Kinsley as she continued to glide into her flesh.

"Oh, God, Nev," she breathed. "Feels so good. Mm. God. You're so wet, love. So, so wet. Am I as wet as you are?"

"God, yes. You're all over my fingers and I love it, love you."

"Ah, God, Nev. What you're doing to me, oh, God, what you're doing."

She clamped her mouth around her nipple again and this time sucked. Hard.

Nev hissed. "Christ, Kinny, yes. Jesus Christ, yes."

And that's when Nev could take no more. In one swift motion, she lifted Kinsley up and deposited her on the bed, onto her back, and she climbed on top of her.

"Together," Kinsley said, wrapping her hands around Nev's ass.

"Okay," Nev said, understanding at once. She maneuvered her thigh between Kinsley's legs while she rubbed her own flesh against Kinsley's thigh. Then she began to move, and their bodies began to flow in unison much like the creek right outside the door. Kinsley clung to her back, whispering sweet nothings into her ear, and Nev devoured her neck, nibbling and sucking, relishing in the taste of her just below her ear.

"Nev," she breathed. "Are you close?"

Nev drew back, looked into her eyes. "Yes." She pumped her hips, kept her thigh firm against Kinsley's wet flesh.

"Come with me?"

Nev swallowed. Groaned. She nodded and they locked eyes and rocked. Rocked until their cries grew louder, rocked until the pleasure mounted, rocked until they exploded together in a cataclysm of cries and thrusts and guttural groans. Until they could rock no more, Nev collapsing in her arms, Kinsley holding her tight as Nev cried into her shoulder.

"Shh, it's okay, love," Kinsley said, kissing her ear. "I'm right here."

Nev pulled away and looked down at her. Tears stung her eyes, but she didn't care. She smiled, and felt it break through the pain that was now dissipating. "I'm okay," she said, meaning it.

"Yeah?"

"Yeah. I'm better than okay." Nev kissed her long and soft and then repositioned herself to rest fully between her legs. "I'm the best I've ever been."

CHAPTER TWENTY-EIGHT

Kinsley awoke to flickering candlelight, wrapped in Nev's arms. She smiled and kissed her upper arm, thrilled to be back where she'd been days before, only this time all the better. They'd just spent the better part of the night making love, touching each other carefully, drawing out the pleasure, giving and taking. Never had she had a lover who was so attentive, so curious and eager to please her, to learn her body like it was the absolute best thing she'd ever discovered.

Nev was a gracious and thorough lover, making sure to cover every square inch of her, touching and caressing, all for the sake of her cries, for her pure pleasure. And Kinsley had done the same in return. Sometimes touching Nev alone, sometimes the two of them touching together. The touching always leading to mind-bending, soul-crashing orgasms, however.

But there was still so much more to explore, so much more pleasure to ignite and fan the flames of. She turned into her arms and kissed her chest, garnering a low growl.

"Mm, what are you doing?" Nev asked, her eyes blinking open.

"I'm kissing on you."

"Mm, again?"

"I can't seem to stop."

"I know what you mean."

Kinsley propped herself up on her elbow.

"You do?"

"Uh-huh. There's so much more to do." Her eyes glinted as if reflecting the wickedness in her statement.

"Funny, I was just thinking the same thing."

Nev tugged her closer. "Oh yeah?"

"Uh-huh."

"What did you have in mind?"

Kinsley traced a finger down her lips to her neck to her chest. "Actually, I was going to let you decide."

"Oh, really?"

"That okay with you?"

"That's more than okay with me."

She flipped Kinsley onto her back and settled down atop her, causing Kinsley to laugh.

"You're in for it now," Nev said, already planting kisses along her chest and shoulders.

"Am I?"

"Oh, God yes."

"And why is that?"

Nev paused and looked at her. "Because I'm insatiable."

"Oh, no, I guess I'm in for it, then. But God help me, I know I'm going to love it."

"I hope so." Nev started kissing her again, quickly leading down to her breasts where she took her nipple into her mouth and swirled with her tongue. Kinsley came up off the bed and ran her nails through her hair.

"Nev," she let out. "God, yes." They'd yet to use their mouths on one another, with the exception of Kinsley's first caresses of Nev's breasts, both agreeing to only touch using their hands. The tasting, as they'd called it, had been saved for later. And now later was here and Kinsley was just about to die it felt so good.

"You like it?" Nev asked, teasing her this time instead of the other way around.

"Oh, yes. Very much."

Nev laughed. "Very much, huh?"

"Mm-hm." She ran her nails through her hair, clawing gently at her scalp as Nev continued, first saturating one nipple with her heavy tongue and then the other. Then she took both in her mouth and sucked, pulling them in until Kinsley writhed and begged her to stop. Leaving her panting, Nev moved lower, inching her way down, making a long, wet trail with her tongue. And when she came to her center, she maneuvered between her legs and settled, kissing her inner thighs.

She didn't speak, just looked up at Kinsley and singed a heavy look of love and desire straight into her before she lowered herself and fed. Kinsley moaned, threw her head back, and opened herself wider, wanting, needing more of her hot mouth. Nev moaned in return and delved deeper, swirling her tongue in and around her folds, paying careful attention to her clitoris. Making sure to circle it again and again, driving Kinsley mad, before diving in and taking it into her mouth. She sucked it much like she had her breast, tugging on it repeatedly until Kinsley clawed at her head, begging her to stop.

Until eventually, Kinsley begged, and this time Nev didn't stop, and Kinsley came up off the bed, held fast to her head, and exploded into her, fucking her hard and fast, never wanting it to stop. Her cries were deep and throaty, her body in a frenzy, taking all that it could. She bucked into her wildly and cried until she went hoarse and her body went limp back against the bed. At some point she felt Nev nuzzle her inner thigh. It caused her to twitch and jerk. She covered her eyes and laughed, a little embarrassed at how strongly she'd climaxed. At how ravenously her body had reacted.

Nev seemed to have loved it.

"God, you are something, Kinny," she said from her position between her legs. "I think that was the most beautiful thing I've ever experienced."

Kinsley laughed again. She couldn't look at her. "I was a little out of control." Her voice was rough, a mere whisper. She'd climaxed numerous times already and it seemed her voice could take no more.

"I think that's kind of the point," Nev said with a laugh of her own.

"I know, but I'm not used to it."

"Yeah, I gathered that."

Kinsley looked at her. "You did?"

"Uh-huh. It's a little obvious."

"It is?"

"Kinny, come on. You like to be in control. I noticed it right away, from day one. And even from when we were kids. It's just who you are."

"You're okay with that?"

Nev grinned. "As long as you give up some of that control every once in a while, yes."

"Like now?"

"Like with what just happened, yes. Definitely, yes."

"What if I don't want to?"

"Are you saying you didn't enjoy what just happened?"

"Mm, no."

"Didn't think so. Besides, I'm bigger than you, so I'll just do my best to try to convince you otherwise."

"Really?"

"Yes, really."

"Like how?"

Nev raised an eyebrow at her. She sat up and crawled up her body. "Like this." Quickly and with surprising expertise, she took both her hands in hers and pinned them up above her head. Kinsley squirmed playfully, loving the feel of being held captive beneath her.

"You like this," Nev said.

"I do."

"You bad girl, you."

"I guess I am."

Nev held her hands together with one hand and then ran her other down the length of her body to her center, where she maneuvered her thighs open with her knee. Then she traced her curls with her fingertips and Kinsley writhed again, loving it.

"You bad, bad girl," Nev said, kissing her.

"Mm, yes, I am." They kissed again and Kinsley tried to move, to outmaneuver her. But Nev held firm, her eyes flashing.

"No, you're mine."

"Then make me yours," Kinsley said, so turned on she surprised herself.

Nev dipped into her folds and then very quickly and smoothly slid her fingers up inside her.

Kinsley threw her head back and cried out in ecstasy. God, it felt good. Nev witnessed her pleasure and fucked her right away, deep, long strokes, making her cry out again and again, until her strained voice could do nothing more than rasp.

"Nev, Nev, Nev," she pleaded as best she could, her eyes doing most of the talking for her.

"Tell me, Kinny. Tell me what you want."

"I want you to fuck me."

"Say it again."

"Fuck me, Nev. Now. Harder." It hurt her throat like hell to say it, but she didn't care. She'd never wanted anything so badly.

Nev kissed her and increased her speed. She fucked her harder, faster, and Kinsley writhed and bucked, loving every second, loving the hot searing swords of her fingers. She told Nev as much as best she could, but soon she was not only hoarse, but breathless as well. So completely caught up and consumed by pleasure.

Her eyes fell closed, and Nev told her she loved her and then took her breast into her mouth, and sucked nearly the whole thing in. She sucked her hard and fucked her hard, inserting another finger.

Kinsley's eyes flew open and she watched Nev feed from her as she continued to fuck her, and Kinsley broke loose and came all over her hand, thrusting like a madwoman into her, arching her breast up into her mouth, begging to be taken in both ways. She came as hard as she'd been fucked, her body racked with pleasure, convulsing with it until she cried out to Nev that she loved her and came down, a lone feather drifting slowly to the ground.

Nev fell atop her, fingers still nestled deep inside her. Kinsley lay there in heaven, their sweaty bodies meshing together, their breathing falling into sync. She'd just had the fuck of her life and it had been incredible. Given to her by the one and only person she'd ever trusted to do so.

Nev pushed up to her elbows and looked into her eyes. "You look so beautiful right now," she said. "So spent."

"Pleasantly spent. Pleasantly fucked."

Nev laughed. "Good."

"No, not just good. Fucking outstanding."

"Really?" She laughed again.

"I've never let anyone do that to me before. Hold me down and take me like that."

Nev seemed to soften. "But you let me."

"Let you? I wanted you to. Told you to. God, Nev, I think you're right. I think I'm a control freak and you just conquered the hell out of me."

"But you told me to."

"Because I was getting off on you having control. God, that was incredible. You, Nev Wakefield, are the best lay of my life."

Nev laughed and rolled them until Kinsley was on top of her. "If you weren't such a control freak I'd say that's hard to believe."

"But you know me, and you know it's true, don't you?"

"Yes."

Kinsley pushed up and straddled her waist. Nev touched her face. "I've never had an experience like this either," she said. "It is pretty fucking incredible."

"It is isn't it?" Kinsley held her hand. Kissed it.

"I think I was waiting for you."

"We were waiting for each other."

Nev smiled. "Yeah. I like the sound of that better."

"It's true."

"Yes, it is."

"It's funny," Kinsley said. "The curveballs life throws at you."

"Not always so funny."

"No, but they all mean something. And they all lead you somewhere. Look where ours led us."

Nev closed her eyes and Kinsley touched her lips. "Hey."

Nev opened her eyes.

"Where did you go?"

"Nowhere. For once, I went nowhere. I stayed right here, knowing when I opened my eyes I'd see you."

"I know what you mean," Kinsley said. "For the first time ever, I know what it means to be present. And more importantly, I know what it means to want to be."

Chapter Twenty-Nine

Nev bolted upright and scanned the darkness, unsure at first where she was. Then, a tentative hand on her arm.

"What is it? What's wrong?" It was Kinsley. They'd fallen asleep again after making love.

"I'm not sure." Her heart was racing, and she had the feeling that something was wrong. Then her phone vibrated. She snatched it up and saw that she had a voice message and a missed call. There were also two texts from Louise informing her of an emergency.

"Shit." She slid out of bed and fumbled around for her clothes. She squinted as Kinsley turned on a lamp.

"Nev?"

"Something's up with Arthur. Louise texted and said there's an emergency."

"Oh, no." Kinsley got out of bed and joined her in her hurry to dress.

Nev pulled on her sweater and stepped into her jeans. She sat on the bed and dialed into her voice mail. Louise sounded distressed, her voice tight, which was unlike her. The woman usually took everything as it came, keeping her cool even when things got hairy. The tone of her voice alone put Nev on high alert. Her message nearly sent her over.

Nev ended the call and stood. She scrambled for her socks and boots.

"Nev?" Kinsley said again, coming to stand beside her, already dressed in a pair of worn jeans and a soft looking T-shirt.

Nev moved past her to sit on the bed again and yanked on her socks and boots. Her heart was still thrumming, her mind flying.

"He's at the hospital. He fell again while getting up to go to the bathroom. Hit his head."

Kinsley covered her mouth. "Oh, my God. Is he—does she—"

"I don't know. You now know as much as I do."

Kinsley blinked, as if in shock, and then hurried toward the closet where she retrieved her trainers. She slid them on and then shrugged into Nev's shirt. Nev stood and crossed to her.

"I need to go," Nev said.

"I'm coming with you."

"No," Nev said, her voice strained with emotion. "I don't know how bad it's going to be. Louise sounded—she didn't sound good, and that's not like her. I don't know what I'm going to walk into."

"All the more reason for me to go," Kinsley said, touching her arms.

Nev shook her head, the fear already rising in her, closing up her throat. She couldn't have Kinsley there seeing her like this. She'd already witnessed enough for one evening.

"I need to do this alone." Arthur was her dearest friend, her mentor. Her family. If something bad had happened, it was for her to deal with. On her own.

Kinsley looked defeated, disappointed. Even hurt. But Nev didn't have time to reassure her.

"I'll call you," she said, kissing her quickly on the lips.

"Promise?" Kinsley followed her to the door.

"I do."

Kinsley grabbed her and turned her to face her once again.

"Please, don't forget. You can just text if you want. But please let me know how he is."

Nev nodded once. "I will."

Kinsley stroked her jaw and then planted a soft kiss on her mouth.

Nev wanted to melt into it, get lost in the warmth of her tantalizing lips and pretend none of this was happening. That the phone call never came. But she couldn't. Arthur was hurt and he needed her. She had to go.

"Drive safe," Kinsley said as Nev hurried out the door. She made her yet another promise she hoped she could keep just before pulling it closed behind her.

"I will."

Nev nearly sprinted once she was inside the hospital. She got to the glassed-off reception area in the emergency room and asked for Arthur.

She rushed through the doors when they swung open and hurried through the maze of curtained rooms. When she got to number ten she stopped and took a deep breath before pulling back the curtain. She nearly gasped when she saw Arthur in the bed, head wrapped in white gauze, with a sizable red stain above his temple in his hairline.

Nev held herself together and eased the curtain open farther. Louise saw her and stood.

"He's okay."

"Is he—awake?"

"I'm right here," he said, opening his eyes, his voice so low it was barely audible. "And yes, I'm awake. My head hurts like hell."

His speech was slurred, and he'd had trouble getting the words out. His face was expressionless, and a small trail of drool trickled down from the corner of his mouth.

Louise dabbed it away with a tissue.

"What happened?" Nev asked. Arthur waved her off, indicating that what had happened was no big deal, and that he wasn't interested in filling her in, but Louise did.

"I was in the living room reading and Mr. Independent here decided to get up without ringing his bell for me like we'd all discussed. He tried to make it to the bathroom on his own."

"I don't need your damn help," he said. "I made it just fine."

Louise continued. "He did make it to the bathroom, but then he fell and hit his head on the counter. I heard the commotion and ran in and found him on the floor."

Louise glanced at him before she spoke again. Then she whispered to Nev, "He didn't know where he was. Didn't know who I was."

Nev nodded, confirming she'd heard and understood. Arthur might be alive and breathing, but the situation was far from okay.

"What about his injury? They said anything?"

"A couple of doctors have already examined him. They're worried about a concussion and sent him for a CAT scan. We'll know more soon."

Nev exhaled. "The one night I choose to stay out…"

"Don't you go doing that now," Louise said. "You did nothing wrong."

"I should've been there."

"Honey, I *was* there and it still happened, and I'm better trained for this than you are."

She gripped Nev's forearm and stared into her eyes with a look of grave concern. She lowered her voice again, her back to Arthur.

"I think he's progressing quicker than we thought. We may not get good news from the doctor. Are you prepared for that?"

Nev swallowed but nodded. Louise gave her upper arm a squeeze. "Come sit down. You look like a ghost."

Nev sank into the chair closest to Arthur and held his hand. His eyes drifted over to hers and he clenched them closed, causing a single tear to escape. She wiped it away.

"I'm gonna go get some coffee," Louise said. "Nev? You want anything?"

"No, thanks." Louise left them and Nev looked back to Arthur. "How you feeling? You still hurting?"

"Yeah. Damn doctors."

"You want me to call someone?"

"No, I'll live."

"Tough guy, eh?"

He licked his lips, struggled to speak. "I'm getting worse."

"No, you're no—"

"Nevaeh," he said, stopping her. His tone was louder than usual, and she closed her mouth and listened.

"You need to prepare. For the end."

"Arthur, I—"

"I mean it. I'm not going to be around forever." His blue eyes bored into hers, watery with tears. But he kept on. "You need to be ready. Need to be ready to move on."

"What is it you want me to do?" He already had an advance directive and she was his power of attorney.

He swallowed, but it seemed difficult. "Live."

Nev teared up and looked away. She felt him grip her hand.

"Look at me."

She shook her head. "You're going to be fine. Just a bump on the head. We'll get you home—"

"Stop!"

She tensed.

"Damn it, look at me, Nevaeh."

She slowly turned, fighting back tears. His were running down his face. She didn't have the strength to wipe them away for him this time. He didn't seem to care.

"You know I love you like my own."

"Yes," she managed.

"Then you need to listen to me. I want you to live. Live. Get out of the house. Do things. Go places. Meet people."

"I'm happy at the ranch and you—"

"I'm not going to be here."

"Arthur—"

"Nevaeh, if you love me you'll promise me."

Nev sighed, her breath shook in her chest. "I've already made enough promises tonight."

"Promise one more time."

She rubbed her brow, the conversation one she'd never wanted to have. She wasn't ready for it. It was too soon. He was being overly dramatic. Sure, he may be getting a little worse, but there was still time. It wasn't the end.

"Nevaeh, I'm dying," he said.

Her eyes shot to his. His were steely and serious. He wasn't bullshitting her. He wasn't being overly dramatic. He really thought he was dying.

"I know my body. And I still have some of my mind. But both are going fast. Too fast. My end is near."

Nev tried to speak but broke down instead. His last few words tore at her heart, and she imagined him in a box, like Viv, being put into the ground, forever. It ravaged her and she didn't want to think about it. Didn't want to face it. Why was he doing this? Why couldn't they just go home?

"You need to listen to me, Nevaeh. You need to have a life."

"I have one," she said. "On the ranch, with you."

"I'll be gone," he said. "And when I'm gone, I want you to let others in. Let someone special in."

Nev bowed her head.

"Kinsley," Arthur said, "is special."

"Yes, we've already agreed on that."

"Then let her in."

"I am. I have."

"All the way."

"I'm trying, Arthur."

"Try harder."

His hand shook as he raised it to wipe away a tear. "Were you with her earlier?"

"Yes."

"Then why isn't she here?"

"Because I told her I needed to come alone."

"See what I mean? You haven't let her all the way in."

"But you're my friend, my family. It's my business, not anyone else's."

"Kinsley is my friend too. She cares about me."

Nev couldn't argue. "You're right."

"Do better," he said. "Don't be afraid."

Nev brushed away tears. "It's so hard to not be afraid."

"I know. But you have to try. For your own sake. Let Adrianna and Kinsley help. They'll listen, they'll be there. If you let them."

Louise pulled back the curtain. "Nev, can you come out here for a second?"

Nev started to stand, but Arthur stopped her, squeezing her hand. "Promise me," he said.

Nev nodded. "Okay. I promise."

He seemed pleased and relaxed against the pillow. Nev followed Louise out into the hallway.

"What's up?"

"The doctor wants to speak to us."

Louise led them down the hall to an empty room on the end. The doctor was waiting.

Nev extended her hand. "Nev Wakefield. And this is Louise, Arthur's caregiver."

"Yes, we've met," he said, referring to Louise. He shook Nev's hand and motioned toward two chairs. Nev sat, along with Louise.

"Arthur has sustained a concussion from his fall. But that's not what I'm concerned about."

"What are you concerned about?" Nev asked, fearing the answer.

"It seems that his Parkinson's has progressed to the final stage."

"Stage five," Nev said, mostly to herself. She choked up. "What does this mean?"

"It's no longer safe for Arthur to try to walk. It's time for him to start using a wheelchair."

Nev rubbed her brow, leaned forward, and rested her elbows on her knees.

"No, not yet."

"I'm afraid it's time," he said. "We don't want a repeat of tonight where he could possibly get hurt worse. And Louise tells me he had a previous fall a short time ago?"

Nev nodded.

"His balance issues are now significant, and his legs lack the mobility needed for him to sustain walking. And I'm told his memory loss is becoming more significant as well. Arthur now needs full-time assistance."

Nev struggled to breathe. Louise rested a hand on her shoulder.

"I'm keeping him for a night, possibly two for observation. His neurologist, Dr. Grimes, is wanting to see him tomorrow, and I'd like to keep an eye on that concussion. With his other issues I think it would be a good idea. It will also give you some time to decide about his full-time care."

"He's staying at home. That's what he wants."

"Whatever you decide. We have someone here who will go over all your options with you and discuss palliative care. I'd say, considering his relatively minor injuries from his two recent falls, that he's one lucky man."

The doctor shook their hands. He left them.

Nev sat with her head in her hands.

"He is lucky," Louise said. "We're lucky. He could've been hurt a lot worse."

Nev stared down at her feet. "The last thing I feel right now is lucky."

CHAPTER THIRTY

K insley didn't bother asking whether or not she could visit Arthur. She just called an Uber and got herself to the hospital. Nev hadn't said much in her text. Just that he had a concussion and was stable and was being held overnight for observation. Kinsley had tried to call her, but Nev wasn't picking up. She wasn't answering texts much either. She had been lucky to get yes or no answers.

Kinsley now knew that that was how Nev dealt with stressful situations. She shut everyone out and focused on what needed to be done. Kinsley tried not to take it personally, but it was difficult. She wanted to be there for Nev and her pushing her away hurt, no matter how she tried to look at it.

Kinsley got the directions for Arthur's room and found him next to ICU. His room had no curtains or walls, just a glass partition that could be seen through from the nurse's station. She knocked softly on the partition and Arthur turned his head from the window. His eyes seemed to light up when he saw her.

"Miss Kinsley," he said. He raised his good hand to her as she came to the bed. She took it and gave it a squeeze.

"Arthur, it's good to see you."

"Well, I am rather handsome," he said, making her laugh.

"That you are."

He struggled to speak. "How are you?" Kinsley's heart warmed. The man was in the hospital and his first thought was to ask her how she was.

"I'm good now that I'm here with you. I was worried."

He seemed to scoff, turning his head. "I'm all right."

"Are you? Nev said you took a fall?"

She reached up and touched his bandage. "It looks painful."

"Doesn't hurt anymore."

Kinsley patted his hand. "That's good." She turned and dug in the gift bag she'd brought with her.

"You bring me flowers?" he asked, obviously teasing her.

"No, sorry. But I did bring you a little something." She pulled out the gift box and held it out for him. "I'll hold the bottom if you just want to lift the lid."

He did so with an unsure hand but managed to loosen the top and pull it off. His blue eyes danced as he looked inside.

"A bolo tie," he said.

"Yep." Kinsley smiled and took out the jade bolo tie she'd bought for him at a local gift store in Cypress Creek. "I saw that and thought how good it would look on you."

She held it up for him. "Do you like it?"

His eyes brimmed with tears and he licked his lips. "You didn't have to do that."

"I wanted to do it." She rested her hand on his and smoothed his skin with her thumb. "I wanted to get you a little something to help cheer you up."

A tear slipped down his cheek. She leaned toward the bedside table and grabbed a tissue. She wiped away the tear for him.

"Does this mean you don't like it?" she teased him, trying to lighten the mood.

His eyes crinkled. "I like it. I—" More tears came. "Thank you."

"You're welcome," she said. "Would you like to try it on?"

"What? Here?"

"Sure, why not?" She loosened the tie and slipped it on over his neck. Then she adjusted it so that it fit him just right. "There," she said. "You handsome devil, you."

She could tell he wanted to smile. She dug in her purse for her phone. "Say cheese," she said. Arthur managed to give her a thumbs-up and she snapped the picture. She showed it to him. "See? I told you you were a handsome devil."

"I am," he said, looking at the picture.

Kinsley laughed. "How about one of us together? A selfie?"

"A what?"

She leaned back and angled the phone just right and snapped the picture. She laughed when she saw it. "I look so ridiculous." She showed him.

"You're beautiful," he said, struggling to do so.

She smiled. "And you're a charmer."

"It's in my blood," he said.

"I don't doubt it. Speaking of which," she said. "When are you going to have me over for some Cajun cooking?"

His eyes clouded momentarily.

"What is it?" she asked.

He tried to speak. "How long you staying?" Though his voice was already low in pitch, she could still hear the emotion that had come over it.

Kinsley eased off the bed and into the neighboring chair. She pulled it closer to the bed. "Well, I've been thinking about that. I'd really like to stay here full-time."

His eyes seemed to light up. "Why don't you?"

"I have a lot to work out. And this is just me thinking aloud. I haven't told anyone. Not even Nev or Adrianna. So this is just between you and me, okay? For now anyway."

"Okay."

"I'd really like to get back to doing what I love," she said. "And that's flying. I'm hoping I can work something out at the local airport here and start offering private flying lessons. Maybe start my own business doing that."

She continued as he watched her closely.

"It would be slow going at first, but I'm okay with that. I have the funds and I'd like to continue to take it easy for a while. I can't tell you how good I feel in having left all that stress and constant traveling behind."

"So, you're staying?" he asked.

Kinsley nodded. "I'd like to."

"Then I'll wear this tie at our next dinner. Whenever that may be."

"Deal." Kinsley stood and leaned down to kiss his cheek.

Arthur looked up at her with soulful eyes and somehow managed to smile at her.

❖

Kinsley handed the driver a ten-dollar bill. "Can you wait here for a second?"

"Sure," he said, happily taking the money.

Kinsley climbed out and walked toward Nev's front door. She

rang the bell but got no answer. She hurried back to the car. "Can you drive around back there?"

He put the car in gear and followed the gravel path that led to the stables and the barn. She pointed at the barn as she spotted Nev's truck. "There."

"Thanks," she said. "I'll be right back."

"Take your time."

She crawled from the car and headed into the shop. The music was loud, almost blaring, and Nev was busy working at her table once again. Only this time she wasn't working on a gate.

"Whatcha working on?" she practically yelled.

Nev looked up and killed the flame to her blowtorch. She pulled off her gloves and switched off the stereo. She ran a hand through her hair.

"I, uh—I'm building a ramp."

"A ramp?"

"For Arthur," she said, eyeing the large pieces she'd already welded together.

"Oh."

"Yeah, I'm going to need a few of them, so I've got a lot of work to do before tomorrow. I'm hoping to have this one done today, in case they let him come home."

She suddenly dug out her phone, as if she'd just realized the hospital might have called. She relaxed when she saw the screen and Kinsley assumed they hadn't called.

"Why the rush? Are you afraid he's going to fall again?"

Nev studied her. "Yes, but—Kinsley he's going to be in a wheelchair from here on out."

Kinsley felt light-headed. "What?"

"I'm sorry, did I not tell you?"

"No, and neither did he. I just came from there."

"You went to see him?"

"Well, yes. Of course."

Nev wiped her face with a towel and tossed it aside. "I wish you would've told me."

"And I wish you would've told me some things too."

Nev crossed her arms but nodded in agreement. "Right. I should have. I've just been really busy."

"I can imagine." Kinsley came closer and touched Nev's arm. "I'm so sorry, I had no idea. I thought he just fell. Does this mean—"

Nev nodded again. "He's progressed to stage five."

Kinsley covered her mouth. "I'm so sorry."

"So am I. That's why I wish you would've told me you were going to see him. I could've warned you of what not to say. He's pretty upset."

"He did cry a lot."

"Did he?"

"Yes."

Nev turned away, the news obviously getting to her. "He tries to be so strong."

"Like you?"

Kinsley touched her shoulder. "Nev?" She turned her so she'd face her once again.

"How are you doing?"

Nev looked at her long and hard. Kinsley couldn't read her eyes. They looked almost…vacant. But when she saw the beginning of tears, Nev walked away.

"I have a lot to do. I've got the ramps and Louise is going to work on the interior of the house when she gets back. Make things he needs more accessible. She's moving in, you know."

"She is?"

Nev busied herself rearranging her hammers. Kinsley wondered if she was purposely putting distance between them by doing something mundane.

"Arthur needs full-time assistance now. And I'm only one person."

"I can help," Kinsley said. "I'm just right next door and I have the time."

"That's okay," Nev said. "I think we got it for now."

"But—"

"If I need something, I'll call. Okay?"

Kinsley's heart faltered. "Okay," she said softly.

Nev came back to the table and slid on her gloves. "I really should get back to it."

"Yeah," Kinsley said, moving out of her way. "I'll see you later."

"I'll call you," she said as she turned on her blowtorch and got back to work.

Kinsley left her without saying good-bye and headed back out to the waiting car. She'd expected the conversation to be a short one, knowing Nev was stressed, but she had not expected what she'd just encountered. It seemed Nev was stressed beyond what she'd initially thought. She understood why. What she didn't understand was Nev declining her help.

Was she pushing her away all over again?

Kinsley ducked her head and spoke to the driver once she reached the car.

"Go ahead and go, I'm going to walk from here."

"You sure?"

"Yeah."

He saluted her and drove away, and Kinsley headed for the distant trail that led back to Peace of Life. As she walked she thought about Arthur and Nev and her future. When she'd decided she was going to stay, they hadn't been her main reason why. But now, on hearing the situation and the way it was affecting her, she wondered if that was really true.

Had she really made such a big decision without Nev in mind?

She also wondered, regardless of her reason for staying, if Nev and Arthur would allow her to help at all? They were both very strong, proud people.

Arthur had seemed eager to have her over, but that could've been a front, him merely being polite. The man was going through a lot and she hadn't known that at the time.

God, she must've sounded so insensitive.

And how could Nev have forgotten to tell her he could no longer walk?

There was so much to wrap her head around and she wondered, lastly, if any of it would need sorting out at all, or had Nev just pretty much told her good-bye?

CHAPTER THIRTY-ONE

Nev put the car in park and glanced over at Arthur. "You ready, old man?"

"Damn right, I'm ready. Anything to get me out of this car. You drive slower than I do."

"I was trying to be safe," Nev said. "I have delicate cargo."

"Delicate my ass," he said.

Arthur hadn't exactly been in the best mood since they'd left the hospital, which surprised her a little. She'd thought he'd be happy to leave and get home. But it seemed the doom and gloom of his advancing disease had taken precedence and soured his mood.

Nev opened the door to Louise's car and climbed out. She had taken it instead of her truck, knowing the truck would be too difficult for Arthur to get in and out of due to its height. She'd have to get something else to drive if she wanted to take him places on her own. Just one more thing she needed to take care of.

She opened the trunk and pulled out the folded wheelchair. It was a rental, one they'd only use temporarily until they could get him a motorized one. With his limited mobility and stiffness, it would be difficult for him to use his arms to move a regular wheelchair. Nev had already found a couple of prospects for motorized chairs online. She just needed Arthur's final approval. She wanted him to have a say in almost every aspect of his care. His final directive, thankfully, had covered most of it, but there were a dozen little things they couldn't possibly have thought about beforehand. Those little things were now what she and Louise were doing their darnedest to take care of.

Nev unfolded the chair and rolled it up to his door. She helped him into it with a few grunts and grumbles from Arthur and then wheeled him up to the house.

"Check out the ramp," Nev said. "Made by yours truly."

"You made that?"

"Yes, sir."

"Doesn't look fancy enough to be yours. Not artsy enough."

"Ha ha. Glad to see your sense of humor has returned."

"Someone has to have one around here."

Nev pushed him up the ramp and opened the front door. Then she wheeled Arthur inside.

"Surprise!" Louise said as they entered.

"What the hell?" he said.

"Welcome home," Nev said, pointing to the banner that said the same and the clusters of colorful balloons.

Louise came up and kissed his cheek. "I even baked you a cake."

Arthur just sat and stared, taking it all in.

"And we got everything ready for you. As much as we could anyway. You shouldn't have trouble reaching most things. And in case you do, there's this."

Nev handed him an extended grabber. "This thing can grip just about anything."

Arthur pushed it away. He tried to wheel himself away but couldn't. Nev looked at Louise with concern.

"Arthur, what's wrong?"

"This," he said waving his arm. "All this nonsense."

"It's not nonsense. We're glad to have you home."

"It's nonsense. Plain and simple. Looks like a damn clown exploded in here."

He tried to wheel himself again, so Nev tried to help him, but he waved her off.

"I don't need your damn help, Nevaeh. I don't need any of this. I can do it myself."

Nev backed away. "Okay."

He continued to struggle.

"Would you like me to help you?" Louise asked.

"No."

She looked to Nev.

Just then the doorbell rang. Nev threw up her hands, exasperated, wondering who it could be.

She opened the door and found Kinsley standing there, looking expectant.

"Hi."

"Hi," Nev said. "Now's really not a good time."

"Is that Miss Kinsley?" Arthur said. "Well, let her in, Nevaeh."

Nev pulled open the door and Kinsley came in and headed right for Arthur.

"Hey, you," she said, enveloping him in a hug.

Arthur's eyes twinkled as Kinsley held him. Nev closed the door and crossed her arms, watching the exchange.

"Hey, yourself."

Kinsley straightened and dug in her purse. She pulled out a gift box. "I forgot to leave this with you the other day." She opened it and pulled out a jade bolo tie. Arthur seemed to beam.

"Oh, yes. My present."

"So, it's okay for Kinsley to do nice things for you, but not us?" Nev asked.

"Yes," Arthur said matter-of-factly.

Kinsley looked around. "This place looks great."

"It looks like a birthday party for a three-year-old," Arthur said.

Kinsley eyed Nev before she spoke to Arthur again. "You don't like it?"

"No, I don't like it. I'm not a child."

"Ah," Kinsley said. "I'm pretty sure no one here thinks that about you, Arthur. Looks like they just wanted to give you a warm welcome home."

"Yeah, well."

Kinsley placed a hand on his shoulder. "They're trying to do something nice because they love you. You should probably thank them."

Nev raised her brow at Kinsley's gumption. She waited for Arthur to slam her down.

But instead, the old man looked from Nev to Louise and back again and then said softly as he looked at the floor, "Thank you both."

Nev about fell over. She stared at Kinsley with her mouth hanging open. Kinsley didn't seem to notice. She just slid Arthur's bolo tie over his neck and pushed his wheelchair into the living room.

"So, how about we go get you cleaned up for dinner? You can wear your new tie. How does that sound?"

"Sounds good," Arthur said.

Nev and Louise followed and then waited in the living room as Kinsley took Arthur to his bedroom to help get him ready.

"What just happened?" Nev asked.

Louise laughed. "Uh, that little friend of his just showed us up, that's what."

"Yeah, no kidding."

"She's got a direct ticket to his heart, it seems," Louise said.

"I guess so."

Nev crossed her arms again, still bewildered. Where had Kinsley come from? Had she known she was coming over? Had she forgotten? She checked her phone. There were no texts or messages. In fact, she hadn't even told her exactly when they were coming home.

But she had told Adrianna when she'd called earlier.

Could that be it?

Yes, of course. Adrianna had told her.

Nev slid her phone into her back pocket. "She has a way," she said.

Louise walked to the kitchen. "Mm-hm. His heart isn't the only one she seems to have a direct ticket to, is it?"

Nev flushed. "What?"

"You heard me."

"I don't know what you're talking about."

"Have you forgotten that I know where you were night before last?"

"Oh."

"Yeah. Oh. You were out awful late, weren't you? Probably having yourself a very good time."

Nev bristled. "Yeah, well, there's no time for that now. I have Arthur to think about."

Louise laughed. Nev didn't appreciate the sarcastic tone to it.

"Nev, honey, please. You can't stop love. No matter how hard you try."

"I..."

"You what? Can? Come on. I saw the way you looked at her when she walked in the door. She gets to you, moves you. As for why you two are playing hard to get with each other right now, that is beyond me. My guess is you pushed her away. Probably didn't keep her updated on Arthur. Tried to keep her away. Well, it seems you've finally met your match. This one isn't fazed by your stand-offishness. She just does whatever the hell she wants. And right now, she's all about Arthur, and I think that's tearing you up a little bit, isn't it?"

Nev crossed to the window. "No."

"Nev."

"It isn't. I don't mind if she spends time with Arthur."

"Uh-huh. So you're saying you told her all about today. When you were bringing him home, the little party we had planned?"

"Well, no."

"Uh-huh, didn't think so."

"I just didn't—"

"Want her involved?"

Nev closed her eyes. "Would that make me an awful person?"

"No, not necessarily. You're used to having him all to yourself."

"He's the only father figure I really have, Louise. He's been there for me like no one else has."

"I have a feeling that woman in there is willing to be there for you. She's here for Arthur. And I have a feeling that she cares about you just as much. If not more."

Kinsley and Arthur emerged from the hallway. Arthur had on a crisp white western button-down and a pair of jeans, and he was sporting his new bolo tie. Kinsley had even slicked back his hair for him like he liked.

Nev couldn't help but smile, despite the slight ping of jealousy she felt.

"Look at you," she said, whistling.

"Yeah, look at me. I'm a stunner." Kinsley laughed and pushed him farther into the room.

"He even smells good."

"I can tell," Nev said, smelling his Old Spice.

"You ready for some dinner, honey?" Louise asked from the kitchen.

"Only if Miss Kinsley stays," he said.

"Miss Kinsley can stay," Louise said. "Right, Nev?"

Nev blinked. "Right."

"Good," Kinsley surprised her by saying. She looked right at Nev as she spoke. "Because I'm not leaving. Not this time."

Chapter Thirty-Two

Kinsley tore out the last sheet of paper and held it over the firepit. She read it and then wadded it up in her hand. She looked across the fire to Holly and Adrianna. They both nodded.

"Go on, Kinsley, you can do it," Holly said.

Kinsley closed her eyes. She thought about all the things she'd written down. All the negative thoughts, negative things she'd heard from other people, negative things she'd heard from herself. She'd burned them all, along with all her worries, fears, and doubts, save this last page. Now it was time to let them all go for good.

She dropped the wad of paper into the fire and watched it burn to ash. She held out her hands, warming them from the heat all her papers had created. She was done now. Free. Clear. She'd faced it all, trudged through it and come out the other side, the husk of negativity no longer on her back.

The group clapped and Adrianna rose and enveloped her in a tight hug.

"You did it, love," she said. "You did it."

"I did, didn't I?"

"Yes, and how do you feel?"

"Free," Kinsley said. "I feel free."

Adrianna wrapped an arm around her and led her away from the fire.

"Would you say you've dealt with everything you needed to deal with?"

"With the exception of the investigation into the crash, yes. But that's going to take a while, and I'm pretty sure Marty and I did nothing wrong."

Adrianna looked at her. "You sure that's all, sweetheart?" She fingered a thread of Kinsley's hair.

"I think so. I mean, I got the job at the airport. I start next week. I've got a lead on a new place…"

Adrianna shook her head. "That's not what I'm talking about."

"What are you…"

Adrianna motioned behind her. Kinsley turned. She saw Nev standing along the outer circle of the group. The firelight was dancing upon her angular face.

"Oh," Kinsley let out.

Adrianna smiled.

"Go on ahead. I'll tell the group you had one last thing to take care of."

Kinsley thanked her and crossed to Nev.

"Hi."

"Hi."

"Didn't expect to see you here." She'd just seen Nev earlier, back at the house. Arthur's motorized wheelchair had arrived, and she'd made sure to be there to check it out with him. He'd never seemed happier than he was when he tried out that chair. He had the freedom to move on his own now and there was no stopping him.

"I thought it might surprise you."

"Was that your intention? To surprise me?"

Nev gave a half smile. "I don't know. Maybe."

"Well, you succeeded."

They began to walk back toward the cabins. The creek crawled along next to them, luring them along in its tranquil but hypnotizing manner. The air had a bite to it and the cold stung her lungs as she breathed. She hugged herself even though she was wearing a good-sized jacket.

"Cold?" Nev asked.

"Mm, aren't I always?"

Nev shrugged out of her light jacket and draped it over her shoulders.

"Thanks, but it's not necessary."

"Yes, it is. You're cold. And I couldn't help but notice that you haven't been wearing my shirt anymore."

Kinsley tugged Nev's jacket tighter over her shoulders. "Didn't think you wanted me to."

"Why wouldn't I want you to?"

"Because you barely tolerate my being around, Nev."

"That's not true."

"It is."

Nev sighed. Kinsley fought back tears. It had been difficult the past week to be around Arthur with Nev around. She'd wanted so badly to talk to her, to hold her and comfort her. To tell her it would all be all right. But Nev had kept her distance, speaking only when spoken to, her sole focus on Arthur. It was plainly obvious she didn't want her around. And if it weren't for Arthur, Kinsley wouldn't have kept coming around.

"Maybe it's a little true," Nev finally said.

"Thank you," Kinsley said sincerely. "For admitting that."

Nev shoved her hands in her pockets. "There's a reason."

Kinsley looked at her. "I'd love to hear it."

"It's stupid."

Kinsley laughed. "Okay."

"I'm jealous."

"What?"

"Of you and Arthur."

"Get out."

"No, I'm serious."

"But why?" She shook her head. "Never mind, I know why."

"You do?"

"Arthur is the only father you've known. You're protective of him."

Nev looked up at the sky and cleared her throat. "Yeah."

Kinsley linked her arm in hers, so moved by her honesty and her obvious emotion over the truth. And all this time she'd thought Nev didn't want her.

"You don't have to worry," Kinsley said. "I'm not going to take him from you."

"No, quite the contrary. You make him happy. And that makes him want to be around others. Without you—I think he would've gone into that deep depression that was looming."

Kinsley pulled her close. "That means a lot to hear you say that."

"It's true. He loves you." She stopped and looked into Kinsley's eyes. "And you love him. I don't know how that could've ever bothered me."

"It's okay," Kinsley said. "I understand."

"You always understand." Nev touched her face, and Kinsley

leaned into her hand. "How many times have I apologized to you these past weeks?"

Kinsley laughed. "I don't know. Two or three."

"Well, here's number four. I'm sorry, Kinsley. For being a silly, jealous ass."

"And I forgive you, Nev. For being a silly, jealous ass."

Nev studied her for a long moment. "You really do always understand. Always forgive me."

"Because you're human, Nev. And you've been hurt. A lot."

"Even so."

"I love you," Kinsley said. "Is that a good enough reason?"

Nev smiled and skimmed her cheek with her thumb. "I'd say that tops the list." She touched Kinsley's lips. "I love you, too."

"Does this mean you're done with the whole pushing me away thing?"

Nev laughed. "Yeah, I'd say so. Or Arthur's going to seriously kill me. So are Adrianna and Louise, for that matter."

Kinsley smiled. "Seriously, though. This is the end of that, right? Because I don't think I can take much more."

Nev pulled her closer and held her face. "Kinsley, I'm so sorry. So sorry I've hurt you."

"Just promise me it's the end."

Nev smiled. "I promise, this is the end. But, Kinsley, for us, for our future together, this is only the beginning."

"It is?"

"Yes, because I want you to stay."

Epilogue

One year later

Kinsley stopped brushing Baby and looked up at Nev as she came into the corral. She had a look of concern on her face as she handed Kinsley an envelope.

"What is it?"

"It's for you." She tugged on the brim of her cowboy hat, her green eyes anxious.

Kinsley looked at the envelope. It was from the NTSB.

"Oh." Her hand shook as she tore it open and read. Her heart fell to her throat and then recovered. Just to be sure, she read the letter again.

"Well?" Nev said. "What does it say?"

"It's over," she said, barely able to get the words out. "The investigation is over. Marty and I have been cleared." She covered her mouth as tears came. Nev beamed and picked her up in a huge bear hug.

"That's fantastic!"

"Yeah," Kinsley said, laughing through the tears. Nev set her down and wiped her cheeks for her.

"So, what happened? Do they say what happened?"

Kinsley slapped the paper. "A faulty carburetor part. A part that came with the refurbished carburetor when Marty and I bought the plane. We were given no maintenance instructions on it or anything. So, we're clear."

Nev picked her up again and swung her around.

Kinsley laughed and grew a bit dizzy as Nev set her back down.

"I'm so relieved, I can't believe it. It's finally all over."

"We should celebrate."

"Are you sure you're up for it?" It was wonderful to see Nev so happy for her. She'd been down recently, grieving Arthur, who'd passed away from pneumonia three months before.

"Yes. I'm absolutely up for it." She smiled. "I think it's time we both move forward. I mean we're here, we're together. Your business is taking off, no pun intended, and my artsy-fartsy smithing, as Arthur called it, is as well. We have the ranch, the horses, the canyon, and the creek. It can't get much better, can it?"

Kinsley wrapped her arms around her. "No, I don't think it can."

Nev touched her face. "I'm so in love with you sometimes I think I'm going mad."

Kinsley smiled. "Don't do that."

"What? Go mad? Too late." She kissed her. Lightly, delicately. Kinsley moaned, she felt so good.

"You cold?" Nev asked, pulling her closer.

"Of course."

Nev took her by the hand.

"Where are we going?"

"Shh. Into the stables."

"Why?"

"To warm you up a little."

Kinsley laughed, following her. "Nev, we have a therapy group in fifteen minutes."

"We'll hurry."

They stumbled into an empty stall, laughing.

"Nev, this is crazy."

"Shh." She kissed her. "I already told you I've gone mad for you. So just shut up and enjoy it."

"Oh, how romantic."

Nev laughed and kissed on her neck, causing her to shudder.

"We'll save romance for another time. Right now I've got to have you."

Nev quickly tore off Kinsley's jacket. Her eyes narrowed with desire.

"I see you're wearing my shirt. You know how I feel about you wearing my shirt."

"Yes, you love it."

"I do. And I love seeing you in it."

"But let me guess, you want me to take it off?"

"No, no, no. I want you to leave it on."

"You do?"

Nev tugged her closer and began unfastening her jeans.

"Yes, but we're going to take off all the rest."

"Is that what you want? Me, wearing nothing but your shirt?"

"Yes," Nev said. "That's very much what I want."

Kinsley cupped her jaw, thinking about all the times in Nev's life when she'd put everyone else before herself. Now it was her time. And Kinsley was going to make damn sure she enjoyed her life now, in every aspect.

"Then that's what you'll get."

About the Author

Ronica Black lives in the desert Southwest with her menagerie of animals and her menagerie of art. When she's not writing, she's still creating, whether drawing, painting, or woodworking. She loves long walks into the sunset, rescuing animals, anything pertaining to art, and spending time with those she loves. When she can, she enjoys returning to her roots in North Carolina where she can sit back on the porch with family and friends, catch up on all the gossip, and relish an ice cold Cheerwine.

Ronica is a two-time Golden Crown Literary Society Goldie Award winner and a three-time finalist for the Lambda Literary Awards.